"Stop Attan?" Mid was incredulous. "How are we going to do that?"

"There must be a way!" Cheff said. "Some piece of evidence, some hidden information, some kind of leverage."

"Leverage," Sable echoed.

"Leverage," Buttons said. "The ponies say we must find leverage."

"So," Mid said, "you're saying that all we have to do is"—he enumerated on his fingers—"figure out what Attan is up to, find some leverage to stop him, hand that leverage over to Master Vessslu, stop Attan's takeover of the monastery, and restore the monastery to the control of the real monks of Xanparthur, all without being caught or exposed. Is that the gist of it?"

"That's the gist of it, Old Son," Cheff said. "I believe you've covered everything."

"Oh, great," Mid said.

Buttons held the ponies up to her ear and listened intently. "The ponies say, 'Piece of cake.'"

Mid buried his face in his hands.

# OPERATION SHIFTING SANDS

Book Three

by

## Liam Kincaid

with illustrations by

## Daniel Wood

LBME Publishing

Operation Shifting Sands—Fellstone Tales Book Three
LBME Publishing: http://LBMEPublishing.com/
ISBN: 978-1-64676-014-5 (trade paperback)
ISBN: 978-1-64676-015-2 (ebook)

First Edition



Printed in the United States of America.

This book is a work of fiction. Names, characters, places, and incidents either are products of the author's imagination or are used fictitiously. Any resemblance to actual persons, living or dead, events, or locales is entirely coincidental.

In loving memory of our dear Robert, who created the worlds of Andaran, Worldheart, and Fellstone City.

He'll be forever missed.

# Acknowledgments

Thank you to all who helped create this book, including:

Robert L. Graham, Master World Builder, best friend, my "brother in a time of distress"

Sarah J, Beta Reader Supreme

And my Twitch Crew:
J. T. "Jack" Shennaghy
FemaleWriter
Dear Alisa
EmperorOfFinland
Mayah Robinson
NightWriter
Charlie Stone


And, of course, my grateful appreciation to Lon Böder and Penney Knightly for the many, many hours of brainstorming, encouragement, and support. This book would never have been possible without them.

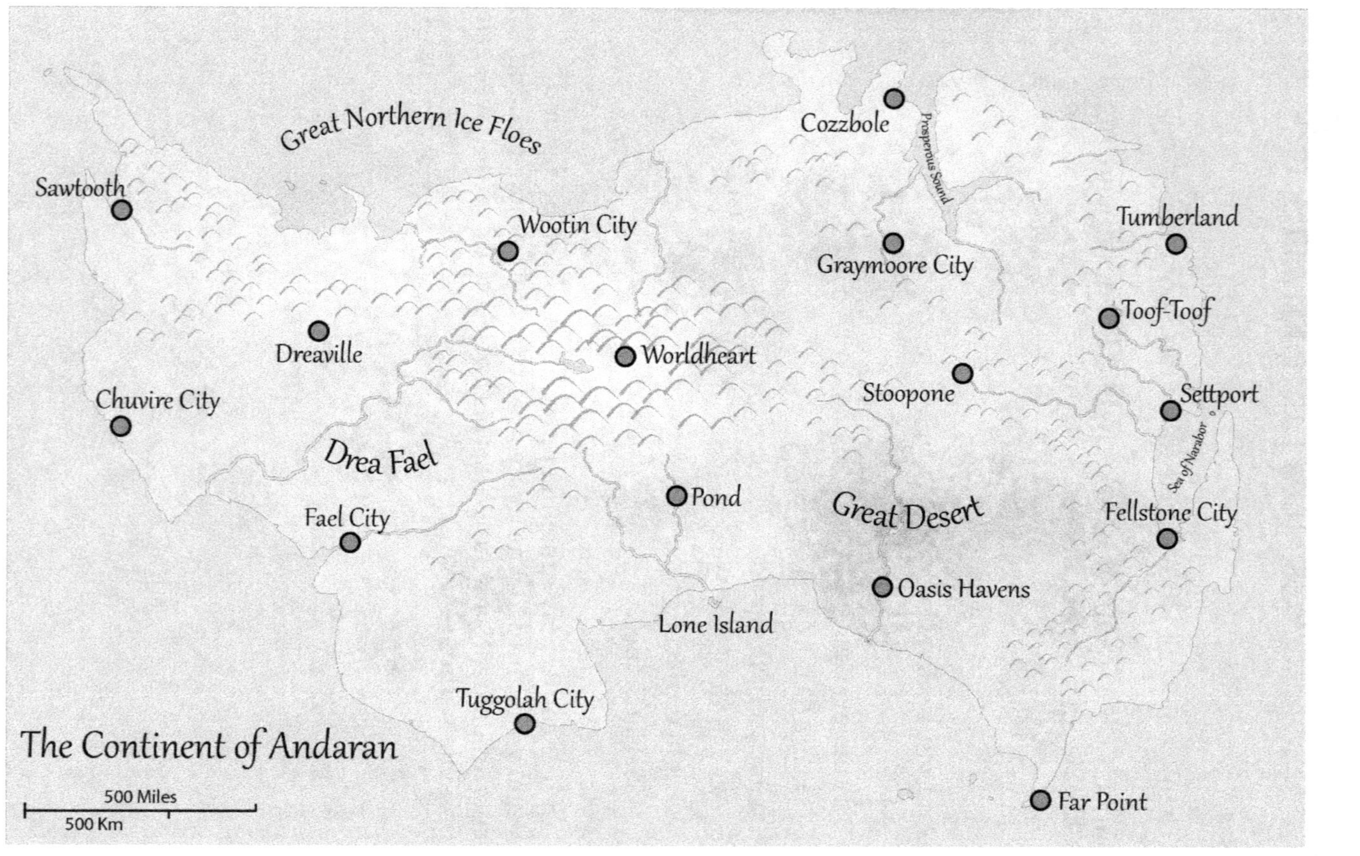

Great Northern Ice Floes
Sawtooth
Cozzbole
Prosperous Sound
Wootin City
Tumberland
Graymoore City
Toof-Toof
Dreaville
Worldheart
Stoopone
Settport
Chuvire City
Sea of Narabor
Drea Fael
Pond
Great Desert
Fellstone City
Fael City
Oasis Havens
Lone Island
Tuggolah City
The Continent of Andaran
500 Miles
500 Km
Far Point

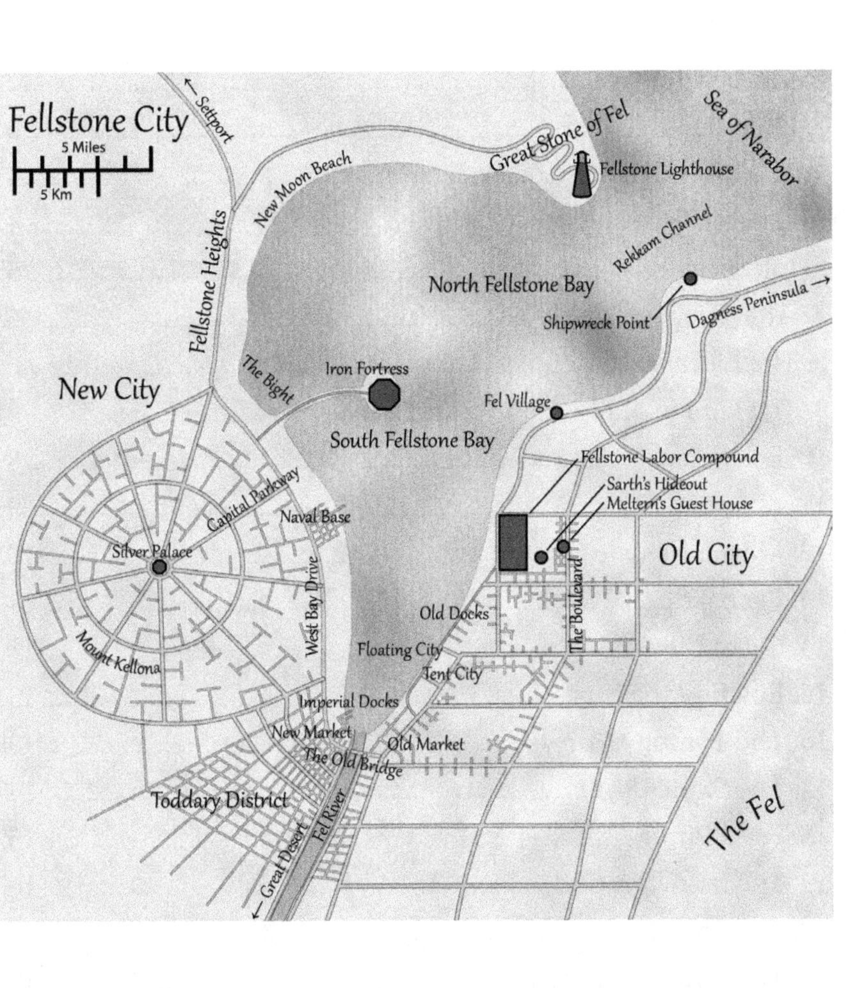

Fellstone City
5 Miles
5 Km
Settport
New Moon Beach
Great Stone of Fel
Sea of Narabor
Fellstone Lighthouse
Fellstone Heights
North Fellstone Bay
Rekkam Channel
Shipwreck Point
Dagness Peninsula
New City
The Bight
Iron Fortress
South Fellstone Bay
Fel Village
Fellstone Labor Compound
Sarth's Hideout
Meltem's Guest House
Old City
Capital Parkway
Naval Base
Silver Palace
West Bay Drive
The Boulevard
Old Docks
Mount Kellona
Floating City
Tent City
Imperial Docks
New Market
Old Market
The Old Bridge
Toddary District
Great Desert
Fel River
The Fel

# Table of Contents


In Memoriam .................................................................5

Acknowledgments .......................................................7

1. The Bus ...................................................................13

2. Jumpoff Jorm .........................................................23

3. Desert's Edge ..........................................................33

4. The Monastery ........................................................43

5. Desert Morning ......................................................47

6. Introductions .........................................................55

7. Attan ......................................................................63

8. The Library ............................................................69

9. The Dining Hall .....................................................81

10. Lost! .....................................................................89

11. Kahph ...................................................................95

12. Master Vessslu .....................................................105

13. Field Trip .............................................................113

14. Great Desert Safaris .............................................121

15. Loading the Bus ...................................................131

16. The Tonton Express ..............................................139

17. The Stone Bear .....................................................147

18. Sand Pirates .........................................................157

19. The Belowground ..................................................167

20. The Tower ............................................................179

21. The Tower Keeper .................................................189

22. Clerment ..............................................................199

23. The Artifact .........................................................207

24. Desert Trek ..........................................................215

25. Battle ..................................................................223

26. Viewpoints ...................................................................... 233

27. Squeaky ........................................................................... 239

28. Dinner with Kahph .......................................................... 245

29. Treason ............................................................................ 253

30. The Unbinding ................................................................ 265

31. With Honors..................................................................... 275

About the Author ................................................................... 298

About the Artist...................................................................... 299

$$-\,1\,-$$

# THE BUS

---

OUR BUS TURNED the corner just across the Old Bridge and ground its way southward on the Imperial Highway toward the Great Western Desert. Before it could gather momentum, it screeched to a halt at the command of a squad of armed Fessal soldiers in the road. The driver pulled our bus to the edge of the highway.

"Look at that!" Mid said, "A Seph Carrier, a big one!"

"It *is* a big one," Cheff agreed. "In fact, I've never seen one quite that large."

"I wonder where it's going?" Buttons asked.

"Monastery," Sable murmured from behind her long, black hair.

"That's where we're going," Cheff said. "With that monstrosity ahead of us, we're going to be poking along for hours."

"Maybe the driver can pass it?" I suggested.

"I doubt it," Mid said. "Look how it's accelerating."

Mid was right. The enormous Seph carrier had rounded the corner and was accelerating rapidly, huge billowing clouds of steam and thick, black coal smoke rising from its smokestack.

A soldier waved our bus on, and we continued on our way down the Imperial Highway along the west bank of the Fel River.

"I don't think it's going to hold us up much," Mid said.

Cheff said, "I had no idea those things could move so fast!"

"It… it's almost… out of sight… already…" Lery said. "That's… amazing."

"The right Seph carrier—" Mid prompted.

"—for the… the right Seph!" Lery finished.

We laughed.

"Who do you suppose is in it?" Buttons asked.

"Old," Sable said.

"Sable is correct," Cheff said. "A Seph big enough to need a carrier that size is certainly ancient. Maybe centuries old."

"So why is an elderly Seph going to the monastery?" Buttons asked.

"I don't know, Sis," Cheff said. "That's probably one of the things the FRM wants us to find out about."

Mid tapped Cheff on the shoulder. "Keep your voice low, Old Man. There are too many ears on this bus." He nodded his head toward the front, where Brex and her bunch of Bluebands sat. "We don't want to give them a reason to be interested in us during this trip."

"Cheff," Buttons whispered, "it looks like our Third Mission has started already!"

"Second mission," Cheff said.

"Second *official* mission," Buttons said. "Third, if you count Operation Break Iron."

"Well, yes, *if* you count—"

"Stop," Sable said.

"Quite so," Mid agreed. "Best not to have that conversation here."

"Right," Cheff said. "Thanks for the reminder, Old Son."

"Don't mention it, Old Man," Mid replied.

We rode along in silence, enjoying the scenery. As political prisoners, we seldom got to see much outside the Fellstone Labor Compound.

We passed through the industrial district that had grown up along the banks of the Fel River since The Fall. Most of the factories along the river had converted to steam power decades ago, though a few still had the dilapidated remains of the huge wooden water wheels once used to harness river power.

Everywhere we looked, people were hard at work. Steam trains puffed alongside factories. Horse-drawn wagons rumbled everywhere, punctuated with officious steam trucks and the occasional sleek, long, black staff car, no doubt filled with fat, pompous officials. On every corner, vendors in street carts sold bowls of steaming soup and grilled fish to hungry workers.

Some dozen miles (19 km) later, the factories gave way to houses, mostly for factory workers, I guessed. "Cheff," I asked, "didn't you live somewhere out this way?"

Cheff nodded soberly. "Pretty close. We lived in the Toddary District. We passed it already, but it was essentially the same as this one."

Cheff's father had been a manager in a factory, until one day the IID, the Imperial Intelligence Division, broke down his door, accused him of treason, and carted him off to prison. Cheff never saw him again.

I patted him gently on the shoulder. I understood. I lost my father in almost exactly the same way, except the soldiers shot him dead right in front of my mom and me. We were no strangers to loss—all of us kids in the Fellstone Labor Compound had lost fathers, mothers, aunts, uncles, brothers, sisters. That's what the Fellstone Labor Compound was for—families of deceased political offenders.

"It seems like another lifetime," Cheff said. "We had a nice house, decent furniture, and best of all, plenty to eat."

"Our mother used to take our extra food to the poor," Buttons said. "Sometimes she took me with her." Her lips set in a grim line. "I can't even remember what our father looked like anymore. But I still miss him sooo much! I mean, the ponies miss him."

"Easy, now." Cheff put his arm around Buttons' shoulders.

Buttons took her two stuffed ponies, Starry Stargazer and Mokacheena, out of their special pony-carrying backpack and hugged them close to her chest. She turned and stared out the bus window.

Sable reached over and patted Buttons' hand. Sable had lost her father, too, to a bogus charge of treason, many years before. Worse, we had learned, only a few weeks earlier, that Sable's father had been eaten by Sephs during a secret ceremony in the basement of the Iron Fortress.

"Okay, people," Cheff said, "we've let a glimpse of our old neighborhood cast a dark shadow on our mission. Let's shake off the gloom as best we can and focus on the things ahead."

Buttons held Starry and Moka up to her ear, listened, then nodded. "Okay, Cheff. The ponies say, onward and upward!"

Cheff tousled her hair. "Onward and upward it is! Well said, good and brave ponies!"

"Look!" Mid said, "It's the old Bulfer Mill." He pointed to an oddly shaped wooden building in the middle of the Fel River. "We studied it in my engineering class."

Mid was on the Engineering and Technology Track at the Labor Compound's Advanced School. We were all students there, except for Lery and Buttons, who attended Regular School in the building next to ours. Buttons would be in Advanced School with us next year.

"What's a Bulfer Mill?" I asked.

"Bulfer was a man who lived through The Fall," Cheff said, "over a hundred years ago. After the battles were over and Pallador proclaimed himself emperor, Mr. Bulfer settled here in Fellstone City. In those days, there was a lumber shortage, for much was needed to rebuild the city after the war. Old Bulfer got the idea that he'd make his fortune in the lumber business.

"He did, too. It seems that all the good places for lumber mills along the river had been taken, but somehow Bulfer managed to wangle a claim on that tiny piece of land in the middle of the river. It was quite a distance from Fellstone City, back in those days. Bulfer figured out how to rig a floating sawmill and anchored it to that tiny island. His descendants are still eking out a living there, cutting logs into lumber."

Mid said, "See how one end of the floating platform is anchored to the rocks on the east bank, and the other end to the island? But the platform with the mill itself is right in the swiftest part of the current, where it can get maximum power. Bulfer figured out how to float logs right down the river to the mill. No trucks needed, see? Once the lumber was cut, they put it on barges and floated it the rest of the way down the river to Fellstone City."

"Smart," Lery said.

"Yes, it is," Mid said. "At the time, no one had seen anything like it before. Bulfer's floating sawmill not only made him rich, it also made him famous."

A short distance from the Bulfer Mill, the Fel River gorge became a deep canyon, with sheer cliffs on each side. The road left the riverbank and wound its way up the steep basalt sides to the west.

"Goodbye, Fellstone City!" Cheff said. "We'll see you in a few days."

Starry and Moka each waved a hoof in farewell. "Goodbye, Fellstone City," Buttons said soberly.

"And hello, Great Western Desert!" Mid said.

Buttons looked up. "The Great Desert? Where? Are we there already?" The ponies peered eagerly out the window.

Cheff laughed. "Not yet. Soon. We have to traverse the Affeltip Gorge first."

"What's the Apple Tips gorge, Cheff? The ponies are exceptionally fond of apples, you know."

"It's '*Affle*tip,'" Cheff said. "Nothing to do with apples."

"Oh." The ponies seemed disappointed.

"The Imperial Highway follows the Affeltip Gorge," Mid said. "It's rough country. I don't know how people got to Fellstone City from the desert before the highway was made."

Cheff asked me, "What about it, Books? Do you have any inside information on the Affeltip Gorge or the Imperial Highway? What does your magic memory tell us, oh Great Reader?"

Cheff was referring to my ability to remember everything I ever read. It comes in handy, sometimes. It's not as easy as it sounds, though. I remember in pictures, not in words, so I have to work at it. First, I have to call up pictures of a book's pages in my mind, then 'read' them to see what they say. I recalled some information I had read once in some forbidden books my father kept hidden in our house. Some of them were ancient, from before The Fall.

"The Affeltip Gorge is a natural geological formation," I read from the picture in my mind, "caused by the meeting of the Theva Range, coming down from Stoopone, and the Minara Range coming up from Farpoint."

"Okay," Cheff said. "How about the Imperial Highway?"

"Before The Fall," I said, "The Imperial Highway was called the Royal Highway, because it was built by old King Maghorn."

"The same one who built the bridge between Old City and New City?" Mid asked.

"The same," I said. "He lived a long, long time before The Fall, hundreds of years. It was his idea to have a road that went all the way from Worldheart, through the Great Desert, to Fellstone City. It doesn't say anything specific about the Gorge."

"So," Buttons asked, "if we kept going on this road, we'd go all the way to Worldheart?"

"Maybe," I said. "I don't know for sure. I've read that Worldheart was destroyed during The Fall. Who knows if the highway still goes there, or if Worldheart is even there anymore?"

"Mmm… Worldheart," Buttons said dreamily. "I'd like to go there someday."

"Perhaps," Sable murmured.

"Do you think so?" Buttons asked.

"You never know," Cheff said. "It could happen, I suppose."

"How wonderful!" Buttons said. "Princes and princesses, carriages, stores and shops everywhere!"

"Lots… lots of… of food," Lery said.

Lery was the BSI's official cook and was always thinking about yummy things to eat.

"Don't get your hopes up," Mid said. "Worldheart is gone now, probably in ruins. The Fall was a long time ago."

"Only a hundred years ago, and a little more," Buttons said. "I learned it in school. Fellstone City is a lot older than that and it's still there."

"True," Cheff said. "Well, in that case, go ahead and get your hopes up! Maybe someday we'll see for ourselves."

As we climbed the Affeltip Gorge, the road got curvier and curvier. The old steam bus lurched from side to side as it made the hairpin turns of the winding road. Before long, Mid looked a little green.

"I don't feel so good," he said. "I think I'm going to… to…" He clamped his mouth shut and swallowed hard several times.

"Easy does it, Old Son," Cheff said. "Take long, slow, deep breaths."

"Distance," Sable said.

"Right," Cheff said. "Look out the window at the distance, as far away as you can."

"And move with the… the bus," Lery said. "Don't try to… to fight… the motion. Relax."

"Okay, okay," Mid said. "The breathing seems to be helping. A little, anyways."

Sable smiled. "Ocean."

Mid glanced at her, then looked out the window again. "It's not the same as what being seasick feels like. I never got seasick when I worked on the fishing boat, and sometimes the seas were pretty rough. This is something else: bus sickness. Arrgh! What a horrible feeling!"

I didn't feel anything, myself. Buttons and Cheff looked fine. Lery looked the same as ever, as did Sable. Of course, Sable came from a long line of sailors. Her father had been the captain of an Imperial Navy heavy cruiser before he was arrested. I thought it might help to change the subject. "Cheff," I said, "Brex and her Bluebands seem pretty occupied up front there. Do you think it's safe to brief us on our mission?"

"I think so," Cheff said. "Gather 'round. I don't have a lot of details, but the substance of it is this: the old Seph Monastery on the edge of the Great Desert is called 'Xanparthur.' It's been there a long time, longer than anyone can remember."

"But isn't a monastery a religious thing?" Mid asked. "Emperor Pallador has outlawed all religions."

"Xanparthur isn't religious," Cheff said. "It's more like a retreat or refuge."

"For whom?" Buttons asked.

"It seems," Cheff continued, "that throughout the ages there has always been a group of Sephs committed to peaceful co-existence with the other species."

"Peaceful Sephs?" Mid asked. "Pah! I don't believe it."

"Me… neither," Lery said. Before we met him, Lery had been cruelly treated by Sephs.

"It doesn't sound likely to me, either," Cheff said, "But that's what Zeek told me at the briefing."

Zeek Bonnovus operated the Fellstone Labor Compound's scrapyard. More important, he was an FRM agent, the BSI's liaison with the Fellstone Resistance Movement's headquarters in Old Fellstone City. And our friend.

"Zeek said that the FRM has recently learned about changes happening at Xanparthur and wants to know more about what's going on there and why Pallador is so interested."

"So they sent us?" Mid asked. "How… convenient. For *them*."

"There's more to the story," Cheff said. "The FRM has known about the monastery for some time. Apparently, the FRM has connections in the nearby resort town. Lately, it seems that there has been a major increase in activity at the monastery. Lots of Sephs being transported and convoys full of trucks. That sort of thing."

"That Seph carrier we saw must be one of them," Buttons said.

"I believe it was," Cheff agreed. "If so, we'll see it again, I'm sure. Anyway, as of a few weeks ago, as part of Emperor Pallador's 'Path of Enlightenment' program, the Imperium has been sending buses of school kids on excursions to Xanparthur. It's supposed to be proof that Sephs are peaceful and benevolent and well-meaning."

"But… they're not…" Lery said.

"Of course they're not," Cheff said. "We've seen that for ourselves. And the FRM knows it, too. That's why—"

"That's why they're sending the Bayside Insurgents up for a look-see, right, Cheff?" Buttons asked. "The BSI does jobs only kids can do!"

"Exactly right," Cheff said. "We're supposed to act like normal school kids on a normal school trip and look around, see what we can see. Nothing dangerous, this time."

"We *are* normal school kids on a normal school trip," Mid said. "We were going to go to Xanparthur anyway. Our whole school is on this trip."

"Right," Cheff said. "So there's nothing suspicious at all. We go along with the other kids, learn what we can, then report back. Nothing to it."

"Yeah." Mid frowned. "Nothing to it. Right."

"There's one more thing," Cheff said. "Zeek submitted our proposal of Lhuk as a prospective BSI member, and it went all the way up to Madame Entigy herself. Lhuk's been approved. We can approach him about it when we feel the time is right."

Buttons clapped her hands. "Yay! That makes the ponies happy!"

Lhuk was a Torph boy about Buttons' age and her special friend.

"Not so fast," Cheff said. "Madame Entigy had a look into Lhuk's family. Remember how Lhuk told us his folks had been sent to a Torph Camp somewhere out West? And do you remember, on our last mission, that Rayce told us that there are no Torph Camps, that the Torphs are simply killed, or maybe even eaten?"

Buttons nodded soberly.

"Well, Madame Entigy verified that Lhuk's parents have both been dead for some time. We're supposed to tell Lhuk that, too."

Buttons' face lost all expression. "I don't want to do that."

"Me neither, Sis, but it looks like we're going to have to."

# — 2 —

# JUMPOFF JORM

---

FTER ANOTHER TWO hours, the bus driver stopped at a rest stop on the top of the mountain pass. "Twenty-minute break, everybody off. Stretch your legs, use the facilities, and admire the view."

We were in the parking lot of a small way-station carved out of a tall cliff. A sign said:

## JUMPOFF JORM SUMMIT
### 7239 FEET (2200m)

I wondered who Jorm was and what prompted him to go over the edge. I searched my memories, but found nothing. I couldn't see the bottom of the gorge, as it was obscured by mist. The mist was a long way down.

Another bus had arrived right before us. A number of the kids sat on the low rock parapet that ringed the edge of the parking lot. A few even dangled their legs over the side. I shivered.

"Yeah, me too," Cheff said. "Not that I'm afraid of heights, you know. I just don't see any reason to hang myself half off them! Let's go find a snack or something."

As soon as Cheff uttered the word 'snack,' Buttons appeared at his elbow as if by magic. "Snack? Did you say we could get a snack, Cheff? The ponies would like that!" Starry and Moka glanced eagerly toward the food stands. "Wherever did you find the money? The ponies demand to know!"

Cheff laughed. "Sure, let's all get a snack, ponies included. As it turns out, I have a few small coins left over from selling meat I hunted. Also, Zeek gave me some money for 'BSI expenses,' or so he said."

"Ha!" Mid said. "That's a fib if I ever heard one. More likely, he dug into his own pocket on our behalf."

"He gave… gave me a… a little bit of money, too," Lery said. "He's a… a good… boss."

Lery worked for Zeek at the scrapyard every afternoon after school, his mandatory labor assignment at the Labor Compound. Zeek had arranged it that way, and it worked out well for us.

Without comment, Sable handed Cheff a fistful of coins, too, then wandered off toward the restrooms. Sable always seemed to have a little spending money. She never told us where it came from, but we assumed it came from her occasional job in Fellstone New City, helping a well-to-do woman tend her house.

Except for Buttons, who was in her last year of Basic School, and Lery, who was in Regular School, we were all in Advanced Secondary School, and exempt from mandatory work assignments. We were supposed to spend our afternoons working on our various school projects. Students from Regular Secondary School, like Lery, either had mandatory labor assignments in one of the many factories in the Fellstone Labor Compound or else joined the Bluebands and later the army. As bad as that sounds, it was worse for adults. Adult mandatory labor was a ten-hour workday.

Buttons pointed toward Lhuk, who stood alone near the parapet, gazing over the cliff. "Look, Cheff! There's Lhuk, all by himself. He looks lonesome. Is there enough money to get him a treat, too? If not, he can have mine. I don't mind."

"Why, Buttons, that's most kind of you! Sure, I think we can afford to include Lhuk. Would you like to ask him to join us?"

"Thank you, Cheff! That makes the ponies happy! We'll meet you there." Buttons and the ponies ran off to fetch Lhuk.

Brex and her Bluebands were already at the food stands. Brex narrowed her eyes and glared at us, particularly Cheff, as we approached, but didn't say anything—yet.

Lhuk and Buttons joined us at the snack shop. Lhuk smiled at us shyly. We each picked our treats from the surprisingly large selection. I picked a pastry with a kind of creamy filling. It was sweet.

We ambled back to the parapet, partly to enjoy the view, and partly to put a little distance between us and Brex's Blueband gang. It wasn't wise to attract the interest of those snoops, but, unfortunately, we had. Brex gave the six of us plenty of special attention.

I took off my glasses to wipe them on my shirttail as I did often, but then noticed that my glasses were clean—no grimy soot like they accumulated in the Labor Compound. I inhaled a deep breath of the pure mountain air. Delicious! "Hey, guys! Look how clean the air is here. My glasses aren't even dirty!"

Mid took a few whiffs. "That beats the smoke and soot in Fellstone City, for sure."

As we finished our treats, Brex's number-one admirer and Blueband subordinate, Tocette, shuffled over. As usual, her Blueband uniform shirt was spotted and wrinkled, and her stringy, greasy hair was tangled into rats' nests. She smacked Cheff on the back so hard that the last bit of his sweet roll flew out of his mouth and over the parapet, into the void below. Cheff watched it fall, wistfully. Tocette stuffed the last of her own sweet roll into her mouth and brayed, spraying Cheff with a shower of crumbs, "Hiya, Cheff! How's things?"

"Why, it's the Beautiful and Intrepid Tocette! Nice to see you. Are you having a good trip so far?" Cheff brushed the crumbs off his vest and edged away.

"I sure am, Cheff! I love bus rides." She grabbed me and crushed my face into her chest in a huge hug. "Hiya, Booksie! How's my little Booksie Buddy doing?"

Now I, too, was covered in crumbs. "Um, hi, Tocette. It's, um, good to see you again. I'm doing great. How's Miss Brex treating you these days?"

"Brex? Oh, well, you know Brex. She's always—" Brex, though out of earshot, glanced our way and transfixed Tocette with her infamous Glare of Daggers. "Er, that is, I mean, um, well, Brex is fine. Wonderful. Like she always is." Tocette shuddered, then turned her back on Brex and walked away along the parapet.

"Is that the Great Western Desert down there?" Buttons asked, pointing to the hazy, greenish-brown landscape, stretching off into the distance toward the western horizon.

"I think it is," Mid said. "It's hard to tell from here."

"It is," Lery said. "I was… was here one time… a long time… ago." He looked pretty uncomfortable, and Cheff didn't pursue it.

Our bus's horn sounded three long blasts.

"That's it," Cheff said. "Time's up. Everybody have a chance to use the facilities? Great! Let's get on board. Lhuk, how would you like to come sit with us?"

Lhuk glanced up at Cheff, the ghost of a smile playing about his mouth. "Okay."

Cheff directed us to the back of the bus, as far from Brex's group as possible. We settled in for the next leg of the trip: winding down the Gorge to the desert below.

When the bus was underway and making enough noise that our conversation would be inaudible to Brex, Cheff motioned Lhuk to come close. We put our heads together.

Cheff whispered, "Lhuk, there are a few things we need to tell you. But first, we must have your guarantee of complete silence, for your safety as well as ours."

Lhuk nodded. "Of course."

"The six of us," Cheff continued, "are members of a secret organization called the Bayside Insurgents or BSI. It's a small, but official, part of the FRM. So far, we're the only members: me, Mid, Lery, Sable, Buttons, and Books."

"And Starry and Moka, don't forget!"

"Right, Starry and Moka, too."

Lhuk smiled a little. He'd been friends with the ponies for a while.

"One of the things we're supposed to do," Mid said, "along with bringing down Pallador's government and locating the True Heir to the Sixth Kingdom, is to recruit other members."

"And that's where you come in." Cheff smiled and patted Lhuk on the shoulder. "We proposed you for membership. We only found out yesterday that you passed your background check, and we're directed to invite you to become a member."

Lhuk stared at Cheff.

"Come on, Lhuk," Buttons urged. "Don't you want to bring down Pallador and his Imperium and find the True Heir?"

Lhuk shrugged. "Not especially, but thanks for thinking of me."

"Not especially?" Buttons asked. "Not *especially*? Why in Andaran not?"

Lhuk smiled sadly. "What's the point? Besides getting yourselves killed, or worse, what good can you do? The Imperium is the Imperium. It's just how things are."

"But of all people—" Buttons started.

"Because I'm a Torph? Because the Empire hates Torphs? That alone is an excellent reason not to draw attention to myself. I'm the only Torph in the Labor Compound. That gets me way too much attention as it is."

"Brex," Sable said.

"That's right," Cheff said. "Brex is a Torph, and she's in the Labor Compound."

"True," Lhuk said. "But look at what she has to do to be accepted. She's the very model of a loyal Blueband and future soldier of the Empire." He made a sour face. "Makes me sick."

"Of course it does," Cheff said. "The whole Torph situation is sickening."

"I just want to keep quiet and out of sight until I'm old enough to join my parents at the Torph Camp out west."

"I understand." Cheff stared at his lap. The rest of us looked away.

"What?" Lhuk asked. "What is it?"

Cheff shook his head.

"Tell me, Cheff," Lhuk insisted. "Is it about my parents? Did you learn something? If you know something, Cheff, you *have* to tell me."

Cheff looked Lhuk in the eye, then took a deep breath. "Okay. You're right, of course. We did learn something about your parents, and we do have to tell you about it. But…"

"But what? I have to join your ISB first?"

"No, of course not," Cheff said.

"And it's BSI, not ISB," Buttons added.

Cheff signaled her to keep quiet.

"Rayce," Sable said. "Fel village."

"Who's Rayce?" Lhuk asked, his voice becoming shrill. "And what does he have to do with my parents? Does he know them?"

"We'll tell you everything right now," Cheff said. "But keep your voice calm. No point in alarming Brex."

Lhuk composed himself. "Okay, Cheff. I'm calm. Now tell me."

"Our last mission for the FRM—"

"—Which was our first *official* mission—"

"Buttons, *please.*"

"Sorry, Cheff."

"Our last mission for the FRM took us deep into The Fel. We found a village of people living out there. A Torph man named Rayce is their leader. They've been out there for decades, some of them. Most of them are Torphs, but the other Peoples are represented, too. They are there because they learned that they were to be sent to the Torph Camps. Only, there aren't any Torph Camps."

"Of course there are Torph Camps!" Lhuk said. "My parents are in one, out west."

"I'm sorry, Lhuk, but it's certain—there are no Torph Camps. When we got back from the mission, when we proposed you for membership in the BSI, we asked if what Rayce said was true. The answer came down from Madame Ent—er, from the highest levels: Rayce was right—there are no Torph Camps."

"Then where are my mother and father?" Lhuk asked. "In prison somewhere? In the Iron Fortress?"

Cheff hung his head. He couldn't bring himself to say the words.

Sable put her hand on Lhuk's shoulder.

"No!" Lhuk said. "No, it isn't true! It can't be true! I'm supposed to join them there when I'm of age. Out west!" Lhuk looked at each one of us in turn. "You're... you're only saying this so I'll join your little club!"

Cheff looked up, tears streaming from his eyes. "I'm so sorry, Lhuk. I didn't want to have to tell you, but you deserve to know the truth."

Lhuk looked deep into Cheff's eyes until he could see the truth of the matter for himself. Then he buried his face in his hands and wept bitterly. We comforted him as best we could, which wasn't much.

After a while, Lhuk stopped crying and wiped his face. "I don't care. I'm still not joining your stupid club!" And he stomped off to the middle of the bus and found a seat by himself.

After a while, Mid said, "That went well."

Buttons glared at Mid, then stomped off to sit with Lhuk, but Lhuk turned away and stared out the window.

"Necessary," Sable murmured.

"I know it was," Cheff said. "But it still stinks. Sometimes I wish someone else was in charge."

"You… you did… good…" Lery said. "There's no… no nice way… to tell something… rotten."

"Lery's right, Cheff," I said. "You did as well as could be done."

"I know, Books, but thank you for saying it. It's a shame he didn't want to join us, though."

"Time," Sable said. "Patience."

"True," I said. "He's had a shock, the worst shock anyone can have. Let's concentrate on being his friend for a while, like Buttons is doing. Maybe, in time, he'll come around."

*Lhuk and Squeaky*

# OPERATION SHIFTING SANDS

## — 3 —

## DESERT'S EDGE

---

OVER THE NEXT few hours, our bus wound its way down the western slope of the Affeltip Gorge. It was slow going, as the road was narrow in spots with many hairpin turns. Gradually the grade grew less steep and the turns less severe, until, at last, we found ourselves on a long, straight stretch of highway.

"This is it," Cheff said, "the Great Western Desert. I've never seen it before. In fact, this is the farthest west I've ever been."

"Me, too," Mid said. "I wasn't prepared for just how…"

"Magnificent," Sable murmured.

"Yeah, that's it," Mid said. "Magnificent!"

"I wish Lhuk could see it with us," Buttons said. She had returned to sit with us, though Lhuk stayed where he was, scrunched down into his seat, staring straight ahead.

"Me, too," I said. "This is interesting. I always thought that the desert would be nothing but sand, but it's full of things. A *lot* of things."

"Things?" Lery asked. "What kind of… things?"

"Well…" Cheff surveyed the landscape. "There are a lot of plants."

"Funny-looking plants," Buttons said. "No grass, no leaves, only those funny-looking things. The ponies say they don't look good to eat."

"Too many… stickers…" Lery said.

"They're called cacti," I said. "I saw a book, once, back in Tumberland. It was a little kids' book called *The Great Western Desert*. It was mostly pictures. I recognize some of these cacti, like that one there, with the tall, grooved stalks. The book said that cacti are specially designed to live where there is little water."

"Makes sense," Cheff said, "since there isn't much water here, yet there are plenty of cacti."

"What about animals, Books?" Buttons asked. "The ponies want to know what kind of animals live here."

"I don't… don't see any… animals," Lery said.

"The book said there are lots of animals," I said, "but they mostly come out at night, when it's cooler."

"What kind of animals, Books?" Buttons insisted.

I closed my eyes and brought up images of the old book's pages. "Well, let's see. There are snakes and lizards, several kinds of small rodents, like mice and such, and something called a desert pup that lives in holes in the ground."

"Birds," Sable said.

"Are there birds, Books?" Buttons asked. "What does the book say about birds?"

"Yes, there are many kinds of small birds and a few species of large birds. Carrion eaters."

"What's a… a carrion eater?" Lery asked.

"It eats dead things," Cheff said.

"Yuck!" Buttons stuck her tongue out. "That's disgusting."

"Depends on how you look at it, Sis," Cheff said. "We eat dead things almost every day, don't we? When the hunting is good."

"Well, I guess so… but we cook 'em first."

"And I'm grateful for that," Mid said. "Think of carrion eaters as the desert clean-up crew. Without them, the desert would be full of dead things."

"Okay," Buttons said, and shuddered. "Cleanup crew is good. But I don't have to like them."

Cheff pointed out the window at a large, dog-like animal. It stood motionless in the shade of a desert bush, watching our bus go by.

The ponies waved. "Hello, doggy," Buttons said. "I hope you're friendly."

"Easy does it with the wildlife," Cheff said. "You need to remember that desert animals aren't pets—they're wild and can be dangerous."

"Mr. Grumbles was wild, and he was nice."

Mr. Grumbles was a Fel bear that took a liking to Buttons during our mission in The Fel. He followed us around for a while and even saved our lives once.

"That's true," Cheff said. "And I'm truly glad I didn't have to tell Aunt Dee how you were torn to bits by a savage wild beast. Still, you can't count on all wild animals being as friendly as Mr. Grumbles. So be careful, okay?"

"Okay, Cheff. I'll be careful." Buttons picked up Starry and Moka in one hand, and wagged the forefinger of her other hand in their noses. "I've explained it to the ponies, and they agree to be careful, too."

"Glad to hear it," Cheff said.

"There's one more thing," I said. "The book has pictures of spiders."

"Sure," Mid said. "Spiders are everywhere."

"Not like this one," I said. "This one's big."

"Ugh!" Mid made a face. "I don't like spiders, especially big ones."

"Really, *really* big," I said.

"Double ugh!" Mid said. He wrapped his arms around himself. "What's it called?"

"The Colossal Jumping Spider," I said.

"Oh, great," Mid said. "Colossal *Jumping* Spider. What could possibly go wrong?"

Cheff laughed. "Maybe Buttons can find you a friendly one, Mid. You can name it Mr. Jumpers."

"Not funny, Old Man," Mid said.

"Maybe that's what happened to old Jumpoff Jorm," Cheff said. "I can see him now, sitting on the ledge, maybe nibbling an apple or a sweet roll, and a Colossal Jumping Spider comes along, and—"

Lery reached out and grabbed Mid by both shoulders.

"Arrgh!" Mid jumped out of his seat, frantically brushing invisible spiders off his clothes.

We cracked up.

"What's going on back there?" the bus driver called.

"Nothing, sir, sorry," Cheff said. "Minor spider problem."

Mid fisted Cheff in the ribs. "Andaran's bones, Cheff."

Cheff laughed.

"Sit down and keep it quiet back there!" the bus driver yelled.

"Yes, sir," Cheff said, pulling Mid back down into his seat. "Sorry, sir." But he didn't look all that sorry to me.

We rode a long way through the desert. This section of the Imperial Highway was flat, straight, and long. Eventually, far off in the distance, a white blur appeared on the western horizon. As we approached, the blur became a cluster of small white buildings around a little pond. Behind that, high on a hill, a ghostly, sand-colored building was silhouetted against the brilliant orange sunset. It had many levels and terraces, pillars, spires, and domes. A majestic golden dome crowned the top. A high wall enclosed the entire structure. It was big, much bigger than the Iron Fortress in Fellstone City. But while the Iron Fortress was dark and forbidding, this one seemed warm and inviting.

"Look, Cheff!" Buttons said. "That must be the monastery!"

"Seems likely," Cheff agreed. "I didn't expect it to be so big!"

The highway curved around the north side of the cluster of small buildings, which turned out to be a pleasant-looking little town shaded by hundreds of palm trees. A gravel road turned off the main road and led up to the monastery.

We made good time. About an hour before sundown, our bus pulled into a large, graveled yard in front of the immense building we'd seen at sunset. The other bus, the one we'd seen at the wayside rest stop, was already there, disgorging its cargo of tired children.

"Xanparthur Monastery," the bus driver called. "Everybody out. Be sure to get all your gear. I'll be back to pick you up in four days. Make sure you're here—it's a long walk back to Fellstone City."

We gathered our gear and got off the bus. No one was in the graveled yard to meet us, so we milled about, waiting for something to happen. Our bus closed its doors, blew its whistle, and rolled out of the yard, returning the way we came. We watched it until it disappeared into the distance. Complete silence reigned. At the far end of the parking area, a gate broke the continuity of the wall. The outer wall and the walls of the buildings were the same color as the desert sand, but their roofs were made of what appeared to be baked red-clay tiles. We saw no sign of movement.

"Look!" I whispered, although I didn't know why I was whispering. "Parked over there, by the wall. Isn't that the huge Seph carrier that passed us at the beginning of the trip?"

Cheff walked a short distance toward it to get a better look. The rest of us followed him, taking care to walk softly. It was so quiet out there in the desert that it seemed somehow wrong to disturb the silence.

"I think it's the same one," Cheff said. "Makes sense. Giant Seph carrier takes a giant Seph to the Giant Seph monastery. Works for me."

"Do you think we'll meet him?" Mid asked. "Could he be part of Emperor Pallador's enlightenment program?"

"He must be quite old, like Sable mentioned," Cheff said. "I wonder what things he could tell us."

"Do you think he'd know about Worldheart, Cheff?" Buttons asked.

"Maybe," Cheff said. "Tell you what—if we meet him, feel free to ask him."

"I… I don't… don't want to… meet any… any Sephs," Lery said. "I… I don't like… Sephs."

Lery had grown up among Sephs and their Fessal Facilitators. He didn't talk much about his past, but we knew that they had mistreated him cruelly. Once he was beaten so badly that his foot became permanently lame.

"I'm afraid we'll have to meet some Sephs at some point," Cheff said. "After all, that's supposedly why we're here, right? To be 'enlightened' by 'peaceful' Sephs?" He put his arm around Lery's shoulders. "Don't worry, Friend Lery. Stick close to us, and you'll have nothing to worry about."

"Okay… Friend Cheff, if… if you say so."

Out of the corner of my eye, I saw a flicker of movement in the brush near the edge of the parking area. I squinted into the half-light. There was another tiny movement. "There's something over there, in the brush." I pointed.

Cheff and the others peered in the direction I was pointing. There was another rustle of brush, and a small creature emerged. He was about the size of a large cat, but built more along the lines of a mink or a weasel. He stood up on his hind legs and sniffed the air, then dropped to all fours and came toward us.

"Look, Cheff, he's so cuuute!" Buttons ran toward the little creature.

"Buttons! Wait! Stop!" Cheff said. "What did I just say about being careful with the wildlife?"

But it was too late. Buttons was already on her knees, offering the little creature some crumbs left over from our snack. The creature accepted the crumbs, then sniffed around Buttons' backpack and pockets for more.

"He's adooorable!" Buttons said. "What is he?"

"It's one of those desert pups I mentioned before," I said. "Don't worry, Cheff—the book says they're not aggressive, and that they're smart."

Buttons bent over and spoke to the pup. "You're not aggressive, are you?"

Brex appeared out of nowhere, Tocette right behind her. "And exactly what is going on here?" Brex demanded.

The desert pup vanished into the brush, confirming his intelligence.

"Hello, Miss Brex," Buttons said. "You look lovely today."

"Never mind that!" Brex snapped. "I want to know the meaning of this!"

"The meaning of what, Miss Brex?" Cheff asked innocently.

"Why are you interacting with the indigenous fauna?"

"Fauna?" Mid asked. "You mean that little desert pup? He's harmless. Came looking for a handout, is all."

Brex stuck her flushed face right into Mid's. "Do you mean to tell me that you actually *fed* that wild animal?"

"Why, no, Miss Brex," Mid said. "I only meant to tell you that it was *looking* for a handout. I didn't feed him anything."

Buttons surreptitiously replaced her bits of food into her backpack, then looked off across the desert.

"And you'd better not, either!" Brex growled. "In fact, you'd all better be on your best behavior while we're here. This is a Extremely Special Privilege, visiting this monastery, and you'd all better act like it. We represent the Fellstone Labor Compound. We're supposed to be examples of the results of Pallador's 'Path of Enlightenment' programs."

"Yes, Miss Brex," Cheff said.

"Do you think the lot of you, just this once, can spend the next four days being examples and not bring shame or embarrassment on me, or the Labor Compound, or the Emperor? For a change? Well, do you?"

"Yes, Miss Brex, of course we can," Cheff said, "and we will. We promise."

The rest of us agreed enthusiastically.

One by one, Brex pierced us with her icicle eyes. "You'd better. You'd all better not embarrass me, or, by Andaran's Bones, when we get back to the Labor Compound I'll make your lives a living nightmare! Why is it that everywhere you go, you—"

Brex's eyes unfocused and she stared off into the distance until a trickle of saliva leaked from the corner of her mouth and ran down her chin. She came back to herself abruptly and wiped the spittle with the sleeve of her immaculate Blueband uniform.

"What is it, Miss Brex?" Cheff asked. "Are you okay? Is there something we can help you with?"

"What? Oh, er, I'm, uh, fine. For an instant, I thought... I saw..." Brex pulled herself together. "Of course I'm fine, you ninny. You'd better be sure you do as I say. I don't want any trouble from you or your grubby friends on this trip. Remember, I'll be watching you."

She spun on her heel to stalk back to her squad of Bluebands, but her knees buckled and she almost fell. Tocette rushed over and took her elbow. "Are you okay, Miss Brex? Did you hurt yourself? Let me help you."

"Of course I'm all right! Leave me alone, you idiot. Unhand me at once!"

Brex drew herself upright, mustered what little dignity she could, and marched back to her group.

Tocette exchanged a look of concern with Cheff, started to speak, thought the better of it, and lumbered off after Brex.

We stared after them, then Mid asked, "What just happened?"

"Memory," Sable said.

"Memory?" Mid asked. "What did she remember?"

"I couldn't say for sure," Cheff said. "But if I had to guess, I'd say that The Forgetting didn't work as well as we'd hoped."

On our last mission, Brex had inadvertently followed us to a Fel village. To protect their secrecy, the Fel elders had performed an ancient technique on Brex called The Forgetting. It had seemed to be working—until now.

"Not good," Mid said. "Not good at all. What do you think she'll remember? Everything?"

"Dreams," Sable said.

"That's right," Cheff said. "The Fel healer told us that if she does remember anything, it will be like remembering a dream. It won't seem real, she said."

"Let's hope that's the case," Mid said. He looked all around. "What do you think is supposed to happen? Are they going to leave us out here all night?"

"I hope not," Cheff said. "We're at a pretty high altitude, I think, maybe as much as five thousand feet (1500m). Mr. Rishten said that it gets exceedingly cold after sundown in the desert."

Mr. Rishten was Cheff's and my Civilian Leadership instructor. I was learning Archiving and Library Management, while Cheff was studying Factory Management. Mr. Rishten had briefed us on what to expect on this field trip.

"Well, he was right," Mid said. "I'm already starting to get cold."

A door opened in the side of the building, spilling yellow light into the growing darkness, then closed again. Shortly, a Fessal Facilitator, resplendent in his red and gold uniform, approached our group, looked us over, then addressed Brex.

"Good evening, Miss...?"

"Brex."

"Good evening, Miss Brex. I am Snard, one of the chief Facilitators here." He signaled for all the children from both buses to join us. "I would like to welcome you all to Xanparthur Monastery. I apologize for the delay in greeting you, but we were unavoidably delayed by the arrival of a V.I.S."

"A V.I.S., sir?" Brex asked.

"Very Important Seph." He nodded toward the huge Seph carrier. "He's old and wise. If you are most fortunate, you may meet him while you're here, but I can't guarantee anything. He went directly to his quarters and requested seclusion."

Snard walked toward the building. "Now, if you will all be so kind as to follow me, we can see about getting you some supper and a place to sleep for the night."

# — 4 —

## THE MONASTERY

---

SUPPER SOUNDED LIKE a great idea to me, until Cheff said, "Don't eat anything that looks like it might have a lot of jexan in it."

"Do you think there's jexan in use here at the monastery, Old Man?" Mid asked.

"Probably not," Cheff said, "but let's not take any chances."

Jexan was a drug that we, I mean the BSI, with the help of To-cette, discovered on our first unofficial mission. Pallador's government used it to 'adjust' the mood of its citizens. Which is to say, to make them more pliable, easier to convince to support the Emperor. A mostly tasteless white powder, jexan was added to all kinds of powdered products, such as flour and sugar. We needed to stick with meats and vegetables, and avoid breads and sauces. And, unfortunately, desserts.

Snard the Facilitator proudly led all the children from both buses through the magnificently sculptured wooden doors into a large room with a high vaulted ceiling. The inside walls looked the same as the outside walls: sand-colored stucco with a swirly texture.

Two long wooden tables ran the length of the room. It looked like they were designed to seat fifty people each, twenty-five on a side, which was about right. Our two buses totaled a shade under one hundred children. At the far end of the room were two identical food lines, mirror images of each other, one for each table.

Snard said, "Well, line up, children! No point in letting it get cold!"

Cheff waited until he saw which line Brex and her Bluebands got into, then led us to the other one. We loaded up our trays and found seats together. After Cheff's reminder about jexan, I felt a little guilty about choosing three desserts, until I looked around and saw that all our gang had the same idea, except for Cheff. He had four.

He saw me looking at his tray and the expression on my face. "Well, Books, a *little* you-know-what won't brainwash us, will it? After all, we get a little every day in our regular food, right?"

I took my seat. That sounded fine to me.

"Reasonable," Sable said quietly.

"*Very* reasonable, Cheff," Mid said through a mouthful of apple pie. Like the rest of us, Mid had opted to eat his dessert first. "It's good to be reasonable." He took another huge bite. "We always want to be reasonable." A shower of pie crumbs covered the table.

"Reasonable is… is good… Friend Cheff." Lery laughed so hard he could barely speak.

Buttons elaborately fed both Starry and Moka hearty helpings of a cupcake, then made them dance on their hind legs, front legs spread wide. She made the ponies sing. "We're just like Tocette, but please don't you fret. We thrive on jexan, so don't you be— Cheff? The ponies can't think of a rhyme for"—she lowered her voice—"jexan."

"Brexan," Sable said, deadpan.

"Brexan, Brexan," Buttons recited quietly, "the opposite of jexan. Jexan makes you feel good, but Brexan is always quite rude. Wait, that doesn't quite rhyme." She frowned.

We laughed heartily.

"It almost rhymes," I said. "Close enough, anyway."

Buttons and the ponies took a bow.

"You'd better stop, Sis," Cheff said when he could talk again. "It's probably not a good idea to mention the J-word too much around here, even quietly."

"Right, Cheff." The ponies continued their dance in silence.

We ate until our plates were clean, then went back for seconds and ate until our bellies felt like they were going to burst. There isn't much food in the Fellstone Labor Compound. The occasional field trip or other outing is about the only time we ever get enough to eat. So, of course, we make a point of taking maximum advantage of Pallador's Bounty, whenever we encounter it.

When we finished eating, Snard marched us through a maze of corridors to a large hall full of beds. It was a little bigger than the dining hall and had a row of windows along one side. "Choose your own sleeping arrangements, children. All the beds are exactly the same. Necessary facilities are through the doors on each side of the room, girls on my right, boys on my left. The lights will go out in about a half hour. I'll be back for you bright and early. Sleep well!" He closed the door behind him.

Cheff chose our beds well away from Brex and her gang. Lhuk chose a bed as far away from us as possible. I looked around the room. I only knew a few of the kids, the ones from class, but that's all. But then, I was a relative newcomer to the Labor Compound. Cheff, on the other hand, had been at the Compound for years.

I asked Cheff, "Who are all these other kids? Do you know them?"

"Most of them look familiar," Cheff said. "Quite a few I recognize from Basic School. The rest are probably new since I started Advanced School. It looks like the entire Fellstone Labor Compound student body is on this trip. I think the other bus was the Basic School students. Some of the kids are pretty young."

"Hey! I'm pretty young!" Buttons said. "And I was on the Advanced bus."

"True, but you're a special case."

"I am?"

"Sure. The Basic teachers asked me to try to keep you from biting the other students, and I told them I could only guarantee your behavior if you rode on the same bus with me. Ooof!"

One of the ponies had kicked Cheff soundly in his belly.

"That's a big fat lie, Cheff! I *never* bit anybody, ever. Well, almost never. But he had it coming!"

After we had used the 'necessary facilities,' while we were getting ready for bed, Brex strode up officiously. "I see you managed to get through the day without embarrassing yourselves or me. Hmmph! Three more days to go. We'll see how long you last. I'd love to report something that would banish you from all future field trips forever! I'm watching you, every single moment." She spun on her heel and marched back to her troops.

"Oh *dear*," Mid said. "She'll be *watching* us. What*ever* shall we do?"

Cheff raised the back of his hand to his forehead in mock distress. "Every moment, no less. Oh dear, oh dear, oh dear." He shook his head sadly.

"No… please… not every… every moment." Lery brushed an imaginary tear from his eye and flicked it away with his forefinger. "I can't… can't… bear it."

Buttons was giggling too hard to talk. Even Sable was smiling. A little. I think. The lights went out. We said our goodnights, and I drifted off to sleep.

# — 5 —

## DESERT MORNING

FACILITATOR SNARD HAD been sincere in his promise to return bright and early—I could still see stars shining through the windows. "Wake up, children, wake up! It's time to get ready for the day. And what an exciting day it will be! How fortunate you children are to have been chosen to visit Xanparthur Monastery, the shining star of our beloved Emperor Pallador's 'Path of Enlightenment' program. I'll be back in a half-hour to take you to breakfast."

A half-hour later found us not only ready, but eager and willing. We followed Facilitator Snard through the maze of corridors, drawn to the enticing odors of traditional Fellstone breakfast meats, smoked fish, and grains. The day promised a fine start.

"Thirty minutes!" Facilitator Snard announced as he held the door open for us. "Don't overeat! You'll want to be bright and attentive for the educational program today."

Exactly thirty minutes later, Snard returned to the dining hall. "Time's up! Let's go! Quickly, quickly!"

"He wasn't kidding about the half-hour, was he?" I asked.

"A most precise fellow," Mid said, in an exaggerated Fessal accent.

"I, for one, am feeling both bright *and* attentive," Cheff said. He yawned, then stretched elaborately.

"I can see that, Old Man," Mid said. The room was nearly empty. "Shall we be going?"

"Absolutely we shall be going, Old Son," Cheff said.

He and Mid flashed Facilitator Snard big grins as they passed through the double doors.

We followed Snard through a new and different maze of corridors. This time, we filed past dozens of closed doors. "Quietly, now, children," Snard advised. "Each of these rooms belongs to one of the Seph monks. We do not wish to distract them from their studies and contemplations."

Lery sniffed, then wrinkled his nose. "Seph." He shivered. "I don't… like Sephs."

"Steady, Brother Lery," Mid whispered. "These Sephs aren't likely to be ones you've met before. And even if they are, I doubt they'll recognize you. You look the perfect Regular Secondary School student."

Lery smiled, then frowned. "Except for… for my…height. And… my age. I'm much too old… to be in… Regular Secondary School."

"True," Cheff said. "But you don't look old, you see, because you're in Regular Secondary School. So you can't be the Lery who used to work at the Iron Fortress, right? That wouldn't make sense."

"I… know, Friend Cheff… That's… why I'm… so worried."

"No need to worry," Cheff said. "Follow along quietly and try to look younger. And try not to limp, if you can."

"Okay… Cheff. I will try. The… brace that… Mid… made me… helps a lot. And you can't… can't even tell I have it… have it on under… my pants."

"It's true, Cheff," Buttons said. "Lery walks so well now that the ponies say they forgot he even had a limp."

Lery reached over and petted Starry, then Moka, who rode proudly in their special pony-carrying backpack. "Good… ponies."

Buttons sparkled.

"Come along, you in the back!" Facilitator Snard waved us on urgently. "No dilly-dallying!"

From time to time we passed an open doorway, through which we peered eagerly for a sight of a Seph monk. Mostly the rooms we could see into were empty, except, perhaps, for a Fessal Facilitator fluffing the huge, elaborately decorated cushions the Sephs preferred.

Through one such door, however, we caught a glimpse of a giant Seph, coiled on his big pillow, being groomed by a Facilitator, a Fessal woman. She took one look at us, then gently kicked the door shut.

"Did you see that?" I asked. "That Seph was enormous!"

"Bigger than any we've ever seen before," Mid said.

Cheff said, "Mr. Rishten told us that most of the Sephs here at the monastery are extremely old. Hundreds of years old, some of them. I should have realized they'd be correspondingly large."

"Because why, Cheff?" Buttons asked.

"Because Sephs never stop growing," Cheff explained.

"You mean they keep growing bigger and bigger?" The ponies exchanged an incredulous look.

"Right," Mid said, "They keep growing until they die. The same as trees."

"Are there going to be any girl Sephs here?" Buttons asked.

"I don't know, Sis. I've never seen a Seph female that I know of."

"I don't know how you'd even tell," Mid said. "Do the females look different from the males?"

"No one knows," Cheff said, "or so I've heard."

I raised a pedantic forefinger and adjusted my glasses. "That, gentlemen, is a matter of interest only to other Sephs."

Everyone laughed.

We emerged from the corridors into a large, green, well-tended, grassy field, maybe a half-acre (.2 ha) in size, ringed by a series of six lushly planted flower gardens. A seventh garden, right in the middle and surrounded by pools of water, lay fallow. A reflecting pool ran the length of the courtyard, dividing it in two. On one side was a raised, wedge-shaped platform, or dais.

Sable looked stunning in her full-dress uniform. I don't know how she kept it so neat—there wasn't a wrinkle to be found. Maybe it's a trick they teach Naval Officers. Her bright green eyes twinkled behind her long, black hair, which shimmered in the morning light.

The rest of us looked shabby beside her: Lhuk in his baggy, oversized coat and patched trousers, Tocette spotted and wrinkled as usual. I tried to smooth my clothing as best I could, but to no avail.

Cheff and Mid looked like they looked: Chef wore his 'vest of many pockets.' Mid, in his rope belt and sandals, had his tech bag slung over a shoulder.

Mid squinched his eyes shut. "This desert is too bright for my tastes." He took a pair of dark glasses out of his tech bag. "These should help." He put them on and opened his eyes wide. "Much better."

Snard ushered us to the opposite side of the reflecting pool and arranged us so that we faced the dais. "Welcome to Xanparthur Monastery. Xanparthur means 'place of repose' in the ancient Seph tongue. This is the Courtyard of the Seven Gardens. Each garden contains native flora from one of the Six Regions of Andaran," Facilitator Snard explained. "The western three gardens, the ones on the left as you enter, represent the Western Regions: Drea Fael, Sawtooth, and Pond. The three on the right are the Eastern Regions: Cozzbole, Tumberland, and Fellstone." He waited, expectantly. "Well, isn't anyone going to ask about the center garden? The empty one?"

Gerina, a girl from our Civilian Leadership class obligingly asked, "Mr. Snard, please, what does the center garden represent?"

Facilitator Snard smiled gratefully. "Well. The center garden stands for Worldheart, the legendary capital of the distant past."

"Hear that, Cheff?" Buttons hissed. "Worldheart!"

"Why is it empty, then?" asked a student I didn't know. "Didn't Worldheart have any plants that grew there?"

"Perhaps it did, once upon a time," Snard said. "But legend has it that since The Fall, Worldheart is desolate and barren. Still, it is fitting that we honor its memory." Snard consulted his timepiece. "The Master should be here presently, children. Please wait patiently."

So we waited patiently, the already hot desert sun causing beads of perspiration to form on our foreheads. Snard kept checking his timepiece, then looking toward the big double doors.

As we waited, I noticed a woman of the Frae People, or perhaps she was a Fruen—it was hard to tell at that distance—carrying a tray of blue and white flowers in tiny little pots. Her wide-brimmed straw hat made it impossible to see if she had a Fruen stripe in her hair. I wished I had one—a straw hat, I mean, not a head stripe. I had enough trouble with my spiky Lildur hair.

She carried the flowers over to the garden bed Snard had identified as representing Drea Fael. She set the tray down at the edge, then knelt beside it. She put on a pair of gloves she took from her apron pocket, then placed the flower in the moist rich soil using a small trowel.

A few long, hot minutes later, a man, also Frae or Fruen, wearing loosely woven white pants and shirt, brought the woman two more trays of flowers, then turned and left.

Facilitator Snard saw me watching them and asked, "What are you looking at, young man?"

"The gardener, sir. She's planting flowers in the Drea Fael bed."

"Ah! So you *were* listening when I identified the gardens. Hmmph! Anyway, so what if she is? What of it?"

"Why, nothing, sir. I was just thinking that Drea Fael must be a beautiful place."

Snard looked thoughtful. "Maybe it is, maybe it isn't. I was there, once, on behalf of my Seph, many years ago. I don't remember much about it. I do recall, however, that there was a forest there, right on the border of Drea Fael and the Pond region. Krag Forest, or Klag—something like that. Nasty place. Made me weak at the knees, looking at it." He shivered, remembering.

He glanced at his timepiece again, then at the doors. "Oh, where *is* the Master? He should have been here by now."

Before he'd finished speaking, the great double doors opened. Slowly, silently, majestically, even, a huge Seph emerged, slithered across the grass, and came to a stop before us. Snard bowed, then left to wait by the monastery wall.

The enormous Seph looked us over, taking time to make eye contact with each one of us. He seemed satisfied with our appearance. He curled himself into a coil on the dais and raised his massive head. "Greetingsss, children. Welcome to Xanparthur Monasssstery. I am Massster Vessslu. I am 471 yearsss old. I have lived here at Xanparthur for over four hundred yearsss. I will be your Inssstructor today."

*"The enormous Seph looked us over…"*

54

**OPERATION SHIFTING SANDS**

# — 6 —

## INTRODUCTIONS

As Master Vessslu entered, we caught the distinctive odor of Seph musk, though it wasn't overpowering.

"Friend Cheff," Lery whispered. "I don't... don't like this... at all." He was shaking.

"Easy, Lery. I don't think this one means us any harm."

"I know... Cheff... but I still don't..."

"Let usss begin with the purpossse of Xanparthur," Master Vessslu said. For asss long asss anyone can remember, the Seph have been the enemiesss of the Ten Peoplesss. No one alive today can remember why thisss isss ssso. The Seph have alwaysss used membersss of the other species as Facilitatorsss.

"We mussst, you sssee, becaussse we have no feet, no handsss. Without Facilitatorsss, we would be as beasssts of the field, naked, without toolsss, other than our teeth.

"We Seph also have the ability to influence, or even control, membersss of the other speciesss. Thisss, too, has been true sssince before living memory. I will demonsssstrate, for those of you who do not yet know what it is to be touched by the Seph."

"Friend Cheff! He... he's going to..."

"Hang on, Lery. Don't do anything. Close your eyes, hold still, and wait." Cheff put his hand on Lery's shoulder.

Lery shivered, but stood stock-still.

On his other side, Sable put her hand on Lery's arm. "Steady," she murmured.

Master Vessslu became motionless and closed his eyes. I closed mine, too. I felt the most wonderful, warm feeling, deep inside. It was the best feeling I'd ever had—like being drowned in honey. Right then, I would have done anything Master Vessslu desired.

I glanced around at the others. Lery stood perfectly straight, completely rigid, but he wasn't bolting. Cheff, Sable, Mid, and Buttons looked like I felt. Lhuk, on the other hand, was staring off across the lawn, seemingly unaffected.

Master Vessslu opened his eyes. The warm feeling vanished in an instant.

"Now you all know what it isss to be kisssed by the Seph," Master Vessslu said. "For mossst of you, it was pleasant, yesss? For the Fessalsss among you, even more pleasant, yesss?"

Lery looked puzzled, but vastly relieved. "That… that wasn't what… what I was… expecting… The other Sephs… in… in the Fortress… and the Hunting Lodge…"

"Okay, Lery," Cheff said. "It's all right, now. Please be careful what you say out loud in this place."

"Of… of course… Friend Cheff…" Lery looked embarrassed. "I… I don't… know… what I was… thinking…"

"It's all good," Cheff assured him, glancing around at the other students. They were all absorbed in their own reactions to the experience. "No worries, Lery. No one seems to have noticed. Okay?"

"Okay… Friend Cheff."

Master Vessslu gave us time to compose ourselves, then continued, "The Seph Ability affectsss different speciesss to different degreesss. Fessalsss are the most sensitive to our Ability, while Torphsss are barely affected at all. The ressst fall somewhere in-between. We do not know why this isss.

"We Seph are born with the ability, need, and desssire to dominate the other intelligent speciesss of Andaran. Throughout hissstory, as far back as anyone knowsss, the Seph have used thisss power to manipulate the other speciesss into ssserving them. Mossstly for ordinary day-to-day purposesss and needsss, but sometimesss for evil purposesss, and to dominate and exploit the other speciesss, even dessstroy them.

"We Seph here at Xanparthur believe sssuch domination isss wrong. We believe that even when used for beneficial purposesss, sssuch domination isss wrong. We have overcome our nature through meditation and long ssstudy of the mission of our Monasssstery. But no day goesss by when I am not tempted to return to my inborn nature. What do you think, young onesss—which isss better, to be born good, or to overcome one'sss evil nature through great effort?" He paused to let that sink in. "But, you may asssk, aren't there Facilitatorsss here at Xanparthur? Yesss, of coursssse there are. Even here, we Seph require Facilitatorsss that we may live like sentient beingsss. Neverthelesss, every Facilitator here at Xanparthur is here of hisss or her own volition. It isss forbidden to use the Seph Ability to control othersss here at Xanparthur. All Seph who live here have taken an oath to that effect."

A ripple went through the students. Could this be true?

"I senssse that sssome of you are wondering why we Seph would choose to live thisss way, contrary to our naturesss. It isss becaussse we have come to believe that every sentient being, of all the Peoplesss, including the Seph, hasss the right to self-determination. We, ourselvesss, would not want to be controlled or even influenced. Therefore, we, in turn, do not wish to control or even influence, othersss. Is this not the esssence of goodnesss?"

Sephs' faces are rigid, immobile, so they can have no facial expressions. Even so, in my mind, Master Vessslu seemed to be smiling.

"But you are hot," Master Vessslu said, "perhapsss too hot. You are not accussstomed to the desssert. Won't you join me in a cooler place, where we might enjoy some refreshmentsss? Pleassse, Facilitator Snard, lead our guestsss to my audience chamber."

Snard rejoined us, smiling. "Come along, children. This way, please."

The coolness of the monastery was most welcome. Snard took us to a medium-sized room full of chairs, with a refreshment stand along one wall and a Seph cushion on the other. A pair of Fessals in chef's hats and aprons were serving cups of an unfamiliar fruit juice. I tasted mine, then drained my glass and went back for another.

"Say, Cheff," I said. "This juice is fantastic! What is it?"

"No idea," Cheff said. "But it sure is good."

One of the servers, a kind-looking Fessal woman, overheard us and volunteered, "This, young sir, is the juice of the fruit of the tonton cactus. It grows everywhere in the desert. Several times a year, it sets fruit. They are not much good for eating, but we harvest them and press them for juice."

The second server, a man of the Lildur People, added, "It's the finest juice in all of Andaran. One of the Five Great Flavors, you know! Nothing like it anywhere else. Enjoy!" He filled our glasses once again.

"Take your seats, Children," Facilitator Snard called out. "Master Vessslu will arrive momentarily."

As soon as we were all seated, a pair of previously invisible doors opened behind the giant cushion, and Master Vessslu entered. He coiled himself on the cushion and drank through a straw from a rather large vessel of tonton juice held by a Facilitator.

"Ah, tonton juice," he said. "The finessst juice of all." He smacked his scaly lips a few times, then cleaned them with his forked tongue. "Now, children, I'm sssure you have many, many questionsss. I'll answer as many asss I can in the time we have this morning."

A girl I didn't recognize raised her hand. "How many Sephs are there here at the monastery?"

"Good quessstion, little one. We number three hundred sssix-ty-ssseven."

A boy asked, "Where do you all live? The monastery doesn't look that big."

"Above ground, the monastery is only as big as it seemsss, but underneath it is connected to the Belowground."

"For those of you not acquainted with the Belowground," Facilitator Snard added, "It is a series of natural and man-made caverns that run all throughout Andaran, mostly under mountain ranges. This particular system is isolated from the main Belowground, but is still fairly large."

Tocette raised her hand next. Brex glared, but Tocette ignored her. "Please, Master Vessslu, sir, may I ask Facilitator Snard a question?"

"Of courssse, little one. Proceed."

"Um, Mr. Facilitator Snard, sir? Um, why do you do it?"

"Do what, Miss…?"

"Tocette, sir."

"Why do I do what, Miss Tocette?"

"Well, Mr. Facilitator Snard, sir—"

"'Mr. Snard' will be sufficient."

"Yes, sir. Um, well, Mr. Snard, if they don't *make* you do it, why *are* you a Facilitator? I mean, well, um, I'm a Fessal, too, you see, and um, well, I don't think I'd like it very much."

A flood of giggles ran through the room. Tocette looked around nervously but bravely pressed on. "What it is, sir, is that I don't like it much when people make me do things. Um, I guess most of us don't. But even if they didn't make me, I still don't think I'd like to be a Facilitator. And, um, well, Mr. Snard, I'd like to know why you do it."

Master Vessslu raised his enormous head. "A good quessstion, Snard. I'd like to hear the answer, myssself."

"Well, Miss Tocette, first let me say that I agree with you—I wouldn't care to be forced to do anything. However, I'm not forced. I'm not even 'rewarded' with that warm feeling you experienced outside. I serve the Xanparthur Masters proudly and willingly because I believe in what they are doing here."

At this, Lery sat up quite straight and paid careful attention.

"The Seph of Xanparthur have dedicated themselves to high moral principles," Snard continued. "They set a fine example for other Sephs—indeed, for all the Peoples. I'm proud to be a part of that.

"They also treat me exceptionally well. I am not only paid generously, but I have a nice suite of rooms to live in with my family. And you saw last night how we eat here at Xanparthur." He smiled kindly. "A man could do much worse."

"Family, sir? You have a family?"

"Tocette!" Brex snapped. "Enough!"

"It's quite all right, Miss…?"

"Brex."

"Thank you. Miss Brex, all questions are welcome. That is, after all, why you are here—to learn about Xanparthur." He turned to Tocette. "I have a wife and three children. Two boys, one girl. They are enjoying a happy, secure life here at Xanparthur. Perhaps you will meet them during your visit."

"I'd like that, Mr. Snard. But—"

"Another question, Miss Tocette?" asked Snard.

"Um, yes, please."

"Go ahead."

"Well, you're a… a… um… *man*."

"Yes," Snard said. "Thank you for noticing, Miss Tocette."

A giggle ran around the room.

Tocette blushed. "I mean, sir, are there any female facilitators? I saw a lady taking care of a Seph. She was a Fessal, like me."

"Oh, yes," Snard said. "Many. In fact, at this time, I believe that female facilitators slightly outnumber the males."

Tocette brightened.

"Both sexes of all Peoples may apply," Snard said, "but the waiting list is quite long. Nevertheless, we're always looking for qualified applicants. If you'd care to apply, Miss Tocette, please see me after today's session."

"Thank you, Mr. Snard. I think, maybe—" Tocette blushed again, and sat down abruptly. From the look on Brex's face, I guessed there would be some harsh words later.

I raised my hand. "I'm Birn Tylandine, Master Vessslu, but my friends call me Books. It's because I'm studying Archiving and Library Management. I'm curious—is there a library here at Xanparthur? And if so, might I be permitted to visit it?"

"Library Management, isss it? A man after my own heart! Yesss, young Tylandine, we have a library here, a rather extensssive one. I have been Chief Librarian for Xanparthur for over two centuriesss. I would be mossst pleasssed to show it to you." He looked at the rest of the audience. "And to anyone who might be interesssted. Although I mussst warn you, not all booksss are available to the public. Sssome are extremely old and therefore extremely fragile. Othersss have been deemed… unsssuitable… for Emperor Pallador's purposesss."

"I understand, sir. Thank you. I would love to see the library."

"Facilitator Snard will arrange a visit. Speak with him after this morning'sss sssesssion."

The rest of the questions and answers were mostly routine, as far as I could tell, with one exception. Toward the end of the Question and Answer session, Desult, a Fessal girl from my Civilian Leadership class, asked, "Is it hard to be peaceful, sir? I mean, going against your natures and all?"

"Peaceful? I'm afraid you have misssunderssstood, my dear girl. We Xanparthur Sephs are dedicated to the self-determination of all sssentient creaturesss. We don't dominate othersss, but we alsssо do not permit othersss to dominate usss. Politically, we are neutral and render ressspectful ssservice to whatever ruler happensss to be in charge. Usefulnesss to the exisssting government is how we've sssurvived all these centuriesss. At peace? Yesss. Peaceful? No. And asss far asss that goesss, children, let me sssay…"

# Operation Shifting Sands

**— 7 —**

# ATTAN

---

WHILE MASTER VESSSLU was finishing his dissertation, four Fessal Facilitators dressed in green and gold uniforms had opened the doors behind him. They held the double doors open for another Seph as he entered the room. The newcomer, while much smaller than Master Vessslu, was still huge, and his scent was pungent, much more so than Master Vessslu's. He wore the same sort of garb as I'd seen Emperor Pallador wear in pictures, only much less ornate—ceremonial headdress, symbolic dress sword, and tail spikes. The new Seph, without waiting for Master Vessslu to finish speaking, said, "Thank you, thank you Master Vessslu, for that interesting information. I'm sure that's quite enough. I'll take it from here. Children, let's have a big hand for Master Vessslu."

We obliged with a perfunctory round of applause.

Master Vessslu took his leave. "Thank you, children. It hasss been a pleasssure. If any of you hasss more quessstions, I'll be happy to sssee you in my officesss. Asssk any of the Facilitatorsss." He slithered down off his cushion and left through the huge double doors without looking back.

The new Seph disdained the cushion. Without being commanded, the four Fessal Facilitators took it away.

"I am Grand Master Attan, Emperor Pallador's chief representative here at Xanparthur Monastery by special appointment. I am here to see that our Beloved Emperor's wishes are carried out with respect to his 'Path of Enlightenment' program."

A hand shot up in the front row. I couldn't see who it was. Attan said, "No questions until I'm finished, if you please. I will not keep you long. I only wish to assure you of our beloved Emperor's good wishes toward you during your visit here."

Attan's four Facilitators returned and took their stations behind him. Their demeanor was markedly different from that of Facilitator Snard's. They stood quietly, heads bowed.

"You are inordinately privileged young boys and girls," Attan continued. "Emperor Pallador welcomes you to his 'Path of Enlightenment' program and encourages you to take full advantage of your time here.

"The Xanparthur Monastery has a key role in the Emperor's various enlightenment programs, and has had for many, many years. Why, Emperor Pallador himself studied here in his youth! Did you know that?"

Cheff and Mid exchanged a look. It was clear they weren't buying this newcomer's line.

"Emperor Pallador desires that you observe carefully the ways of the Seph Monks here at Xanparthur and carry their message of peace and harmony back to your homes and families. It is important for all citizens of Andaran to appreciate Emperor Pallador's peaceful intentions and lofty ideals. Above all else, our beloved Emperor wishes all the Peoples of Andaran to live in peace and prosperity, with the Seph, of course, taking their proper place as servants of all the Ten Races."

I heard a low, growling noise in the room. I looked around to see what it was and realized it was Cheff. I took Cheff by one arm, Mid took his other arm.

"Steady, Old Son," Mid said. "Let it go by."

Cheff murmured, "Lying Seph toady."

"Of course he is," Mid said. "That's his job."

"Good at it," Sable murmured.

"He certainly is," I said.

"The ponies don't like him," Buttons said.

"I… I don't… like him… either," Lery said.

Lhuk shrugged.

"What is all the commotion in back?" Attan asked.

"I apologize, sir," Mid said. "Our friend, Lhuk, couldn't quite hear what you were saying, sir, so we repeated it for him. We didn't want him to miss out on anything."

"Ah, quite right," Attan said. "No good coming all this way, then missing out. Carry on." He was about to speak again, then stopped. "In fact, why don't you all come up front? That way, you won't miss anything else."

"Thank you, sir," Mid said. "We'll do that."

There were a few giggles around the room as we moved toward the front, but we ignored them. The musky odor of Seph was overpowering so close to Attan.

When we were all settled again, Attan continued, "As I was saying, Emperor Pallador wants you all to pay close attention to everything you see here at Xanparthur, so that you can share Emperor Pallador's grand vision with your schoolmates and family back home."

As he continued his speech, I took a closer look at Attan's Facilitators. They couldn't have been more different from Facilitator Snard. While Snard was proud, upright, and spotless, Attan's four Facilitators were rigid, dejected, and unkempt. They had stains on their uniforms, and their hair was dirty and stringy. They kept their eyes firmly fixed on their shoes.

When Attan finished his speech and invited questions, I raised my hand. "Excuse me, sir. I'm wondering if your Facilitators are completely uninfluenced, like Facilitator Snard. Is that Emperor

Pallador's new policy? To respect the self-determination of all sentient creatures?"

"Let me assure you, young man, that Emperor Pallador values peace and harmony above all things. These Facilitators, like all of Emperor Pallador's Facilitators, serve completely voluntarily. Why would you even ask such a question?"

"Uh, well, in school we learned that being controlled is a great privilege, a goal worthy of a lifetime."

"And it is. The kiss of a Seph is the greatest honor anyone can receive. But only at the request of the recipient, never against their will."

"But—"

"Ask one of my Facilitators. You, Wert, tell the young man that you are controlled by your own request to enhance your service."

Wert shuffled forward. Without looking up, he said, sullenly, "I am controlled by my own request, to enhance my service."

"Tell him it's the highest honor you ever hope to receive."

"It's the highest honor I ever hope to receive."

"Tell him that your family is grateful to you for your willingness to serve, to keep them safe and prosperous."

"My family…"

"Yes, Wert," Attan said. "Go on."

Wert looked up at me, his gaze locking with mine. "My family is grateful to me for my willingness to serve. It keeps them safe and prosperous." He dropped his gaze to the floor again.

"Thank you, Wert," Attan said. "Well spoken!" He turned to me. "Well, there you have it, young man, directly from the Facilitator himself. Satisfied?"

I glanced at Cheff. He was bright-red and his fists were clenched. "Yes, sir," I said. "Thank you. I have no more questions."

"Excellent. Please, all of you children, feel free to ask me anything, anytime. That will be all for now. In fact, it's almost time for the noon meal. Where is Facilitator Snard?"

"Here, Grand Master Attan," Snard said.

"Would you be so kind as to escort these fine young people to the dining hall?"

"Certainly, Grand Master Attan. Come along, children, follow me."

We lined up and followed, but when I got to the door, Facilitator Snard bent over. "Not you, Birn Tylandine. You stay with me. Master Vessslu wishes to speak with you. And your little Torph friend, too, please."

Lhuk stopped dead in his tracks, eyes wide. I looked anxiously for Cheff, but he and the rest of the gang had already left the room.

"Yes, sir," I said. "We'll be happy to, of course."

But Lhuk didn't look all that happy, and, I suppose, neither did I.

## — 8 —

## THE LIBRARY

WE FOLLOWED FACILITATOR Snard into the corridor and down a long, gently sloping ramp. "The ramps are called 'slitherways.' There are no stairs in Xanparthur," he explained. "Stairs are difficult, even painful, for Sephs."

I already knew this from our adventure in the Iron Fortress, but I kept my own counsel. Lhuk didn't say anything, either.

We descended slitherway after slitherway until we were far below ground level. The smooth, stucco walls of the monastery gave way to the rough-hewn stone of the Belowground. After what seemed hours, but in reality was only a half-hour or thereabouts, we came to a vast underground chamber, filled with row after row of bookshelves. I'd never seen anything like it, nor was there anything in my Library Management class that suggested such a thing existed. There were thousands of books, maybe tens of thousands. Many of them looked old, extremely old. I hoped I'd get a chance to examine some of them.

The stacks radiated from an open space. A red and gold Seph cushion dominated the center, surrounded by a long, circular desk covered with books.

"Wait here," Facilitator Snard commanded.

We waited. In due course, we heard the sound of a Seph slithering and smelled the scent of Seph, but much milder than Attan's pungent odor. Master Vessslu appeared and took his place on the cushion.

"Welcome to my Library, young onesss. Isss it to your sssatisfaction, young Mr. Tylandine?"

"I… I've never seen anything like it. I wish you could lock me in, and let me read myself out again! Except I don't think one lifetime would be enough to read all these books."

"Indeed, right you are, Birn, if I may be ssso familiar asss to call you by your firssst name."

"Of course, sir," I said. "The honor is mine."

"You can call me Lhuk, if you want to," Lhuk said.

"Thank you, Lhuk. What do you think of my booksss?"

"There certainly are a lot of them, sir. But what good are they, if no one reads them?"

"Ssso young, yet ssso wissse," Master Vessslu said. "I take it you don't agree with Emperor Pallador'sss viewsss on ressstricting knowledge?"

"Well…"

"Never mind, Lhuk. You need not anssswer that question. What about you, young Tylandine?"

"Well, sir," I said, "my father died for owning 'forbidden' books, among other things."

"Both my parents are dead," Lhuk said. "Not for forbidden books, though. Merely because they are Torphs! What do you have to say about that?"

I put my hand on his arm. "Lhuk, please."

He shook me off. "I don't care! It's true! Grand Master Attan talked all that fancy talk this morning about serving the Ten Peoples, but my mother and father are dead simply because they are Torphs. *Were* Torphs."

"It isss a great sadnesss, Lhuk," Master Vessslu said. "I grieve with you."

"So what?" Lhuk said. "You never even knew them! Who are you to grieve for them?"

"I grieve for all unnecesssary losss of life." Master Vessslu turned to me. "Birn, would you be ssso kind asss to leave the two of usss alone for a little while? Perhaps you would enjoy browsing the stacksss while I ssspeak privately with Lhuk? Ssstay where I can sssee you, though—sssome of the booksss are forbidden. For now."

I moved away, pretending to look at the books, while in reality, I was straining to hear their conversation. I took a book from the shelf at random. Without reading it, I flipped through the pages, using my special ability to 'photograph' each page mentally. There was no need to read it—I could bring up the images and read it later.

In the distance, I heard Lhuk say, "Now what? Are you going to kill me now?"

"Of coursse not," Master Vessslu said. "Why would I kill you?"

"Isn't that the reason you had me brought here?"

"No, absssolutely not!"

"Why, then?" Lhuk asked.

"I brought you here to asssk you a quessstion," Master Vessslu said. "You are one of only two Torphsss in your group, is that not so?"

"Yes."

"The other, Averith Brex, is a True Believer in Emperor Pallador and hisss policiesss, isss she not?"

"She is."

"And you? Are you a loyal follower of Emperor Pallador and a devotee of his 'Path of Enlightenment?'"

Lhuk laughed bitterly. "Sure. Who isn't?"

"And your parentsss—were they also followersss of the 'Path of Enlightenment?'"

"Who knows? They're dead now. What does it matter?"

"Answer the quessstion, please."

"My parents had the Torph Ability. There was no place for them on the 'Path of Enlightenment.'"

"Are you suggesting that Torphsss have no place in Emperor Pallador'sss world?"

Lhuk said nothing.

"And you? Do you, like your parents, have the Torph Ability?"

"I'm too young to know yet."

"Of courssse you are, young Lhuk, of courssse you are. And if, when you're older, you prove to have the Ability?"

"Then I'll die, like my parents."

"And doesss thisss ssseem fair and right to you?"

"It's just how things are."

"But it wasssn't always ssso."

"What?"

"I'm old, asss I told you thisss morning. When I wasss young, it was taken for granted that Torphsss were the ruling classs, not the Sephsss."

"What?"

"I'm telling you that for centuriesss, all the kingsss and queensss of Andaran were Torphsss. *All* of them. All."

*"What?"*

"You can read about it, if you like, and if you can find the right booksss in my library. But I'm telling you—for many, many centuriesss, all the rulersss of Andaran were Torphsss."

"I… I don't understand."

"It seemsss that Torphsss have a natural inclination toward leadership. An inclination that the Sephsss mossst emphatically do *not* have."

"I still don't understand."

"There are Ten Peoplesss, are there not?"

"Yes."

"And there isss the One People, the Seph, in opposssition to the Ten, isss there not?"

"Opposition? I don't understand."

"No one knowsss how all the different speciesss came to be. But one thing we do know, beyond all doubt from hissstory: *Andaran prospersss when Torphsss rule.*"

Lhuk was speechless.

"But there'sss another part to thisss," Master Vessslu continued. "The converssse is also true: when Sephsss rule, Andaran suffersss."

"But… but that's…"

"Treassson? I suppossse ssso. Neverthelesss, hissstory provesss it to be true."

"But… why? Why is that so?"

"It hasss to do with the Ability."

"Torph Ability?"

"Both Torph Ability and Seph Ability. They are the sssame."

"The same! How can that be?"

"No one knowsss how it came to be. The Seph can bend the other speciessss to their will. The Torph alone can resist the Seph Ability. What'sss more, the occasional Torph, extra ssstrong in the Ability, can shield nearby members of the other speciesss from the Ability of the Seph."

"But… Emperor Pallador says that Torphs can control other people, and that's why they must be isolated."

"By isssolated, do you mean dessstroyed?"

"I… I think so. I learned, only yesterday, that my parents are dead. I had been told they were in special Torph Camps in the West, and that I would join them there."

"There are no Torph Campsss. I'm ssso sssorry."

"So I was told. What, then, is there for me?"

"The real question isss, what isss there for all Torphsss?"

Lhuk shrugged. "Okay. What?"

"Torphsss are the rightful rulersss of Andaran, becaussse they, and they alone, can resissst the Seph. Not only resisst them, but in sssome ssspecial casesss, protect the other speciesss from the Seph as well."

"So… I should be King of Andaran?"

"Perhapsss… but not necessarily. At the time of The Fall, the king and queen of Andaran were both Torphsss. There existsss an heir, a True Heir, to the throne of Andaran. A Torph heir."

"'Heir' again." He sighed. "Books' friends were talking about an heir on the bus. Isn't the heir a myth, a folk tale?"

"Perhapsss, perhapsss not. We certainly hope not."

"If he's not a myth, then where is he?"

"Or she, perhaps. We don't know. The heir disssappeared jussst after The Fall."

"If you know all this, why haven't you done anything about it? Why aren't you out looking for the heir?"

"Because Xanparthur Monassstery is dedicated to political neutrality. It cannot ssseek to determine the fate of othersss, not even the true heir. Each individual mussst determine hisss own fate. If we were to interfere, how would we be different from the Seph who ruthlesssly use their abilities to control the minds of othersss?"

"Then what? What else is there for me? Lie down and die?"

"Not at all. There are thosssse, many, in fact, who even now ssseek the true heir, the Torph heir, to the throne of Andaran. When once again a Torph rulesss Andaran, there will be hope for all the Peoplesss."

Master Vessslu turned to me. "Master Birn, if you're not actually going to read any of those booksss, you might asss well rejoin the conversssation."

I blushed and rejoined Master Vessslu and Lhuk.

"I sssee you brought with you the book you were holding," Master Vessslu said.

"I did? Oh, I did. I'm sorry—I'll go put it back."

"What isss the book you have chosssen?"

"The book I have…? Oh, this one? It's, um, I'm not…" I looked at the book for the first time. "It's *The Glorious Exploits of Emperor Pallador in the Dark Times After The Fall*. Oh, hmm, by Emperor Pallador."

Master Vessslu made a series of strange hissing noises while shaking his huge head up and down. I was startled and so was Lhuk, until we realized that Master Vessslu was laughing. *Laughing!* Lhuk and I exchanged a glance. Neither one of us had ever even heard of a Seph laughing, let alone seen one.

"Here," Master Vessslu said. "Put that down."

"Did I do something wrong, sir?" I asked.

"No, not at all. Besidesss the fact that it's a terribly dry read, it happensss to be the biggessst pack of liesss in the entire library." He lowered his head to our level, then whispered, "I'd appreciate it if you didn't repeat that remark."

"Of course not, sir."

"Let's sssee if we can find you sssomething more sssuitable. And factual. Sssomething you could ssshare with your friendsss. Dissscreetly, of courssse."

"Yes, sir, discreetly, of course."

"Go down that aisle over there." He gestured with his nose. "Turn right, and passs four, maybe five, shelvesss. It'll be on your right, on the middle ssshelf, right about your eye-level. It's called *The Life and Timesss of Maghorn I*. You can't misss it—it'sss red. Quite red. Go with him, Lhuk, and help him look. I need a few minutesss to mysssself. You'll undersssstand when you're my age."

"When I'm four hundred seventy-one?" I asked. "I… uh… um." But Master Vessslu was laughing again, so Lhuk and I went down the aisle to hunt for Maghorn I.

When we thought we must be out of earshot, Lhuk said, "What do you think he's playing at?"

"What do you mean?"

"I mean, what's his game, his angle? Everybody has an angle, right?"

"I… don't know? He seemed sincere to me, but I haven't known that many Sephs. One thing, though—he doesn't seem to like Pallador much."

"Neither do I," Lhuk said.

We followed Master Vessslu's instructions, and in due course found the book. Master Vessslu was right—it was red, brilliantly red.

When we got back, Master Vessslu's eyes were closed. We waited quietly, but he didn't move. I opened the book and read the introduction. I said to Lhuk, "I've heard about this Maghorn before. According to some old books my father used to have, Maghorn built a lot of things that Pallador is taking credit for."

"Oh? Like what?"

"Like the Old Bridge between New City and Old City."

"You mean the Bridge of Pallador's Glorious Unification?"

"Yeah, that's the one. If you look closely, you can see where Maghorn's original dedication plaque was removed. But I've seen pictures of the original plaque in some old books my father had."

"So, you're saying that Pallador is taking credit for this Mag… Maghorn's work?"

"Exactly! And I'll bet this book is full of examples."

"Well, let me know what you find."

"Don't you want to read it yourself?"

"Nah. I don't—"

Master Vessslu stirred and took a huge, deep breath. "Ah, you're back. Were you successsful?"

"Yes, sir," I said and held up the book for him to see.

"That'sss the one. I'm sure you'll find it… enlightening."

"Thank you, sir. I'll read it right away."

"It'sss time for you to rejoin your companionsss, young onesss. But before you go, I want to ask Lhuk a quessstion."

"What's that, sir?"

"Do your friendsss know that you have the Torph Ability? Or do you conceal it from them?"

Lhuk looked like he was going to bolt, but decided against it.

Master Vessslu laughed again. "It'sss all right, Lhuk. I could senssse it in you when I demonssstrated the Seph Ability in the courtyard. Also in your companion. The female. Brex."

Lhuk stared.

"She does, Lhuk," I said. "I've seen it in action."

"Brex?" Lhuk asked. "Brex *hates* the Ability. Brex hates *Torphs.* If Brex could grow scales, she'd *be* a Seph. Er, no offense, Master Vessslu."

"None taken. Brex deniesss herssself to essscape the fate of her parentsss. And who can blame her? You, Lhuk, on the other hand, have far more Ability than Brex, far more than most Torphsss, for that matter. Even more than most of the Seph."

"I knew I had the Ability, sir, but I had no way of knowing how strong it is. Not in Pallador's world. Until you told us about Brex, I was the only Torph with Ability I knew of. And yes, my friends know." He glanced at me. "My closest friends."

"Torph Ability comesss with great resssponsssibility, Lhuk. What will you do with yoursss?"

"*Do* with it? Why, nothing, nothing at all. I've always thought that if anyone ever finds out I have it, I'll go straight to a Torph Camp. Except…"

"Except what, young Lhuk?"

Lhuk fought back the tears. "Except, now I know that there are no Torph Camps and my mother and father—" He clenched his jaw shut.

"It meansss that your mother and father are almossst certainly dead," Master Vessslu said, "though no one can sssay for sssure."

Lhuk wiped his eyes on his sleeve and looked up. "You mean there's a chance they're alive?"

"There is alwaysss hope," Master Vessslu said. "The question iss, what are you, Lhuk, going to do about it?"

"What *can* I do about it? I'm just a kid."

"You're not *jussst* anything. Every sssentient being has the potential to be massster of his own fate. That isss what Xanparthur Monastery standsss for, and that isss what I've dedicated my life to. Embrace your Ability, Lhuk. It isss, in part, what makesss you, *you*."

"Yes, sir," Lhuk said. "I… I'll think about what you said, sir."

"Do that, young Lhuk. Think about it, and talk about it with your friendsss. Later, if it isss to be, you and I will ssspeak again. Go, now. I am old and in need of sssleep. If you hurry, you may be able to join your friendsss for the noon meal. Snard!"

"Yes, Master?" Snard appeared out of nowhere.

"Would you be ssso kind as to essscort these young onesss to the dining hall? If it's closssed, have a word with the cooksss."

"Of course, Master. Will there be anything else?"

"No, no, that'll be all for now. I need to clossse my eyesss for a while."

He rested his scaly chin on his topmost coil and closed his eyes.

"Come along, children," Facilitator Snard said quietly. "Let's be off."

*"I pretended to look at the books while I was strainingto hear their conversation."*

## — 9 —

# THE DINING HALL

WHEN LHUK AND I got back to the dining hall, it was empty, except for Cheff and the rest of the gang, who sat together around an empty table. Lhuk and I thanked Facilitator Snard, who went off to have a word with the cooks.

"What are you still doing here?" I asked Cheff.

"We were told to wait here," Cheff said, "but not for what. For you, maybe."

"Did you eat already?" I asked. "Of course you did."

"We did," Cheff said. "Everyone else was dismissed to tour the new museum."

"Museum?" I asked.

"It seems Emperor Pallador decided to build a museum here," Cheff said. "Recently, in fact."

"Pallador has museums everywhere," Buttons said. "The ponies like museums, especially if we can smash the display cases and steal stuff, like last time." Starry and Moka nodded in agreement. "Where were you and Books, Lhuk?"

Lhuk started to answer, but his voice failed him and he turned away.

"Master Vessslu called us to the library," I said gently.

"Library?" Mid asked.

"Oh, yes," I said. "The monastery has an enormous library. There are books there that are centuries old. Look!" I showed him *The Life and Times of Maghorn I.* "Master Vessslu gave me this to read."

"Let me see that," Cheff said.

I handed him the book. He thumbed through it.

"So, what did you and Master Vessslu find to talk about?" Mid asked Lhuk.

Without replying, Lhuk wandered off to a table on the far side of the room.

"What's up with him?" Mid asked.

"Master Vessslu confirmed the death of his parents," I said quietly.

"Oh," Mid said, "no wonder he doesn't feel like talking."

"That wasn't all Master Vessslu had to say, though. He talked about lots of stuff: empire, Pallador, Torph and Seph Abilities, both. And responsibility, self-determination, and purpose."

Cheff's eyebrows lifted. "So, it seems that Master Vessslu has singled you two out for special attention."

I glanced over at Lhuk. Lhuk nodded. I beckoned everyone to lean in close. Lhuk reluctantly rejoined the group. "Master Vessslu sensed Lhuk's Torph Ability. And Brex's, too. He said that Lhuk's Ability is particularly strong and that great responsibility comes with such Ability."

"Is that so?" Cheff asked. "Well, we knew Lhuk had Ability. How come you never told us your Ability was above average, Lhuk?"

"Because I had no idea," Lhuk said. "How could I? I don't even know any other Torphs, except Brex."

"That's all right," Mid said, "no one expected you to sit down and have a cozy little chat with Brex about Torph Ability."

"Lhuk should know about Brex," I said.

No one spoke for several minutes, then Cheff said, "I agree. Tell him about it, Books."

So I explained to Lhuk how we battled a Seph during our last mission, and how that Seph had influenced us all with his Ability, and how Brex used her Torph Ability to help us.

Lhuk asked, "So why doesn't Brex know she has the Ability?"

I explained about The Forgetting, how the Fel People had made Brex forget about everything that happened.

"Is that ethical?" Lhuk asked.

"Not entirely," Cheff said. "But the alternative was to kill her outright. It seemed like the best solution—at the time."

"I see," Lhuk said. "And she has no recollection of any of that?"

"None so far," Mid said. "But yesterday it seemed she might be remembering a little."

"Not good," Sable murmured.

"Not good, indeed," Cheff said. "If she gets her full memory back, we're going to be in a world of hurt."

"There's one more thing," I said. "Master Vessslu said that the Torphs have been, for centuries, the proper rulers of Andaran, because the Torph Ability can protect the other Peoples from the Seph. He doesn't like Pallador, not even a little bit."

Cheff tipped his chair back and stared at the ceiling. He always did this when he was deep in thought—he said that it made the blood run to the back of his head to help him think better. Finally, he rocked forward again. "That Attan fellow, he's not one of the monks here, is he?"

"He said he was the Grand Master," Buttons said.

"Doesn't fit," Sable said.

"That's it!" Cheff said. "Sable nailed it. He's not at all like Master Vessslu."

"And... and his Fessals... weren't like... like Snard," Lery said.

"No, they weren't," Mid said. "That one, Wert, repeated what Attan told him word for word."

"Without ever looking up," Lhuk said. "I'm pretty sure that he was controlled."

"Controlled!" Cheff said. "But that's not permitted here at Xanparthur."

"Apparently it is, Old Man," Mid said, "for some. But I'd bet good money that Attan fellow isn't a real monk. In fact, I don't think he's even from here."

"Maybe he works for Pallador," Buttons said. She consulted Starry and Moka. "The ponies think so, too."

"So," Cheff said, "a fake monk. A fake Grand Master, for that matter. I wonder what he's actually here for?"

"He… he talked a lot… about… Pallador's enlightenment program," Lery said.

"He did, didn't he?" Mid said. "Could he be trying to take over the monastery for the Emperor?"

"That would be a tragedy!" I said. "There are thousands and thousands of books in that library, books that Pallador would certainly destroy if he could. Like that one you're thumbing through."

Cheff lowered his voice. "This one alone, from what little I've seen, would give the lie to nearly all of Pallador's propaganda. And you say there are thousands of them?"

"Many thousands," I confirmed.

"We can't let them fall into Pallador's hands," Cheff said. "We have to stop Attan."

"Stop Attan?" Mid was incredulous. "How are we going to do that?"

"There must be a way!" Cheff said. "Some piece of evidence, some hidden information, some kind of leverage."

"Leverage," Sable echoed.

"Leverage," Buttons said. "The ponies say we must find leverage."

"So," Mid said, "you're saying that all we have to do is"—he enumerated on his fingers—"figure out what Attan is up to, find some leverage to stop him, hand that leverage over to Master Vessslu, stop Attan's takeover of the monastery, and restore the monastery to the control of the real monks of Xanparthur, all without being caught or exposed. Is that the gist of it?"

"That's the gist of it, Old Son," Cheff said. "I believe you've covered everything."

"Oh, great," Mid said.

Buttons held the ponies up to her ear and listened intently. "The ponies say, 'Piece of cake.'"

Mid buried his face in his hands.

A pair of cooks came out of the kitchen bearing trays of sandwiches, cold cuts, sliced fruits and vegetables, and some pastries. Facilitator Snard must have told the cooks we were starving, even though most of us had already eaten. They set the trays on our table without a word, then withdrew to the kitchen.

Buttons nabbed the nearest sweet roll. "Mmm… it's filled with some kind of jam… wait, I know…" She gave Starry and Moka a taste. "What is that yummy jam, ponies?" She listened, then reported, "The ponies say it's tonton jam, the same as the juice we had this morning. Taste it." She broke off a piece of the roll and gave it to Cheff.

"It's tonton, all right," Cheff said.

Mid had a taste, too. "Amazing! If we had a way to sell this in Fellstone City, we'd all become rich in short order!"

"It's… it's rare… Brother Mid," Lery said. "It takes… a lot of tonton… to make a small… amount of jam."

"Well, so what?" Mid asked. "Maybe tonton cactus is rare, but the Great Desert is supposed to be huge, right? I'm sure we could find some if we had a way of scouting around."

"I wonder if it would grow in Fellstone City?" Lhuk asked.

Mid thought that over. "Well, if it doesn't like Fellstone Bay climate, maybe we could rig something up at BSI headquarters."

"Like what?" Buttons asked.

"Like a big box, with sand on the bottom and hot lights on the top. The tonton will think they're still in the desert."

Cheff considered this. "You know, Old Son, I think it could work. I wonder where we'd find some seeds?"

"Maybe we could ask Master Vessslu," I suggested.

"Wait a minute," Lhuk said. "What is this about BSI headquarters?"

"Sorry, Lhuk," Cheff said. "That's need-to-know information, BSI members only. Mid shouldn't even have mentioned it."

"I shouldn't have," Mid said. "Lhuk fits in with us so well that I forget he's not BSI. I'm sorry, Cheff. I'll be more careful."

"Don't worry," Lhuk said. "I won't say anything. It's not like I actually know anything, anyway. Besides, you never know."

"Are you changing your mind?" Buttons asked. The ponies looked at each other, astonished. "Please say you are! Pleeease?"

"Let it be," Cheff said. "Lhuk must decide for himself."

"It's something Master Vessslu said in the library," Lhuk said. "It got me to thinking. He said that every sentient being has the potential to be master of his own fate, and that's what Xanparthur Monastery is all about. He said I should embrace my Ability and determine my own destiny. Or something like that." He looked at me for confirmation.

I nodded. "That's about the size of it."

"He also said that for centuries all the rulers of Andaran were Torphs. He said Torphs are natural leaders, and that they can use their Torph Ability to protect the other species from the Seph."

Cheff hefted the red book. "So, this Maghorn I, he was a Torph, right?"

"Yes," I said. "According to the book, Maghorn and his descendants ruled Andaran for three hundred years, right up to The Fall."

"And there *is* an heir," Lhuk added, looking vaguely embarrassed. "I thought you were making it up. Before, you know, on the bus."

"When we were sworn into the FRM," Cheff explained, "we promised to help find the True Heir."

"Right," Buttons said. "Mr. Meltern said the heir would be a Torph, a boy *or* a girl." The ponies nodded. Starry and Moka were both girl ponies.

"Who's revealing top secret information now?" Mid asked.

"Meltern said we should talk to Lhuk," Buttons protested. "I'm not telling him anything Meltern didn't tell us before we took the oath."

"True," Mid said. "Carry on."

"Lhuk," Cheff said, "one of the main purposes of the FRM is to find the true Torph heir to the Sixth Empire, and restore him—"

"—or *her*—"

"Thank you, Buttons. Uh—restore him or *her* to the throne."

"Interesting," Lhuk said. "So, if I had lived a long time ago, I might have been royalty."

"Well," Buttons said, "not all Torph have the Ability."

"Mind your words, minion!" Lhuk said, feigning a lofty demeanor. "Or it's off with your head!"

Buttons' jaw dropped, and she stared at Lhuk.

Lhuk stared back for as long as he could keep a straight face, then cracked up, which cracked us all up.

"I may have to give this FRM/BSI business some more thought. I like the idea of a Torph ruler." Lhuk made sure that no one from the kitchen was watching, then brought his pet mouse, Squeaky, out of his pocket. "Here you go, little fellow." He fed him some bits of meat and pastry, then scratched behind his ears. "Is it yummy? Huh? Is it? Mmm, good!" When Squeaky was done eating, Lhuk said, "So far, I've only used my Ability to teach Squeaky a few tricks. Right, Squeaky?" Squeaky stood up on his hind legs and bowed, then went back to his nibbling. "I never tried to do anything else with it."

"Master Vessslu said that the Torph Ability and the Seph Ability are the same thing," I said.

"I thought Seph Ability was about controlling, but Torph Ability was for protecting," Mid said.

"Same," Sable said.

"Maybe they are different aspects of the same thing," Cheff said.

"Could be," Mid said. "There's so much we don't know."

"But, only a few floors below us," Cheff said, "is an archive of all the knowledge ever learned in Andaran, going back for centuries. Surely we could find out more if we could only find the right books. Right, Books?"

Buttons giggled.

"Right," I said, grinning.

"The right… books for the… the right… heir…" Lery said.

Cheff looked around the empty dining hall. "Where do you suppose all the rest of the kids are?"

"I don't know," Mid said. "Still at the museum, maybe?" He asked me, "Did Facilitator Snard or Master Vessslu say what we were supposed to do after lunch?"

"No," I said, "not a word."

"In that case," Cheff said, "I think we're all due for a little field trip to the library. "Can you remember how to get there?"

"Sure," I lied. "It's right through those doors." I pointed to the end of the room. "Those *are* the doors we came in through, aren't they?"

Cheff laughed. "You don't have a clue, do you? Either of you?"

Lhuk and I shook our heads.

"No," I said. "We were too busy keeping up with Facilitator Snard to pay much attention. He has long legs and walks fast, like Lery."

Lery smiled. "No point in… in… what did Snard call it?"

"Dilly-dallying," Cheff said.

"That's it," Lery said. "No… dilly-dallying."

— 10 —

# Lost!

---

THE SEVEN OF us took our empty trays and plates to the clean-up station, then left through the double doors. We filed into the dimly lit corridor and stopped to listen. There was no sound at all, neither of voice nor of movement. The corridors took off in three directions, all looking very much alike.

"All right, Mr. Books," Cheff said, "which way do we go?"

I swallowed and tried not to look as unsure as I felt. I pointed to the corridor leading straight away from the dining hall. "That way."

"You sure?"

I shrugged. "Sure, why not?"

Cheff took the lead, and we padded softly down the corridor. After a short distance, we came to a sort of junction with corridors and slitherways.

"Which way?" Cheff asked me again.

I was asking myself that same question. "I remember that we went down a number of slitherways. Let's try going down."

"Whatever you say, Books. Down it is."

We descended the long, cool, smooth, stone slitherways.

"The… the Seph smell… is getting… stronger," Lery said. "I don't… don't like it."

"Three hundred sixty-seven," Sable said.

"That's right," Cheff said. "Master Vessslu said there are over three hundred Sephs here. So far, we've only seen two—Master Vessslu and that Attan character. They all must live somewhere, right? So it's no surprise if we smell them. All good, Friend Lery."

"I… I still don't… like it," Lery said. He glanced around anxiously. "What… what will happen… if… if they find us here?"

"Don't worry, Lery," Mid said. "These are peaceful Sephs, remember? We'll tell them we got lost looking for the library, which is true."

"All too true," I said. "I have no idea which way to go."

Cheff laughed. "Don't worry about it, Books. You said the library is truly big, right?"

"It is."

"Well, the bigger it is, the better chance we have of finding it."

"Sure," I said, though I was anything but.

"Meanwhile, let's have a good look around. We're getting the 'inside tour' that most people never see, I think."

So on we went, down corridor after corridor, slitherway after slitherway. We kept finding junctions like the first one and picking corridors and slitherways at random. The corridors were all the same—long, stuccoed walls punctuated with sets of closed double doors, all lit by dim electric bulbs in sconces. I'm pretty sure we went in circles at least twice, maybe more.

Finally, at one junction, we took one more slitherway leading downward and found ourselves at the end of the stuccoed walls and at the edge of the Belowground proper.

"I think this might be it, Cheff," I said. "I think the library is in the big chamber straight ahead."

But when we got to the edge of it, the huge, rock-walled chamber was completely empty, except for a few ineffective light fixtures sprouting from the bare stone ceiling. We stopped dead in the entrance.

"The library was in a room exactly like this one," I said, "only it was filled with books. Rows and rows of bookshelves. Master Vessslu had one of those giant Seph pillows right in the middle."

"Unless the Masked Book Bandit has struck in the last hour," Cheff said, "I'm pretty sure this isn't the library."

Buttons laughed and covered her eyes with her hands to simulate a robber's mask. In a low voice, she said, "I am the Masked Book Bandit! I have come for your books! But your books are not here. Soon, you will not be here."

"Please don't… don't say that," Lery said. "I don't… like this place. I can… can feel… the Sephs… all around."

"She's right, though," Cheff said. "Soon we won't be here, because we're going somewhere else! Come on, let's move."

We started back the way we came, but froze in our tracks when we heard the ghostly whisper, "Are you lossst, children? Come to me. I ssshall help you."

I called out, "Master Vessslu? Is that you? Where are you? We're looking for the library and for you. We have questions."

"Questionsss, have you? Good, becaussse I have answersss. Come to me. Follow my voice."

His voice was clearly coming from somewhere inside the chamber we had just left. We returned to the chamber's entrance and peered into the darkness, but could see nothing.

"If we go to the center of this chamber," Cheff said, "maybe we can tell which direction the voice is coming from."

"I don't… want to… do that… Friend Cheff," Lery said. "I don't… don't like this place." He was shaking. "This reminds… me of… my time in… the Iron Fortress."

Cheff put his hand on Lery's shoulder. "I understand, Friend Lery. You don't have to go anywhere you aren't comfortable.

How about you wait here at the entrance? Then, if we get lost, you can guide us back. How's that?"

"F… fine… thank you… Friend Cheff."

"Hurry, children," the ghostly whisper came again. "I'm waiting for you. Go into the chamber, now."

We took a few dozen steps toward the center of the pitch-black cavern.

Cheff called out again, "Where are you? Say something, so we can follow your voice."

"Thisss way, children," the voice said. "Jussst keep going. That'sss right, you're getting clossser now."

We were nearly all the way across the floor of the dome when Sable pointed ahead and slightly to the right. "There."

We strained to see the dim light.

Cheff called back to Lery, "I think we're almost there, Lery. Wait for us. We'll be back to get you soon."

Lery's voice came through the darkness. "Okay… Friend Cheff. I'm waiting… right… here."

A few yards more, and we reached the mouth of yet another dimly lit corridor.

"That'sss the one, children. Come to me. Only a little farther."

At the end of the corridor was a set of double doors, partially open.

"Open the doorsss, children. Come in. I am here."

We hesitated and exchanged a look. Finally, Cheff drew himself up, opened the door, and marched in boldly, the rest of us right behind. Seated on an extremely large green cushion was the biggest Seph any of us had ever seen.

"Scars," Sable observed.

Scars of all shapes and sizes covered the mammoth Seph's entire body.

"He must have been in some disaster," Cheff whispered.

"Cheff!" Mid said. "This must be the Seph from the giant Seph carrier that passed us in New City."

"I wonder who he is," Cheff said.

"I am Massster Callor," the huge Seph said, his voice still ghostly. "Once known asss Kullor, Qulor, and more recently, Kahph. Welcome. I have been waiting for you for sssuch a long time."

# Operation Shifting Sands

— 11 —

# Kahph

"Waiting for us, Master Kahph?" Cheff asked.

"I knew you would come," he said.

"You knew?" Mid asked. "That someone, anyone, would come, or that it would be us?"

But Kahph was staring at the rock roof of his cave and swaying back and forth rhythmically. He sang,

*"The watersss came,*

*"The watersss went.*

*"All the children's backs were bent.*

*"When I at last to Fellsssstone came,*

*"All the children looked the sssame."*

Every time he finished the verse, he'd start over again, still swaying and staring.

"Master Kahph," Cheff said quietly.

The oversized Seph didn't answer.

"Master Kahph!" Cheff said, a little louder.

Still no answer.

"MASTER KAHPH!" Cheff shouted.

Abruptly, the swaying stopped. Kahph lowered his immense head to Cheff's level and sniffed at Cheff. "A Lora? What's a Lora boy and a—" he sniffed at Buttons "—little Lora girl doing ssso far from the ssssea, away out here in the desssert?"

He sniffed at Mid. "A Troh. Deliciousss! I am fond of Troh."

Mid's eyes opened wide, but he kept silent.

Next, it was my turn. The great Seph turned his head in my direction. "A Lildur! Lovely. Lovely, lovely Lildur."

"I'm Birn," I said, "but my friends call me Books, because I like books."

"Booksss it isss, then," Kahph said, "for I sssenssse that we are to be great friendsss."

"And who isss the tall, dark, quiet one?" He sniffed at Sable. "A Kreff! How delightful! And one more…" He sniffed at Lhuk. "A Torph? A little Torph boy?"

"I'm Lhuk."

"And who isss your little friend, Lhuk? The one in your pocket, I mean."

"That's Squeaky," Lhuk said. "He's a mouse."

"A… moussse? Why would a Torph bring a moussse to a Seph?"

"Well, sir," Lhuk said, "we weren't expecting to meet you to-day."

Kahph closed his eyes, and Lhuk went rigid. Kahph's eyes opened. "A Torph rich in Ability, no lesss. Oh, yesss, I can senssse it. It'sss almossst involuntary in the face of Seph Ability. Did you know that? I can sssee you did not. Well, Lhuk, it isss sssomething you ssshould keep in mind. It might come in handy sssome day."

Lhuk shivered. "Yes, Master Kahph. I will. But we didn't come here to find you, sir."

"Then who are you children and why are you here?"

Cheff stepped forward. "My name is Cheff, this is my sister Mellabee, who prefers to be called Mel, and these are my friends,

Sable, Mid, Books, and Lhuk. We were looking for the library, sir, and got lost. We came to you because you called us."

"I *called* you? *I* called you? I called *you*? Why would I ever do sssomething like that?"

"We don't know, Master Kahph," Mid said. "We were hoping you would tell us."

"HOW DO YOU KNOW MY NAME? NO ONE KNOWSSS MY NAME!"

"You told us yourself only a few moments ago, Master Kahph," Buttons said. "Don't you remember?"

Kahph sniffed at Buttons. "Are you here to feed me or not?"

"No, Master Kahph. I'm sorry. We didn't bring any food with us."

He made that peculiar sound that serves as laughter for Sephs. "Didn't bring any food, that isss funny, little girl. Maybe I should eat you firssst?"

"*Eat* me?" Buttons took a couple of steps backward. "Um, no thank you, Master Kahph, sir. I'd rather you didn't. In any case, we're not here to feed you."

"*Too bad, so sssad,*

"*I really rather wish you had.*"

He resumed staring and swaying.

"*I'm in the mood*

"*For tasssty food,*

"*I surely could*

"*Eat sssomething good.*"

Starry caught Moka's eye, put her hoof up to one ear, and made a circular motion. Moka nodded soberly.

"*You could try to be more hasssty,*

"*And bring me something tasssty.*

"*Maybe a bit of tonton passstry.*"

Buttons stepped forward again and said boldly, "That doesn't rhyme."

Kahph froze and transfixed Buttons with his unblinking gaze. "Of course it does, little girl."

"No sir, I'm sorry. 'Hasty' and 'tasty' rhyme just fine," Buttons said. "But 'pastry' doesn't quite work."

Kahph lowered his head until his nose nearly touched Buttons'. We cringed, expecting those mighty jaws to snap shut around her at any moment. Instead, Kahph said, "You know, little girl, I do believe you are correct. Tasssty, hasssty, passstry… tasssty, hasssty, passstry… No indeed, *not* a rhyme. Clossse, but not a rhyme. Thank you, little one, for your assissstance. Is there sssomething I can do for you in return?"

Buttons glanced inquiringly at Cheff, who shrugged and mouthed the words, "Go ahead. You're on a roll."

"Why, yes, Master Kahph. We've been looking for the library. We're supposed to meet Master Vessslu there, and I'm afraid we're quite late. Would you be so kind as to tell us how to find it?"

*"Would I be ssso kind*

*"As to help you find*

*"The misssing library,*

*"Which isn't very…* sssomething. Hmmm." He shook his head to clear it, then continued, "Sssay, did you little onesss happen to meet a Seph called Attan? Thin fellow. Built like an eel. Needsss to eat more, I suppossse.

*"Of all the Sephsss who need to fatten,*

*"The thinnessst one of all isss Attan."*

"Yes, sir," Cheff said. "We were introduced to Grand Master Attan only this morning."

"Oh, *Grand* Massster, is it?" Kahph threw back his head and laughed again.

*"Nobody gets promoted fassster,*

*"Than Attan, our brand-new Grand Massster.*

*"He came here to bring disassster,*

*"'Cause he'sss a dirty, rotten —"*

"Has he been a monk  for long?" Cheff broke in.

"Monk? MONK?

*"If Attan isss sssome kind of monk,*

*"Then Pallador'sss crown is a heap of junk.*

*"For Attan is a New-City ssskunk."*

"So," Mid said, "*not* a monk then?

"Never!" Kahph said. "Not in my lifetime! Certainly not in hisss lifetime."

"Attan's from New City?" Cheff asked.

"Yesss, from the Sssilver Palace. He worksss for the Emperor. IID, you know—Imperial Intelligence Division.

*"Attan worksss for Pallador,*

*"Never knowsss jussst what he'sss for.*

*"He doesss Pallador'sss dirty deedsss,*

*"Becausse he worksss for the IID.*

*"Watch him and you'll sssee he's very*

*"Keen to ruin the Monassstery."*

"Ruin the Monastery!" I said. "But it's been here for centuries. Why would Pallador want to ruin it?"

*"Pallador'sss reasonsss are no myssstery,*

*"This monasssstery is full of hissstory.*

*"If Pallador can bring it down,*

*"He may get to keep hisss crown.*

*"I don't like to hear the sssound*

*"Of Pallador making my babiesss drown."*

"Excuse me, sir," Buttons said, "But 'sound'—"

Cheff took her arm and pulled her backward. "Not now, Sis."

"But—"

"Not *now!*"

"Okay, Cheff, if you say so, but the ponies are demanding—"

"Buttons." Sable said quietly.

"Okay, okay."

Kahph was swaying and staring at the ceiling again.

When it appeared that Kahph was distracted, Cheff motioned us toward the doorway, then whispered to the rest of us, "Okay, gang, what have we learned here?"

Mid counted on his fingers. "One: we've established that the monastery is a threat to Pallador. Two: Attan is here to neutralize that threat. Possibly by ruining the Monastery, especially the library, the 'history.'"

"Three:" Cheff said, "Attan's not a monk at all, but works directly for Pallador at the Silver Palace."

"Cheff," I said, "it would be a tragedy, a real tragedy, if the monastery's library were destroyed. It may be the last place in all of Andaran with the knowledge of our past. Pallador must believe that there is ancient knowledge here that could cost him his throne."

"You may be right, Books," Cheff said. "That's why he's outlawed old books and declared nearly everything 'forbidden knowledge.' He knows the Truth would end him. Depending on how much true history is here, it could pose a serious threat to Pallador's 'Path of Enlightenment' program."

"No wonder he wants it gone," Mid said.

At the word 'enlightenment,' Kahph abruptly stopped swaying and turned his attention back to us. "Ah, the 'Path of Enlightenment.' What a bunch of hooey!"

I laughed right out loud, shattering the stillness of Kahph's chamber.

"Books!" Cheff hissed. "Stop it!"

"I'm sorry, Cheff. I couldn't help it. I never expected to hear the word 'hooey' from a Seph."

"Focus, Books," Cheff whispered. "We need to figure out how we can stop Attan."

Apparently, Kahph had acute hearing. He intoned,

*"To sstop Attan you'll need the power,*

*"Found in the lonely desssert tower.*

*"You mussst travel there and bring me back*

*"The ssspherical crystal artifact."*

"Spherical crystal artifact?" Mid asked. "What's a spherical crystal artifact?"

Kahph locked eyes with Mid and said in his normal voice, "It isss an artifact, made of cryssstal, in the shape of a sssphere. What did you think it was? Whatever are they teaching children in ss-school these daysss?" He sniffed at Mid again. "Ah… *prey!* The Troh were always my favoritesss for a quick sssnack. There'sss nothing like a plump, tasssty Troh boy.

*"A roly-poly Troh,*

*"Isss the very bessst sssnack, you know.*

*"But he will give you lotsss of grief,*

*"If he getsss ssstuck between your teeth."*

At this, Buttons started to say something, but Cheff gave her such a stern look that she stopped and hung her head.

"Not this Troh boy, if you please," Mid said. "I'm not in a snacking mood. Besides, if you eat me, how will I get you your artifact?"

"*Artifact?*" Kahph reared his head. "What *artifact?*"

"The spherical crystal artifact, of course," Mid said.

"HOW DO YOU KNOW ABOUT THE ARTIFACT? IT ISSS FORBIDDEN KNOWLEDGE."

"It's not forbidden to you," Cheff said smoothly.

"Naturally not," Kahph said in a normal tone. "Nothing isss forbidden to me. I am Kahph."

"If this artifact is so powerful, Master Kahph," Buttons asked, "why don't you get it yourself? Why do you need us?"

"Buttons," Sable whispered again.

"What?" Buttons asked. "I only wanted to know if—"

"Please, Mel," Cheff pleaded, "give it a break before you turn us all into Seph supper."

Buttons' eyes widened, but she didn't say anything further. She hugged Starry and Moka close to her chest.

"Look at my body," Kahph said. "I'm covered in scarsss. Not jussst the onesss you can sssee. I am broken… inssside, too. Alssso, I have been in prissson for nearly a hundred yearsss. I'm not able to leave thisss room on my own power. They don't even bother to lock me in. I would never be able to make a trip into the desssert."

"Where exactly is this 'lonely tower?' Mid asked.

Kahph pondered this.

*"Through the desssert you must go,*

*"On your left, peaksss of snow,*

*"Crosss a river, though it isss dry,*

*"Until the Ssstone Bear catchesss your eye.*

*"Then turn toward the sssetting sssun,*

*"And there'sss the tower, the lonely one."*

We stared at Kahph.

Kahph stared back, then laughed. "Go into the Great Desssert. Go sssouth until you get to the big Ssstone bear. Turn right. You can't misss it. It'sss the only tower out there. Got it?"

"Stone bear?" Mid asked.

"You'll know it when you sssee it, Prey," Kahph said. "Now go, ssshoo, sssscram, beat it. I'm old now. It's time for me to sssleep." He rested his chin on his topmost coil, closed his eyes, and almost instantly began to snore.

We tiptoed out of Kahph's chamber into the dimly lit stucco corridor and gently closed the double doors behind us. We walked as fast as we could back to the big dome where we'd left Lery. When we got to the center of the dome, Cheff called, "Lery! We're back. Where are you?"

There was no answer. Cheff tried again. "Lery! It's us. We're here."

Still no answer.

Cheff asked, "Can anyone remember which way we came?"

"Not me," Buttons said. "We turned around in all directions trying to figure out where Kahph's voice was coming from. How about you, Books?"

"I'm… not sure." I pointed. "That way, maybe?"

"No," Sable said. She pointed in a different direction. "That way."

"Are you sure?" Cheff asked.

Sable merely looked at him.

"Of course you're sure," Cheff conceded. "Lead on."

Sable led. We were soon back in the relative security of a corridor, presumably the one we'd arrived through.

Lery wasn't there.

"Are you sure this is the right corridor?" Cheff asked Sable.

"Yes."

"Lery's not here," Mid said. "We've got to find him!"

"We've got to find Master Vessslu," Cheff said.

"Do we?" Mid asked. "We've already had a lot of Sephs for one day."

"Of course. He can help us find Lery, I'm sure. We don't know enough about the layout of this place to go on another wild-goose chase."

"Artifact," Sable said.

"Or maybe we should find Lery and go get the artifact," Cheff said. "On the other hand, I wonder what Master Vessslu knows about it?"

"Good point," Mid said. "And maybe he's heard something about Lery."

"Fair enough," Cheff said. "Let's see if we can retrace our steps and find our way back to the main floor. Maybe someone there can help us find Master Vessslu. Sable, do you think you can backtrack us out of here?"

Sable smiled a tiny smile.

"Of course you can," Cheff said. "After you!"

*Kahph*

$$- 12 -$$

# MASTER VESSSLU

---

ABLE STRODE RAPIDLY down the long corridor.

The rest of us struggled to keep up. Cheff and I stayed right behind Sable, then Buttons, and Mid puffed along in the rear, his short little legs pistoning away to keep up with Sable's military pace.

"How do you think she does it?" I asked Cheff.

"I don't know, but she always does. I've never known her to be wrong. I never asked her how. I figured it has to do with her Military training."

Sable's school 'Path of Enlightenment' was Military Leadership. She planned to become a Naval Officer like her father was—before he was arrested, and Sable was sent to the Fellstone Labor Compound.

I sped up so I was trotting alongside her. "I'm curious," I said, "about how you always know directions so well. Is it something you learned in Military Leadership School?"

Sable smiled at me. Without slowing down, she reached over and touched the side of my head with her forefinger. "Books," she said, then pointing at her own head, "Maps."

"You mean you remember maps the way I remember books? Like taking photographs?"

She nodded.

I thought about this. "Well, it's a good thing nobody knows about it, or you'd have a nickname even weirder than mine. You'd be 'Miss Maps.'"

Sable stared at me without speaking until I squirmed inside. "Okay, so, maybe not," I said. "At least, not because I told them about it."

She raised her eyebrows.

"I won't, I promise."

She smiled at me. I felt all warm inside—Sable's approval was no small thing.

Sable led us through the maze of little twisting passages, all alike. She turned up slitherways and into corridors without hesitation.

I dropped back to trot alongside Cheff.

"Well?" Cheff asked.

"She didn't say much," I said.

Cheff laughed. "She never does. Maybe someday, when she likes you enough, she'll tell you. Then again, maybe not."

"Do you think she would tell you, if you asked her?" I said. "You've known her longer than any of the rest of us."

Cheff and Sable had been friends for years, ever since Cheff arrived at the Labor Compound as a small boy.

"Probably," Cheff said, "but the thing is, I wouldn't ever ask."

"Why not? She didn't seem to mind that I asked."

"It's how Sable and I are. Always have been. She can do it, and that's all I need to know. If she wants me to know more, she'll tell me."

I was still thinking this over, wondering if I'd committed some Sable faux pas, when Sable abruptly turned into a corridor and led us straight into the dining hall. There was no one there. Our dirty dishes were still where we had left them. Lhuk sat down, brought Squeaky out of his pocket-home, and fed him crumbs from our leftovers.

"Lery's not here," Mid said unnecessarily.

"I can see that," Cheff snapped. He started pacing, always a bad sign.

"Maybe Kahph scared him off," Lhuk said.

Cheff stopped dead in his tracks. "What did you say?"

"I said, maybe Kahph scared him off." He fed Squeaky another bit of bread and cheese. "You know, when he tried his Seph Ability."

"What? When did he try his Seph Ability?"

"Didn't you notice?" Lhuk asked. "It was right about the time he tried to eat Buttons."

"Tried to eat Buttons!" Cheff clapped his hand to his forehead.

Buttons blanched, then took a seat next to Lhuk. She picked up a scrap of cheese and offered it to the little mouse, who sniffed it, then took it in his front paws and nibbled at it.

"Sure," Lhuk said. "You know, right about 'Did you come here to feed me?' Didn't you guys feel it?"

"I didn't feel anything," Cheff said. "This is the first inkling I had of it. How about the rest of you?"

No one had felt anything.

"I could feel his Ability pushing at us," Lhuk said. "I pushed back, only a little, then he stopped. He wasn't pushing hard. I thought you all knew, but weren't saying anything."

"No," Cheff said. "Nothing."

"But," Lhuk asked, "you could feel Master Vessslu's Seph's Kiss in the courtyard this morning?"

"Well, true. We all felt something. It was… nice." Mid said.

"You'll see how nice it is when he tries to eat *you*!" Buttons said. The ponies covered their eyes with their hooves.

"Didn't," Sable said.

"Didn't what?" Cheff asked. "Didn't try to eat Buttons?"

"Maybe not," I said, referring to our previous mission. "At the hunting lodge in The Fel, the Seph lord used his Ability on us, remember?"

"I'll never forget it," Cheff said.

"We all felt *that*," I said, "and no mistake about it. And we could feel it stop when Brex used her Ability. If Kahph had used his Ability in earnest, we would have known."

"Then what is Lhuk talking about?" Buttons asked.

"Maybe he was just testing?" Mid asked.

"Testing what?" Lhuk asked.

"Testing to see how much Torph Ability you have," Mid said, "and how well it's working."

"Oh." Lhuk said. "Well, if that's what it was, he found out what he wanted to know. I hope that's not a problem, Cheff. Anyway, it's not like I did it on purpose. I… well, my Ability kind of turned on all by itself."

"That's good to know," Cheff said. "I guess."

"Yeah, great," Mid said. "You never know when you might need a little Torph Protection, here in the Seph monastery, surrounded by Sephs, one of whom is stark raving mad, and including, as we just found out, a Seph working directly for Emperor Pallador."

"More than one," Sable murmured.

"She's right," Cheff said. "Surely Attan isn't here alone."

"In any case," Mid said, "that would be enough to scare Lery away. He's told me some of the stuff he went through while he was in the army. We talk, sometimes, in the evenings. It's… not pretty."

Lery lived with Mid and Mid's mom. Mid called Lery his adopted brother.

Buttons held the ponies up to her ear and listened. "The ponies have an idea, Cheff." She put both ponies on the table next to Squeaky, who seemed pleased to have some company, then she took off across the room.

"Wait! Buttons! Where are you going?" Cheff yelled.

"I'll be right back," Buttons called, then disappeared through the doors leading to the kitchen.

"Andaran's bones!" Cheff said. "This day is turning into a nightmare!"

"Wait," Sable said.

We waited, holding our breath.

The double doors opened and out came Buttons, towing Lery by the hand. "I found him—exactly where the ponies said I would!"

Lery wore a white apron over his regular clothes and a white food-service cap on his head.

"He was washing dishes," Buttons said happily.

Mid rushed up to Lery and threw his arms around him. "We were so worried! I'm so glad you're all right."

"I'm all... right, Brother Mid," Lery said. "I was... washing dishes. I'm... sorry that you... were worried..."

"What happened?" Cheff asked.

"I... I... felt something... bad..." Lery said. "Seph..."

"It was Seph Ability," Mid said. "We found a big old Seph down there. Probably the one that came here in that big Seph carrier. He said his name is Kahph. Lhuk says he tried to use his Ability on us."

"I... I guess... that... was it..." Lery said.

"How did you find your way back?" Mid asked.

"I don't... know... I... I felt... Seph... Then... I was here... in the... the dining hall. I thought... felt... that I... should hide..."

"And what better place to hide than as a kitchen helper! Well done, Lery!" Cheff patted him on the back. "That was smart, extraordinarily smart!"

"Kahph," Sable said.

"Do you think it was Kahph who directed you here?" Cheff asked Lery.

"I don't… know? Maybe… at first… it must have… been Kahph…But after… it felt… different…"

"Different?" Mid asked. "Different how?"

"It was like… like… like Master Vessslu's… Seph Kiss… this morning…"

"Do you think Master Vessslu was helping you?" Buttons asked.

"I'm… not sure?" Lery said.

"Lhuk," Buttons asked, "did you feel anything like that, anything warm?"

"No," Lhuk said. "Only Kahph."

"Interesting," Cheff said. "If Master Vessslu helped out somehow, wouldn't that violate the sanctity of self-determination?"

"Good point, Old Man," Mid said. "Maybe it's okay for them to help us do something we want to do."

"Maybe so," Cheff said. "I'd sure like to ask Master Vessslu."

"Well," Mid said, "why don't you?"

"How could I? He's not here."

"Ask him anyway, Cheff," Buttons said. "The ponies say, try."

"Um, okay," Cheff said dubiously. "Lhuk, see if you can feel anything."

Cheff stood up self-consciously. He raised his voice and addressed the air. "Um… Master Vessslu, if you can hear us, can you please help us? We have learned something we need to discuss with you."

We waited.

Nothing.

Cheff tried again, "Could you please show us how to get to where you are? Oh, and please, don't frighten Lery. He's had some bad experiences with Sephs in the past."

We waited again.

Lhuk stood up and put Squeaky into his pocket. "I think I feel something, maybe. Oh, yes, there it is! Follow me!" He went into the corridor.

"You okay, Lery?" Cheff asked.

"Yes… Friend Cheff… I'm… okay… I can… feel it… a little… but it's not… not scary."

"Okay, good. Let's go."

So into the maze of twisting little passages we went again. As we walked along, I got to thinking. "Do you suppose a Seph's Ability gets stronger with age? They keep growing larger, so why shouldn't their Ability grow, too?"

"I sure hope not," Buttons said. "The ponies say that would be a Bad Thing."

At the next junction, Lhuk said, "We're supposed to go down this corridor."

"I'm pretty sure that doesn't go to the library," Cheff said.

"Still," Lhuk insisted.

"Sable?" Cheff asked.

She shrugged.

"Okay, then," Cheff said. "Lead on, Lhuk!"

Lhuk led on for another five minutes or so, then stopped in the middle of a long stucco corridor exactly like all the other corridors, in front of a pair of double doors exactly like all the other double doors. "Here. It's this one."

"You sure, Lhuk?" Cheff asked.

"I'm sure."

"Fair enough," Cheff said. "Everybody ready?"

"As ready as we'll ever be," Mid said.

Buttons said, "The ponies say, get a move on, Cheff."

Cheff laughed. "Right you are, Sis." He stepped boldly forward and knocked on the door.

"Come in, young onesss, come in!" came Master Vessslu's voice through the wooden doors.

We heaved a collective sigh of relief. No surprises, this time.

All seven of us entered what appeared to be the foyer of Master Vessslu's well-lit private chambers. They smelled of Seph musk, but not unpleasantly so.

"Welcome, young onesss," Master Vessslu called out. "Come into the main room."

We passed into the main room and stopped dead in our tracks. Next to Master Vessslu, coiled on a second giant pillow, was Grand Master Attan.

"Yes," Grand Master Attan said, "welcome, young ones. We've been expecting you."

## — 13 —

## FIELD TRIP

WE FROZE AND waited. My heart sank into my shoes.

"What is it, young onesss?" Master Vessslu said. "What isss the matter? Come in, sssit down, be comfortable." He indicated seven people-sized chairs placed in a row in front of the Sephs' cushions.

We hesitated at first, until Master Vessslu gave us a private little nod, then we reluctantly took our seats.

"We, uh, have a matter we'd like to discuss with you, Master Vessslu," Cheff said.

"Very well," Master Vessslu said. "Proceed. You have my full attention."

Cheff glanced anxiously at Attan. "We, uh, well…"

"What isss it, young Cheff?" Master Vessslu asked, a note of impatience in his voice.

"You know my name," Cheff said.

"I know all your namesss, of courssse. It isss my busssinesss to know your namesss. Now, what isss your concern?"

"We, um, had hoped to discuss it with you privately, sir," Cheff said.

Master Vessslu looked over at Attan, then back at Cheff. "Whatever you have to sssay, you may sssay it in front of Grand Massster Attan. He isss, after all, the Grand Massster of Xanparthur Monassstery. I'm sure we have no secretsss from him."

"Well, okay," Cheff said, "as you wish. It's like this: we tried to find you, Master Vessslu, in the library where you spoke with Books and Lhuk this morning. Instead, we found ourselves in some other part of the monastery where we met a giant Seph named Kahph."

"Yesss, go on," Master Vessslu said. "What happened next?"

"Well," Cheff continued, "we introduced ourselves. It was hard to communicate with him, sir, because he didn't seem to make sense much of the time."

"He's been… unwell, for quite some time now. That's why we brought him here to Xanparthur, to rest and to be healed. He arrived only yesterday, right before you children. Perhaps you saw his transport vehicle?"

"Yes, sir," Cheff said.

"Did Kahph give you anything, or ask you for something?" Attan asked.

"Well…"

"Tell the truth, Lora boy," Attan snapped, "and be quick about it!"

"What Grand Massster Attan meansss to sssay," Master Vessslu said, "is that you may ssspeak your mind, here in my private chambersss, without fear or concern."

Cheff swallowed hard. Beads of perspiration formed on his forehead. "Of course, Master Vessslu. Kahph, excuse me, *Master* Kahph, asked us to go out into the desert and bring back an artifact for him."

At that, Master Vessslu and Attan both reared their huge heads and exchanged a look.

"An artifact!" they said together.

"Yes, sir, that's what he called it. An artifact."

"What kind of artifact?" Attan demanded.

"Please, Grand Massster," Master Vessslu said. "Allow me to handle thisss my own way."

Attan subsided, but his eyes smoldered.

"Now, young onesss," Massster Vessslu said gently, "did he happen to sssay what kind of artifact?"

"No, sir," Cheff lied. "Only that it was in a tower out in the desert somewhere."

"I sssee," Master Vessslu said. "Mossst interesssting. Did he happen to mention what he wanted it for?"

"No, sir. He did suggest that if we brought it to him, he'd owe us a favor."

Master Vessslu said, "It'sss no sssmall thing to be owed a favor from a Seph." He exchanged another look with Attan. "Well, perhapsss we can help you."

"Help us?" Cheff said. "But… I thought…"

"You thought we'd be angry?" Master Vessslu asked.

"Well… yes."

"Not at all," Master Vessslu said. "We are, however, mossst interesssted in thisss artifact."

"Emperor Pallador hasss been looking for a certain artifact for centuries, Lora boy," Attan hissed sharply. "If you happen to find an artifact of *any* kind, you'll turn it over to me at once. If, that isss, you know what'sss good for you."

I noted that when he was agitated, Attan lost his refined New-City accent—he hissed his S's like all the other Sephs.

"Pleasssse, Grand Massster," Master Vessslu said. "Allow me to continue. Of courssse these young onesss will be happy to bring usss any artifact they may find. Won't you, young onesss?"

The seven of us nodded in unison.

"Sssee there, Grand Massster? These young onesss are loyal subjectsss of the Emperor."

Again, Attan did not reply, only sullenly rested his scaly chin on his topmost coil. Master Kahph was right—Attan was much smaller and thinner than any Seph we'd ever seen. It looked like he could use a whole truckload of tonton pastry.

Master Vessslu continued, "Did Massster Kahph tell you where in the Great Desssert you should look for the artifact? The Great Desssert isss immense."

"He did," Cheff said. "He told us to go south until we come to the Stone Bear, then turn right until we find a tower."

"A tower? Are you certain?"

"Yes, Master Vessslu. He repeated it to be sure we'd remember."

"He called it a 'lonely tower,'" Mid added.

Attan asked Master Vessslu, "Do you know the tower of which he speaksss?"

"No," Master Vessslu said, "but I know ssssomeone who might. Snard!"

Facilitator Snard appeared instantly. "Yes, Master Vessslu?"

"Could you pleassse find Kregg Setnar and Jewell, and bring them to me? And have the kitchen prepare food for ssseven children for several days. Packed, pleassse. Our young friendsss will be going on a little journey."

"At once," Snard said, and disappeared again.

"A journey? Us?" Cheff asked.

"Yesss, young one," Master Vessslu said. "You *do* want to help usss, I mean Massster Kahph, find the artifact, do you not?"

"Well..."

"Excuse me, sir," Mid said. "If I may, I have a question."

"Asssk, young one."

"Well, sir, if this artifact is as important as it seems to be to you and Master Attan, and perhaps even to Emperor Pallador, why not simply send some Facilitators to go get it? Why send us? We're just kids."

Attan, who appeared to have regained his composure, barked, "Keep quiet and do as you're told, Troh boy!"

"Attan, *pleassse*," Master Vessslu said. "That is a good quessstion, young Mid. The artifact isss, indeed, of special interessst to the Emperor. So much so, in fact, that sssecrecy isss a top priority. Were we to send Facilitatorsss, it would attract much attention, do you sssee?"

"Yes, sir," Mid said.

"But if," Master Vessslu went on, "a group of young visitorsss to our monastery happened to go on a sssightsssseeing tour, why, that wouldn't aroussse any sssuspicion at all, now would it?"

"A sightseeing tour?" Mid said. "Well, no, I suppose not."

"What kind of sights would we see, Master Vessslu?" Buttons held up Starry and Moka for the Sephs to see. "The ponies would like to know."

"Oh, for—" Attan began.

But Master Vessslu cut him off. "The ponies asssk an excellent quessstion. There are many interesssting thingsss to sssee in the Great Desert. Strange plantsss and animalsss, rock formationsss, and who knowsss, perhaps a certain… tower. A lonely tower."

"Oh," Buttons said, blinking. "I see."

Facilitator Snard returned, bringing the man and woman we'd seen working in the garden that morning.

"Greetings, Grand Master Attan, Master Vessslu," Kregg Setnar said. "How may we be of service?"

"Greetingsss," Master Vessslu said. "I would like you to meet some young friendsss of oursss. Kregg Sssetnar, Jewell, this is Cheff, Mid, Buttonsss, Booksss, Sssable, Lery, and Lhuk."

"Hello," Cheff said. "We saw you this morning, planting flowers in the garden."

"Hello," Kregg Setnar said. "It's nice to meet you again!"

"That'sss correct," Master Vessslu said, "Jewell and Kregg sometimes work here as gardenersss. The ressst of the time, they give toursss of the desssert to visitorsss." He turned to Kregg.

"I would like you to do me a favor, if you would be ssso kind. I would like you to take these young onesss on a tour of the Great Desssert. It won't be an ordinary tour, ssso we will pay you twice your usual rate. The children are looking for sssomething in particular, ssso the tour might lassst several daysss. Would that be posssible, old friendsss?"

Jewell and Kregg considered this, then Kregg said, "I see no problem. I'm sure it would be fine."

Jewell asked, "When would they like to leave?"

"As sssoon as posssible," Master Vessslu said. "I apologize for the ssshort notice."

"Not a problem," Kregg said. "We'll make arrangements immediately."

"Thank you, my friendsss," Master Vessslu said. "There's jussst one more thing. It would be bessst for everyone if you didn't mention thisss trip to anyone, essspecially here at the monassstery."

"Of course," Jewell said.

"Snard, pleassse inssstruct the kitchen to add food for two adultsss to the package they are making. And caution them to keep quiet about the matter, too."

"I already did so, Master. But I'll remind them again, in no uncertain terms."

"Excellent!" Master Vessslu said. "I believe that concludesss our businesss for today. Thank you, children, that will be all. Pleassse go with Jewell and Mr. Sssetnar."

"Yes, Master Vessslu," Cheff said. "And thank you, sir… I think."

Master Vessslu laughed. "Don't worry, young Cheff. You'll be in good handsss. I'll sssee you sssoon, I hope."

Jewell beckoned to us. "You'll have a few things to pack, I imagine. Follow me to the dormitory, then we'll be on our way."

We followed Jewell and Kregg into the corridor, and the great double doors closed gently behind us. Lhuk and Lery sighed with relief. I hadn't noticed before, but Lhuk looked pale, and Lery's hands were shaking.

Cheff wiped his forehead. "Well. I certainly wasn't expecting that!"

"Me, neither," Mid said.

"The ponies would like to know, Cheff, exactly what it is you've gotten us all into."

"As would I, Sis, as would I." He drew a deep breath. "And I expect we're about to find out."

Kregg took his leave at a junction in the corridor. "I'll fetch the bus," he said, "and meet you in front."

"Right," Jewell said.

When we got back to the dormitory, Jewell said, "Go ahead and get your kits together, children, then find your way to the monastery entrance. Can you do that? If you have trouble, ask a Facilitator, okay? Good. I'll see you in a short while." And she was gone.

Cheff said, "Pack your gear as quickly as possible, before you-know-who gets wind of this."

"Should be pretty quick," Mid said. "I never unpacked, and we're all traveling pretty light."

"Too late," Sable said, and gestured toward the doorway.

Brex strode in, flanked by Tocette and the rest of her Blueband thugs. She marched up to Cheff and stuck her face right in his. "What is the meaning of this, Karfendek? Just where do you think you are going?"

"Why, hello, Miss Brex. You're looking lovely this afternoon, as always."

"Answer my question, Karfendek! I demand to know what's going on."

"It's a field trip, Miss Brex," Buttons said brightly. "We're packing our gear! Isn't that wonderful?"

Brex glared at Buttons, then turned on Cheff again. "Field trip? What is this? Who authorized a field trip?"

"Master Vessslu, Miss Brex," Mid said. "We're not sure why. He said he had something special for us to see."

"Hmmph! I'll be checking with Master Vessslu, you can count on that. I can't imagine that you and your gang running off into the Great Desert can bring anything but trouble and embarrassment." Her eyes glazed over briefly, then she recovered.

"What is it, Miss Brex," Tocette asked. "Are you all right?"

"Of course I'm all right!" Brex barked. "I was remembering riding in that truck…" She blinked rapidly, then drew a sharp breath.

"Truck?" Tocette asked. "What truck, Miss Brex? Are you sure you're okay?"

"What in Andaran are you talking about, cadet?" Brex demanded. "There's no truck. Now, get your gear together."

"My gear? What for?"

"Because you're going with them."

"Me? Go into the desert?" Tocette shuddered. "Wouldn't it be better if you—?"

"Are you deaf, Cadet Moron?" Brex was almost screaming. "Can't you, for once, just follow a simple order? Get. Your. Gear. Together. You know I can't leave my post!"

"Yes, Miss Brex." Tocette trotted over to her bunk and began stuffing her things into her pack.

"When you're finished," Brex went on, "meet me out front. And you'd better be out there before these hooligans, or else! I'm going to arrange things with Master Vessslu." She stormed out of the dormitory in a flurry of indignance. The double doors slammed shut behind her.

"Great," Mid grumbled. "Exactly what we need—a Blueband to watch our every move."

Sable said, "Better this way."

Cheff laughed. "She's right! Tocette will see that we don't get into any trouble, and she'll give the best possible report about us to Brex."

Buttons laughed. "The ponies think that's hilarious, Cheff. I'm going to help Tocette get ready so she can get out front before we do!"

# — 14 —

# GREAT DESERT SAFARIS

BUTTONS AND TOCETTE were ready to go almost immediately and left. Sable changed into her mission outfit but carried her tool belt in a small cloth valise. She tied her long black hair into a ponytail. The rest of us finished packing and we headed out.

Waiting for us at the main entrance of Xanparthur Monastery, where we first arrived, was one of the strangest vehicles we'd ever seen. It was like a bus, but not as big as most buses. The big, wide tires had special tread which I supposed was for driving on sand. Its green and tan exterior paint matched the tones of the desert sand and cacti. Though steam-driven, like most vehicles, the steam engine itself was concealed beneath a long, shiny, tan hood. Where the windows would normally be, the sides were open. The top was made of green canvas that matched the green parts of the vehicle.

Along the side, below the opening, red and gold lettering boasted 'Great Desert Safaris.' Underneath that, in much smaller letters, was 'J. Jorg & K. Setnar, Proprietors.'

Standing by the boarding stairs, located directly behind the driver's compartment, was Mr. K. Setnar, himself, wearing a huge smile. "Welcome, welcome, children, to Great Desert Safaris! Climb aboard, pick your seats, and stow your packs underneath them."

Cheff and Mid sat together, as did Sable and Buttons, and Lery and Lhuk. I sat farther back, all by myself at first, but then Tocette climbed aboard and sadly surveyed the situation. I think she'd been hoping to sit with Cheff or maybe next to Sable and Buttons. I felt a little sorry for her, so I waved.

Tocette lit up and instantly became all smiles. "Booksie!" she brayed, and lumbered down the aisle to me. She jammed her bulging canvas pack under our seat, crushing my own pack in the process, then plopped her enormous bulk down next to me. She wrapped her hairy arm around my shoulders and hugged me so tight that I couldn't breathe. "Booksie, my little Booksie Buddy! I'm sure glad to see you! How are you doing? Are you having a fun trip, so far?"

I turned my face away in a futile attempt to avoid the fallout of food particles when she talked, borne on her foul breath. "Not yet," I said. "We haven't even started moving."

"Haw, haw, haw!" Bits of old food and spittle flew everywhere, but mostly on me. She slapped her thigh. "You're as funny as always, little Booksie Buddy! I know we're not moving yet. I mean the whole trip, Xan… Xanper… Parthur…"

"Xanparthur Monastery?" I suggested.

She clapped me on the back so hard my glasses flew off. I caught them in mid-air and replaced them.

"That's the one! Xan… Pan… well, you know, what you said. How do you like it so far?"

"It certainly has been interesting," I said. "I'm learning a lot of things I wasn't expecting to learn."

"Haw, haw! Me, too. I guess. Maybe. I… I'm not as good at learning stuff as you, Booksie. But I'm still having fun. Say, how come you guys get a special field trip of your own?"

"That's a good question, Tocette. I can't say. Lhuk and I visited Master Vessslu in the library this morning, then later he arranged this trip."

"That's good for you, I guess. You guys, you know, Cheff and all, you always seem to get a little something special. Say, is that Lhuk kid coming, too? Is he one of your gang now?" She lowered her voice to a whisper that could probably be heard all the way back to Fellstone City. "He's a Torph, you know!"

Lhuk turned his head around and gave her a faint smile. "You don't have to whisper, Tocette. I know I'm a Torph."

Poor Tocette flushed deep red. "I'm sorry, Lhuk. I didn't notice you next to Lery. I didn't mean any offense."

"And I take none."

Tocette smiled shyly and dropped her gaze to her lap. She self-consciously wiped a tear away with her sleeve. "You all are so… so nice to me. I don't know why." She wiped her eyes again, then said so quietly that I could barely hear, "No one else is."

"Why shouldn't we be nice to you?" I asked. "You're always nice to us."

She sniffled, then smiled a little. "I guess I am, amn't I?"

"Sure," I said.

She looked up. "Cheff calls me beautiful and intrepid. I like it when he says that, even though I don't really know what 'intrepid' means."

"It means fearless, bold," I said.

She brightened. "It does? That's nice… even though I'm not. I'm not beautiful, either, but it's still nice to hear."

"But you are beautiful, Tocette," Cheff said. "There are many kinds of beauty, and you have a special kind, all your own."

"You really think so?"

"Of course. Cheff never lies, you know," I lied.

She threw her arms around me and tried to crush my chest again. "Awww, that's so sweet!" She was almost, but not quite, beaming. Then her face fell, and the tears started again.

"What's the matter now, Tocette?" I asked.

"It's so sad about Lhuk. I'm glad he got to go with us today."

"Why is that sad?"

"Well, you know," she whispered. "Because he's a Torph. And he's almost old enough to develop the Ability. And then… and then…" She started to cry again, in earnest this time. Her whisper turned into a wail. "And then we'll never see him again!" She buried her face in my shoulder and commenced sobbing.

By now, everyone else on the bus had turned around and were staring at us.

"Stop it, Tocette!" I hissed. "Everybody's looking. Besides," I lied again, "Lhuk doesn't have the Ability and may never develop it. Like Brex," I lied a third time. "She's practically grown up and hasn't shown any symptoms of Ability." I was getting good at lying with a straight face. My mother would have been horrified if she had known—she always insisted that I tell the truth, no matter what. For that matter, I always did, to my mother—she had a right to the truth.

Tocette sniffled and wiped her face with a sleeve, leaving slime trails on her makeshift uniform. "I guess that's true. Thanks, little Booksie Buddy. I'll try to stay positive."

"You do that, Tocette. That's a good plan."

Kregg Setnar came aboard and settled into the driver's seat, followed by Jewell, who took a seat behind Kregg, facing us.

"Welcome, children," Jewell said. "If you're all settled, we'll be on our way. This trip was unexpected, to say the least, and we're not quite entirely prepared. Oh, here comes the food!"

Four uniformed chefs from the monastery kitchen came aboard and handed everyone a parcel, including Tocette, Jewell, and Kregg, then silently disembarked.

Tocette sniffed at her package. "Food!" She began tearing off the wrapper. I wondered how they had known about Tocette—I guessed Brex had made good on her promise to consult with Master Vessslu.

I put my hand on her arm. "Not now, Tocette. You're supposed to save it for later."

She regarded me sadly, then tried in vain to replace the torn wrapper. "Okay, Booksie, if you say so. But it smells so *good!*"

Jewell called out, "Hang on, children! Here we go!"

Kregg shoved the safari bus into gear, and we rumbled out of the monastery parking area.

Jewell said, "Next stop, Kell's Junction."

"What's Kell's Junction?" Buttons asked.

"It's the little town at the base of the monastery. You drove past it on your way up here. I live in Kell's Junction, and so does Kregg. It provides some services for the Xanparthur Monastery, and also has a few hotels for wealthy tourists, down by the oasis."

Starry raised her forehoof and waved it vigorously.

Jewell was nonplussed, but quickly recovered. "Yes, er, Pony?"

"Her name is Starry," Buttons explained. "This other one is called Moka."

Jewell came over and shook each pony's hoof. "Nice to meet you Starry, Moka. Now, what was your question?"

"Please, Miss Jewell, the ponies would like to know what an oasis is."

"Good question," Jewell said. "An oasis is a place in the desert where water is found. It was important in the olden days before steam travel was invented. People, horses, and other livestock all need water. It can be hard to find water in the Great Desert, even when you know where to look. So, whenever a place was discovered that had plenty of water all year round, it often became a landmark along the road. Kell's Oasis is quite large—it's a small lake—and is ringed by palm trees and all sorts of desert plants. A lot of desert animals live there, too."

Cheff asked, "Why is it called Kell's Junction and Kell's Oasis? Was Kell a person?"

"Probably," Jewell answered. "It happened so long ago that no one knows anymore. Legend has it that his name was Kell Solcum, a man of the Sevro People, from Fellstone City. It's almost certainly the reason the old road came this way. Now, of course, it's the Imperial Highway."

"Why 'junction'?" Mid asked. "Is there another road that branches off here?"

"Not anymore," Jewell said. "There probably used to be. It's the first place you come to if you're traveling westward from Fellstone City. Maybe, long ago, other roads branched off. To the south is more desert, a lot more desert. North, if you go far enough, you come to the mountains. Straight west goes all the way across the Great Desert to Feyar City, then continues all the way west to the ocean."

Lery asked, "So… what made… Kell… stop here to… to build… a town?"

"Another good question," Jewell said, "but again I'm afraid that no one knows nowadays. Kell, if he lived at all, lived a thousand years ago or more. Maybe he thought he could earn his living providing hospitality to travelers." She smiled. "There is one legend, though, that seems to have survived the centuries. It is said that after Kell built his town at the edge of the oasis and had lived to see it become a bustling travel stop serving a near-constant stream of travelers, that someone asked him that same question: 'Why did you stop here to build a town?' And Kell replied sadly, 'I was trying to find a little peace and quiet.'"

The Safari bus climbed a little hill, then started downward again. In the distance, we saw the oasis, an azure-blue lake surrounded by emerald-green palm trees.

"Beautiful," Sable said.

"Can we go swimming?" Buttons said. "The ponies love to go swimming."

"They do?" Tocette asked.

"They sure do!" Buttons said. "That's how Starry's stuffing got shriveled. I gave her diving lessons in the bathtub one day."

"Oh." Tocette said. "I like swimming. At least, I think I would. There's no place to do it in the Labor Compound. But I wouldn't want my stuffing to get shriveled."

"There is a place to go swimming," Jewell said, "but we won't have any time for that today. We're going to load some fuel and supplies, and be on our way."

"Awww," Buttons said. "That's too bad. The ponies love the water!"

But Starry gave me a look that said otherwise.

The Great Desert Safari bus wound its way down the hillside, and soon we came to the outskirts of town. There was a hand-made wooden sign driven into the sand by the side of the highway. It read:

KELL'S JUNCTION
POPULATION: 1,893
ELEVATION: 5,746 FEET. (1,751m)

"That's pretty high!" Buttons said.

"More than a mile (1,600m)," Cheff said.

"Sometimes," Jewell said, "people who live at sea level have a hard time catching their breath up here. If that happens to you, slow down and breathe deeply. Also, it helps to drink lots of water. Does everyone have a canteen?"

We all did.

"Good. Be sure to take them with you at all times, and sip a little water frequently. When they get half empty, you can fill them from the water barrel in the back." She pointed to a large barrel strapped into a rear corner of the bus, next to a tiny kitchen. "We'll fill that before we leave. Also, and again because of the altitude, even though it's usually pretty hot in the daytime, it can get extremely cold at night. So be sure to take your jackets everywhere with you. It's important to be prepared."

Kregg eased the bus to a stop in the front drive of a large, tan house. It was the same color as the monastery walls, and it looked old.

"Here we are, kids! Welcome to Setnar's Mansion, your home away from home, where hospitality is king. We'll only be a few minutes. Maybe you kids can give me a hand with the supplies?"

When we had followed Kregg off the bus, he said, "Cheff, maybe you and Mid can fill the coal box? You'll find it all the way in front, under the hood. The coal is in that bin there, against the wall. Books, you can go with them, too. The rest of you can help Jewell with the food. And Lery, maybe you can help me load the equipment chest." He pointed to a rather large, heavy-looking, wooden box.

Lery said, "Okay."

"You take one end, I'll take the other," Kregg said.

"That's… okay… Mr. Setnar… I've got it."

Lery bent down, wrapped his long arms around the equipment chest, and picked it up. Kregg dashed ahead of Lery to open the big doors at the rear of the bus. Lery easily lifted the chest and slid it inside.

Kregg stared, eyebrows raised. "Right, then," he said. "Nice work, Lery. If you ever need a job…"

Lery smiled. "It was… was nothing. I'm happy… to help."

"Climb aboard, pick your seats, and stow your packs!"

## — 15 —

## LOADING THE BUS

"**G**REAT," KREGG SAID. "Let's find a hose and top off that water barrel. Can't ever carry too much water in the desert."

"Okay," Lery said, and followed him to the house.

Kregg handed Lery the end of a rubber hose. "Stick that into the barrel and holler when you're ready. I'll turn it on."

"Okay." Lery dragged the hose to the back of the bus, then called out, "Ready!" When the barrel was nearly full, Lery called out again. "It's… full."

Kregg shut down the water. "Good, now take the hose around and fill the boiler, would you, please?"

Lery dragged the hose around to the front of the bus. Cheff and Mid had opened the hood and were inspecting the Safari bus's innards. Lery, hose still in hand, stuck his head under the elegant tan hood with Cheff and Mid.

"Look!" Mid said. "This is amazing! Brilliant design!"

"What… what is that… for?" Lery pointed at a series of silver chambers, each larger than the previous one.

"Those are expansion chambers," Mid said. "It's a way of getting more out of your steam."

"I… I don't… get it," Lery said.

"Well," Mid said, "it's like this: the steam comes out of the boiler under pressure, right? It goes into the cylinder, then expands to make the piston move. After that, where does it go?"

"Into… the air… I guess," Lery said.

"Right!" Mid said. "Usually. But not in this engine. In this engine, it goes into another cylinder, a larger one, because the steam is already partially expanded. In the larger cylinder, it has room to expand even more, so it's used to push another piston. I've seen steam engines with two chambers before, but this baby"—he patted the bus's fender—"this baby has *four* chambers, the main cylinder plus three expansion chambers."

"That must be how such a small engine can power such a big bus," Cheff said.

"You got it, Old Man," Mid said, "but the extra power isn't all. This engine will use less coal and less water, too. And that makes it perfect for long-distance travel where there are no fuel or water stops."

"Like… like the Great… Desert," Lery said.

"Right again!" Mid said. "But wait—there's still more. See this funny-looking metal tube? It has a kind of screw inside that moves coal from the coal bin to the boiler's firebox automatically. And this"—he indicated another component attached to the coal bin—"I'm pretty sure is a coal grinder to make the autoloader work more smoothly."

Cheff said, "So, no shoveling coal in the hot desert, then?"

"Exactly!" Mid said. "Whoever invented this arrangement is a true genius!"

"Why, thank you, Mid," Kregg said. He'd left his post at the water faucet to see what the holdup was. "It's nice to meet someone who appreciates good engineering."

"This is *your* invention?" Mid asked.

"Mine and Harleen Beeker's," Kregg said. "He's a friend of mine, keeps the tavern in Kell's Junction. He has a little shop in his back room and likes to tinker. I think it up, and he builds it. A genius with his hands. Makes good tonton cider, too."

Cheff grinned. "The thinker and the tinker! Sounds like another tavern keeper we know. His name is Meltern, and he has a guest house in Old City. He's not a tinkerer—"

"—that we know of—" Mid said.

"—but he's justifiably proud of his cider. Apple, though—not tonton."

"It's the best in all Fellstone City," I said, "according to Mr. Meltern. Buttons says that the ponies can't seem to get enough of it."

"Speaking of cider," Kregg said, "We need to load some supplies, too. Are you boys nearly done here?"

"Yes, sir," Cheff said. "All except for the water."

"Well, you and Mid can finish that up, then join Lery and me in the cellar. Walk right on in and go through the kitchen. You'll see the stairs. Can't miss them."

I helped Cheff and Mid fill the boiler tank, then the three of us went to find Lhuk and the girls.

Inside Setnar's Mansion, our eyes took a few seconds to adjust to the cool darkness inside. Mid took his dark glasses off. "Ahhh, that's more like it!"

"Yeeeeow!" Cheff yelled, nearly scaring my pants off. "Andaran's Bones! What is it?"

"What is what?" Mid asked.

Cheff stood absolutely still in the middle of the room. "My shoulder," he whispered.

A furry little animal, a little bigger than a cat, perched on Cheff's shoulder, sniffing at his ear. Cheff started to turn his head to look, then thought the better of it. "Get it off!" he hissed.

Kregg came back to see what the matter was, then laughed. "That's Mr. Kip. He's a desert pup. He won't hurt you."

"Maybe not," Cheff said, scowling, "unless you count heart attacks. He scared me half to death!"

Mr. Kip gently took Cheff's face in his soft forepaws and turned Cheff's head around to peer intently into his eyes. "Treeeeeats?" he begged. "Caaaaandy?"

Buttons, who, along with Jewell and everyone else, had come running when Cheff yelled, clapped her hands. "He talks! How wonderful!"

"He knows quite a few words," Jewell said. "You'd never know it, though, because he mostly asks for treats and candy."

Buttons approached Mr. Kip slowly. "Treats? Are you looking for a handout, Mr. Kip?"

Mr. Kip let go of Cheff's face and turned to Buttons. "Treeeeeats?" he asked her.

Buttons giggled and dug around in her pockets, but found nothing. Jewell passed her a couple of slices of tonton fruit. Buttons held them out. "Do you like tonton fruit, Mr. Kip?"

Apparently, he did, because he leaped from Cheff's shoulder into Buttons' arms. "Here you go," she said.

He took the slices from her with his tiny paws and nibbled them.

"I guess you do," Buttons said and giggled. "He's cute."

"Mr. Kip," Jewell said, "what do you say?"

"Taaaaank youuuuuu."

"Why, you're welcome!" Buttons said.

The slices of fruit had vanished. Mr. Kip licked his paws clean, then looked up at Buttons. "Treeeeeats? Caaaaandy?"

"That's all for now, Mr. Kip," Jewell said. "Jump down—we have a lot to do."

Mr. Kip reluctantly jumped to the floor.

"Anyway," Jewell said to the fuzzy little creature, "we're getting ready to go on safari."

"Safaaaaaari?" Mr. Kip asked.

"Yes," Jewell said. "Would you like to go, too?"

"Safaaaaari!" Mr. Kip dashed out of the house and leaped into the Safari Bus. He took up what I guessed was his usual station on the bus's dashboard. "Let's goooo, Boss! Hurry! Safaaaaari time!"

"Pesky little creature," Kregg said, "One of these days I'll have him stuffed and mounted for a hood ornament."

Jewell punched him gently on the shoulder. "Oh, you're *such* an old meanie! You wouldn't know what to do without him. Well, come on, everyone, let's get this show on the road."

Jewell led us to the cellar and pointed at a stack of crates. "That's the last of it. Everyone grab what you can, and let's be off."

Mid took the time to look over Kregg's workbench, his eyes glowing with delight. "I wish we had more time to talk shop with Kregg."

Lery spotted a rather large pipe wrench at the far end of the workbench. He picked it up and hefted it. "Brother Mid?"

"Maybe. Ask Kregg when we get back upstairs."

"Okay."

After we loaded the crates, Lery approached Kregg. "Mr. Kregg? Do you… think that maybe… maybe I could… borrow… this pipe wrench? They… they wouldn't… let… let me… take mine… on the bus…"

Kregg frowned and glanced at Cheff, who nodded almost imperceptibly. "Well, um, sure, I guess so, Lery."

"Thank you… Mr. Kregg. The… the right… tools…" Lery hooked it to his belt and sighed contentedly.

We climbed in and found our seats. Kregg closed the doors and took his place at the wheel. The Great Desert Safari bus was on its way!

As we rolled slowly through town, nearly everyone we passed stopped to wave. It seemed that Kregg and Jewell were both well-known and well-liked in Kell's Junction.

We passed a sprawling building with a big sign that read:

## Kell's Junction Guest House

"That's Harleen's place," Kregg said. "It's not as elegant as the tourist hotels, but it's a lot less expensive. And, if you ask me, the food is a lot better. Harleen found a cook who can only be described as legendary."

"Our best cook is Lery," Cheff said. "He's something of a legend in his own right."

"I'm glad to hear it," Kregg said. "Lery, if you'd like, you can be our official cook for this expedition."

"Okay," Lery said. "I… I would… would like that."

"Excellent!" Kregg said. "Jewell usually does our cooking. She'll appreciate the break." He lowered his voice. "Frankly, so will I. Not that she's a *bad* cook, mind you, but, well, let's just say she's a long way from legendary."

"I heard that!" Jewell called from the back of the bus. "One more crack like that, *Mister* Setnar, and you'll never taste my farnam soup again!"

This cracked Tocette up, and she laughed like a donkey braying in the morning.

As we left the little town, we passed the three tall, elegant tourist hotels by the edge of the oasis.

"They were built before The Fall," Kregg said. "I don't know how they remained standing all these years. I suppose it's because the fighting never reached this part of the Great Desert. Although, I've heard that in the years immediately after The Fall they were used to billet soldiers. Anyway, that was long ago. I think it's interesting to see how intricate and elegant the architecture is, compared to the little concrete ovens we live in nowadays. My house is old, too, and well-built. I'm sure you noticed how cool it is inside?"

"We did," Mid said. "Same as the monastery."

"And for much the same reason," Kregg said. "The walls are made of something called adobe, which is basically mud, shaped into bricks and dried in the sun. They soak up the heat in the daytime, keeping the house cool. Then, at night, they slowly release the heat, which keeps the house from getting too cold. Adobe is another reason the oasis was so important—it's where the old-timers got the water to make the adobe mud."

"I didn't see any bricks," Buttons said. "Not at your house, and not at the monastery. All the walls were made of some kind of scratchy plaster."

"That's called 'stucco,'" Kregg said. "It's made largely of sand, which is why it's that color, and also why it's scratchy. It goes on the bricks after the building is built."

"To make it pretty?" Buttons asked.

"Partly," Kregg said, "and partly to keep the little rain we get from melting the adobe bricks. But you have to be careful not to rub against it, because it's abrasive."

"Sandpaper," Sable said.

"Exactly," Kregg said, "except without the paper."

We drove on until we were out of sight of the hotels, then Kregg checked the road ahead and behind. Satisfied that no one was in sight, he turned the bus southward, off the Imperial Highway, straight into the desert.

"No point in advertising what we're doing out here," Kregg said. "The fewer who know about it, the better off we'll be. If things go well, we'll be out and back before anyone's the wiser. Meanwhile, it's time to take care of an important matter."

He set the throttle and clipped a lanyard to the steering wheel to hold it in place, then got up and went to the back of the bus where Jewell was still arranging our supplies. Mr. Kip jumped from his dashboard perch onto the steering wheel.

Tocette was amazed. "You're going to let Mr. Kip drive?"

Kregg called back, "Why not? There's nothing out here to hit. All he has to do is go in a straight line. Anyway, it seems to make him happy."

He opened a cabinet mounted in the back of the bus near the water barrel and turned a knob inside. He waited a few seconds, then lit a match and a small flame appeared inside the cabinet. "In the Great Desert, we light a fire when we want to make things cold." He turned a valve on the tube leading from the water barrel to the cabinet. We heard the sound of running water, then it shut itself off. "Good, that's started. Let's give it twenty minutes or so." He consulted his timepiece. "Good."

"What's in the box, Mr. Kregg?" Tocette wanted to know.

"All in good time, Miss Tocette, all in good time." He waggled his bushy eyebrows at her, which made her giggle.

"I think I might know," Mid said. "I read something about this a while back."

"Well, for Andaran's sake, don't say anything!" Kregg said. "You'll spoil the surprise. Meanwhile, if I'm not mistaken, Jewell would appreciate a hand. Miss Tocette, would you care to help Jewell?"

"Me? Help?" A smile spread slowly across her face. "Sure! What do I do?"

Jewell pulled a crate out of storage and opened it. It was chock-full of tonton fruit. "The monastery is paying us a bonus for taking you kids out, so I splurged a little." She got a knife, a bowl, and a funny-looking tool out of a drawer and placed them on the counter of the tiny little kitchen. She found a large pitcher and put it on the little counter, too.

"What's that weird tool?" Buttons asked. "It looks like a nutcracker that got into a fight with a pincushion."

Jewell laughed and held it up. "It does, doesn't it? This is one of Kregg's marvelous inventions. It's a tonton squeezer."

She handed it to Tocette, who examined it carefully. "What do I do with it?"

"I'll show you in a minute, dear. We're going to make an assembly line."

## — 16 —

# THE TONTON EXPRESS

---

"Hurray! An assembly line!" Tocette said. "What's an assembly line?"

"Yes," Buttons said. "The ponies aren't sure, either."

"Well, it's like this," Jewell said. She filled the bowl with water about halfway, then placed it at the end of the table closest to the crate of tonton fruit. "Buttons, you take a tonton fruit from the crate and wash it off, then hand it to Sable."

"Okay."

Jewell handed Sable the knife. "Sable, you slice it in half and give the halves to Tocette."

Sable did so.

"Okay, Tocette, your turn. You put half a tonton into the squeezer, like this, see? Then you hold it over the pitcher and squeeze as hard as you can."

Tocette stuck a tonton half into the squeezer and squeezed. A little stream of tonton juice ran into the pitcher, filling the bus with the most tantalizing scent of fresh fruit.

"Hey! I did it!" Tocette said.

"You certainly did!" Jewell said. "And a fine job you did of it, too."

"Oh." Tocette glowed. "What next?"

"Next, the three of you keep doing that until the pitcher is full."

For the next quarter of an hour, the assembly line ran at full speed until the crate was empty and the pitcher was full.

"Done!" Buttons said.

A few seconds later, Sable murmured, "Done." She handed the last two tonton halves to Tocette.

Tocette gave a mighty squeeze, then another, then shouted triumphantly, "I'm done, too!"

"Excellent!" Jewell said. "Good work, everyone!"

"Now what?" Tocette asked.

"Now, we wait," Jewell said.

"What are we waiting *for*?" Buttons asked.

"You'll see," Jewell said, "Give it time to work."

Sure enough, we soon heard a loud crash from inside Kregg's mysterious cabinet.

"What was that?" I asked.

Jewell took a small metal bucket from the cabinet, filled to the brim with little cubes of ice.

"I knew it!" Mid said. "I knew it was an ice maker!"

"Yes," Kregg said. "You're very smart. Now, how about you fill these glasses with ice, eh?"

"Sure," Mid said, looking smug.

Shortly, we were each holding a frosty glass of fresh tonton juice with ice. It was wonderfully cold and delicious!

Mr. Kip decided to join us. "Treeeeeats?"

Jewell filled a little glass with juice and gave it to him.

"Taaaaank youuuuuu." The little fellow drained the glass in one gulp. "Treeeeeats?"

"More treats?" Jewell asked. She gave Mr. Kip an affectionate pat on the head. "Who's the most spoiled little desert pup in all of Andaran?"

"Miiiiister Kiiiiip!"

"It's no wonder he's getting so fat!" Kregg said.

We laughed. Sable picked up a couple of the squeezed tonton halves and looked inquiringly at Jewell. Jewell nodded, and Sable gave them to Mr. Kip, who immediately got to work removing the pulp with his long fingers and popping the bits into his mouth. "Treeeeeats good! Taaaaank you, Saaaaable!"

Sable gave him a pat.

"How does he know her name?" Buttons asked.

"I told you," Jewell said, "he's smart. And he knows how to listen. In fact, I'll bet he knows all your names by now. Let's see." She pointed at Buttons. "Mr. Kip, who's this?"

"Buuuuuttons!"

"And this?"

"Tooooocette!"

Jewell pointed at each of us in turn.

"Cheeeeeff! Boooooks! Lhuuuuuuk!" He was clearly enjoying this new game. "Miiiiid! Leeeeery!"

Lery took another tonton half from Sable and handed it to Mr. Kip.

"Taaaaank youuuuu."

Jewell pointed at herself. "And who am I?"

"Beeeeeautiful Laaaaaady!"

"That's right, excellent!" She pointed at Kregg.

"Meeeeean Ooooold Maaaaaan!"

We cracked up.

"Hey!" Kregg said. "Who taught him that?"

Jewell looked intently out the bus window at the Great Desert. "I'm sure I don't know."

"Aha! It *was* you. I knew it! Anyway, it's a wicked, wicked lie. I'm not so old."

We laughed again.

Kregg gave Mr. Kip a cheerful pat on the head, then said, "I'm going back up front. *One* of us ought to be driving." He called behind him, "I'll be thinking up your punishment, *Beeeeeautiful Laaaaady*! Don't go anywhere until I get back."

"Wouldn't dream of it," Jewell said. "I can hardly wait."

Mr. Kip finished his tonton, handed the peels to Mid, stood up on his hind legs, and bowed.

Mid stared at the wet, chewed, empty tonton halves in his hand. "Taaaaank youuuuu," he said quietly, and dropped them into the waste bin. Which cracked us up again.

"That's odd," Jewell said. "I've never seen him bow like that before."

"He looked exactly like Squeaky!" Buttons said. "Squeaky is Lhuk's pet mouse. Lhuk taught him to bow like that."

Cheff shot Lhuk a look, but Lhuk was busy inspecting his glass of juice. Cheff frowned.

"I'll bet Squeaky would like tonton fruit, too." Buttons said.

Lhuk looked at Cheff, who shrugged. Lhuk set Squeaky on the countertop. Squeaky stood up on his hind legs and bowed. Lhuk handed him a piece of the tonton fruit. Squeaky sniffed it all over, then nibbled enthusiastically. Mr. Kip hopped up next to Squeaky and looked him over. Lhuk said, "Mr. Kip, meet my friend Squeaky. Squeaky, this is Mr. Kip."

With his tiny paw, Squeaky nudged the tonton fruit toward Mr. Kip. Mr. Kip broke it in half and gave one half back to Squeaky. "Taaaaank youuuuu, Squeeeeeaky."

Mid put some more ice in each of our glasses, then Jewell filled them to the brim again. "This is the life, isn't it?" she asked. "Ice-cold tonton juice in the heat of the Great Desert, good friends, good kids." She sighed contentedly, then gestured toward the front of the bus. "You'd have to search a long time to find another man like that one. He's the best man I ever met."

"Are you married?" Buttons asked.

"Oh, no, of course not," Jewell said. "He's a Fruen, I'm a Frae, so romantic feelings are impossible. I've never been married. He was married once, a long time ago, but that's another story."

"I knew Kregg was a Fruen," Buttons said, "by the white stripe in his hair. I thought you might be a Fruen, too, but I wasn't sure, because your hat covers your hair. I hope that wasn't a rude question?"

"Not at all. I wish I could have romantic feelings for Kregg—he's a fine man, but it's simply not possible between species. So, Kregg and I are content with being friends. And business partners, of course. Couldn't ask for better."

Kregg rejoined us and refilled his tonton juice from the pitcher. Mr. Kip promptly seized the rim of Kregg's glass and slurped loudly.

"You're going to spoil him," Jewell said.

"Too late, you beat me to it!" Kregg replied.

They smiled at each other.

"Kregg," Cheff began, "I've been wondering. How much do you and Jewell know about why the Sephs sent us out into the desert?"

"Well," Kregg said, "They sent me and Jewell because it's too far for you kids to walk. I don't know why they sent you. Master Vessslu only said to drive south until we get to the Stone Bear, then turn right, which is west, until we come to a tower. You're supposed to fetch something from there. Master Vessslu didn't tell me what it was, and I didn't ask. With the Seph masters, it's usually best not to ask too many questions."

"I see," Cheff said. "Well, we're supposed to find an—"

Kregg held up his hand. "Stop right there. I don't need to know, and I don't want to know. Some things are better left unsaid."

"Yes, sir," Cheff said. "I understand. Well, do you know anything about this Stone Bear we're supposed to find?"

"Is it a Fel bear?" Buttons asked.

"Of course not," Cheff said. "If it was any kind of bear, it would have to be a Great Western Desert bear."

"That's right," Kregg said. "Except that there aren't any bears in the Great Desert. Bears like a wetter climate, I think. In the desert, the wildlife tends to be smaller. It's easier for smaller animals to survive where there isn't much food or water."

"Are there any other larger animals in the desert?" I asked. "Besides desert pups, that is."

"Desert pups are about the largest creatures out here," Kregg said. "There's only one species larger, a kind of wild dog. You can hear them howling at the moon, sometimes. They survive out here because they will eat almost anything, alive or dead, plant or animal. There are lots of smaller animals, though, like desert mice, moles, snakes, lizards, and a number of bird species, too."

"And bugs!" Jewell said. "Zillions and zillions of bugs!"

"Do they bite?" Buttons asked.

"A few, but not often. The only insect you have to worry about is the jumping spider."

"Spiders aren't insects," Lhuk said.

"Well, they're *bugs,* anyway," Jewell said.

"Are they poisonous?" Buttons asked.

"Yes," Jewell said, "but only to other bugs. They don't bite people that I ever heard of."

"Then why do we have to watch out for them?" Mid asked.

"They're big," Jewell said. "And they jump. They won't hurt you, but they can scare the stuffing out of you." She put her hands together and made a jumping motion at Buttons. "Woohoo!"

Buttons jumped away, then laughed. "I see what you mean."

"Not yet you don't," Kregg said. "But you will. They're big and black and hairy, and they have fearsome jaws." He put his hands to his mouth and demonstrated spider jaws.

Buttons shivered. "Yuck! I hope they don't jump on me!"

"Some people catch them and keep them as pets," Kregg said.

"Not me," Jewell said. "Not ever!" She turned to Kregg. "And not you, either!"

Buttons asked, "If there are no bears in the Great Desert, what's the Stone Bear we're supposed to find?"

"How long have we been on the road?" Kregg checked his timepiece. "A few hours. Hmmm. It should be coming up any time, now. Let's go see." He got up and went to the front, and we followed him. He scanned the horizon, then opened a small compartment under the dashboard and retrieved a pair of binoculars. He scanned again using the binoculars, more slowly this time. "Sure enough, I can barely make it out." He passed the binoculars to Cheff. "Can you see it?"

"All I see is a big rock."

"Yep, that's it," Kregg said.

"Lemme see, Cheff!" Buttons said.

Cheff handed her the binoculars.

"You can't tell from here," Kregg said, "But when we get closer, you'll see that the rock is roughly in the shape of a bear."

"Oh, that's exciting!" Buttons said. "How long before we get there?"

"Another half hour, maybe, at this speed."

"In that case," Jewell said, "I'm going to get us another glass of juice. I'll be right back." Instead, she called from the back of the bus, "Kregg, can you come back here? Bring your binoculars."

He raised his eyebrows but said nothing. Buttons handed him the binoculars, and he joined Jewell at the rear.

"What is it?" he asked her.

"I'm not sure," she said. "Maybe nothing. Look way out to the horizon. What is that, do you think?"

He studied the desert through the binoculars. "Plume of dust, maybe?"

"That's what I thought, too," Jewell said. "I've been watching it for a while. At first, I thought it was a dust spiral, but it didn't go away. In fact, I think it might be getting closer."

"Not good, not good at all," Kregg said. He abruptly returned to the front of the bus and cranked up the steam valve.

As the Great Desert Safari bus moved faster, the ride became far less comfortable. A glass slid off the little countertop and crashed to the floor.

"We'd better batten the hatches," Jewell said. "Give me a hand, kids."

Lery picked up the broken glass. Buttons and Sable stowed the empty tonton crate. Tocette and Jewell hastily washed up the glassware and the pitcher. Lhuk put Squeaky back into his jacket pocket.

"All clear," Jewell called to Kregg.

Kregg opened the steam valve and increased the coal flow to the firebox. The Great Desert Safari bus groaned as it picked up speed.

Jewell had another look through the binoculars, her forehead furrowed.

"What is it?" Cheff asked. "What do you see?"

Jewell didn't answer. Instead, she went to the front of the bus, then spoke in Kregg's ear. She slipped into the driver's seat as Kregg rose, took the binoculars from her, and came to the back.

He scanned the horizon again. "Oh, *seriously* not good!"

"What is it?" Cheff asked again.

Kregg handed him the binoculars. "See for yourself—the dust plumes on the horizon."

"I see them," Cheff said. "What are they, a sandstorm?"

"Worse," Kregg said. "We're being followed. And not by one vehicle. Two plumes, two vehicles." He turned to Cheff. "I think maybe it's time that you tell us what you've gotten us into."

— 17 —

# THE STONE BEAR

---

CHEFF SILENTLY CONSULTED the rest of us. No one objected. Sable flicked her eyes toward Tocette.

Kregg noticed Sable's gesture. He put a hand on Tocette's shoulder. "Jewell and I need to have a word with your friends, Tocette. But we can't leave the bus without a driver for long, at this speed. Would you mind driving for a while?"

"Me? You want me to drive the bus? Really?" She was beaming all over. "I'd love to! But… I don't know how to drive."

"I'll show you," Kregg said. "Come with me."

Jewell left the driver's seat and came to the rear. Kregg ensconced Tocette behind the wheel. "All you do is keep it pointed straight at the big rock on the horizon. If it swerves, turn the wheel until it's pointed again. Can you do that?"

"Sure I can!" Tocette said. "Thank you for asking me. I never got to drive anything before. Zeek taught me how to shift the gears, though. He taught Buttons, too. We're shifter sisters."

"I'm sure you'll do fine. If you need help, call me. But I'm not worried."

147

I wasn't worried, either—I'd noticed that Kregg hadn't un-clipped the lanyard that held the wheel straight for Mr. Kip.

Kregg came and sat down with the rest of us in the back. We put our heads together.

"Okay," Cheff said quietly. "I'll tell you what we know, but it isn't all that much. This morning we were… drawn… to a Seph in the Belowground beneath the monastery."

"Drawn?" Kregg asked. "As in…?"

"Seph Ability," Cheff said.

"Are you sure? The Xanparthur monks don't permit the use of Ability within the monastery."

"Yes, sir, we understand that, but we're sure. Lery and Lhuk could both feel it. And in any case, this Seph was no monk. Plus, he was old, extremely old. He said his name was Kahph."

"He had scars all over!" Buttons said.

"Wars," Sable said.

"He definitely looked like he has been through more than one war," Mid said.

"We think he arrived yesterday from Fellstone City," Cheff said, "on that extremely large Seph carrier. Anyway, we were looking for Master Vessslu, but instead, we found this big old Seph—the biggest we've ever seen."

"The ponies say that he was not right in his mind," Buttons said. Starry made the 'crazy' gesture with her forehoof again, and Moka nodded sagely.

Kregg smiled. "I see. Those ponies are pretty astute observers, aren't they?"

Moka and Starry exchanged a look, then both nodded.

"They sure are," Buttons said. "I don't know what we'd do without them!" She picked up both ponies and gave them a hug.

"Kahph was acting peculiarly," Cheff said. "He kept singing little rhymes he made up about the conversation."

"And sometimes he seemed to drift off," Mid said.

Cheff continued, "He asked us to find a way to go out into the desert and retrieve an artifact."

At the word 'artifact,' Kregg's ears pricked. "An artifact you say? Did he say what kind of artifact?"

"He called it a 'spherical crystal artifact,' and said it was 'forbidden knowledge.'"

Kregg exchanged a glance with Jewell. "Interesting."

"Do you know something about it?" Cheff asked.

"Maybe," Kregg said. "But first, tell us the rest of the story."

"Right," Cheff said. "When he dismissed us, we went to see Master Vessslu to ask him about it."

"Smart," Jewell said. "What did Master Vessslu have to say?"

"That's the strange thing," Cheff said. "When we found Master Vessslu's office, Grand Master Attan was there with him, and they were expecting us. They questioned us briefly, and we told them what we just told you—mostly. We didn't mention Kahph using the Ability."

"Probably for the best," Kregg said. "Continue, please."

"There's not much more to the story. Attan seemed keenly interested in the artifact. He practically demanded that we go out to the Great Desert and retrieve it for him. Master Vessslu agreed and called for you and Jewell. You know the rest."

"Why send a bunch of kids?" Jewell asked. "No offense."

"None taken," Cheff said, smiling. "We *are* a bunch of kids. In fact, Mid asked Master Vessslu that same question."

"And?" Kregg prompted.

"He said no one would suspect a bunch of kids as anything other than an innocent sightseeing trip."

"I see," Kregg said. "Sensible. And Tocette? She doesn't quite… fit… with the rest of you, does she?"

Cheff chuckled. "That's another story. Tocette's okay, in her own way. She's a member of the Fellstone Labor Compound Blueband troop. Her squad leader is convinced that we're always up to something and ordered her to keep an eye on us."

"I see." Kregg chuckled, too. "And are you?"

"Sir?" Cheff asked innocently.

"Are you always up to something?" He looked hard at Cheff, then at the rest of us.

Cheff met Kregg's gaze. "Who, us? Up to something? Why, I have no idea what you mean."

They stared at each other, then Kregg laughed. "Of course not! Whatever was I thinking?"

Cheff laughed, too.

"I've heard a little about life in the Labor Compound," Jewell said. "You youngsters have had some tough times, haven't you?"

"Some," Mid said, "but it could be worse."

"It can always get worse," Jewell said. She sighed.

"So that's what we know," Cheff said. "What do you make of it, Kregg? Jewell? Any idea who's following us?"

Kregg frowned. "I do have an idea, but it's not a happy one. I think the Sephs know more about the artifact than they let on. I'm guessing that Master Vessslu was acting against his will, under the constraint of that crooked Attan character. 'Grand Master' indeed! He's no more a monk than my grandmother's pet puppy! I think Attan sent a truck full of Fessal Facilitators, or, more likely, soldiers, to follow you. They probably have orders to wait for you to find the artifact, then kill us all and take it."

Buttons' eyes grew wide, but she kept silent. Lhuk took Squeaky out of his pocket and fed him a small piece of tonton fruit. No one else moved.

After we'd all had time to let that sink in, Cheff broke the silence. "I'd rather they didn't."

"They'll make it look like an accident, I'm sure," Kregg said. "Lots of bad things can, and do, happen in the Great Desert. It's beautiful out here, and I love it, but it's not… friendly. You have to respect it, or it'll hurt you, even kill you."

"Ocean," Sable murmured. "Same."

"Interesting," Jewell said. "I'd like to see the ocean someday."

"Those Fessal soldiers," Cheff asked, "do you think they know the Great Desert well?"

"Them? Pah!" Kregg said. "They'd be doing well to find their way out of a paper bag with a flashlight and a blowtorch!"

We laughed.

"They're city born and bred," Jewell said. "Straight from Fellstone City. New City, probably."

"Silver Palace, even," Kregg said. "I have it on good authority that faker, Attan, is a member of Pallador's own Palace Guard. I'm sure his fake Facilitators are Palace Guard soldiers, too. Some of them, anyway."

"We're not supposed to know," Jewell said, "but we overheard that Attan is here to bend Xanparthur and the Seph Monks to Pallador's will." She smiled. "There are no secrets in the monastery."

"We figured as much," Mid said. "He kept on about Pallador's 'Path of Enlightenment' and how the monastery played a key role in it."

Kregg laughed again, bitterly this time. "Is that his line? What a load of… well, what I put on my flowers to make them grow! If Pallador has his way, he'll exterminate the monks and burn Xanparthur Monastery down to the sand. Pallador's idea of enlightenment is to pull the veil of darkness over all of Andaran. Xanparthur is the last holdout of true knowledge."

"Then," Cheff said, "we must do all we can to preserve it."

We cheered, quietly, but Tocette overheard.

"Thanks!" she called back. "I *am* driving good, amn't I?"

"You sure are!" Cheff said. "From now on I'll have to call you the Beautiful, Intrepid, and Great Driver Tocette!"

Tocette said, "Don't distract me, now. I have to keep my eyes on the road, you know!" But she was smiling.

"Wait a minute," Mid said. "If we're being followed by a truck full of soldiers with orders to kill us, then who's in the second vehicle?"

"Good question," Kregg said. "I don't know. If I had to guess, I'd say that after Attan pulled his treacherous stunt, Master Vessslu sent a truckload of his own Facilitators to protect you."

"He may have to feign compliance to Attan, but he'd never agree to the murder of children," Jewell said. "Or of me and Kregg, for that matter."

"You seem pretty sure of that," Mid said.

"We're sure," Jewell said. "We've known Master Vessslu and the rest of the Seph monks for many years. Everything they stand for is anathema to aggressive violence, though I imagine they would defend themselves if necessary."

"And anathema to Pallador's 'Path of Enlightenment' nonsense, too, for that matter," Kregg added.

"That's good to know," Cheff said, "but the problem remains: we're being hunted down like rats. What can we do about it?"

"That a great question, Cheff," Kregg said. "It's not like we have a lot of options."

"I have an option," Buttons said. "Don't get caught! The ponies say that being murdered isn't their first choice."

"Right you are, Buttons," Kregg said. "So, how can we avoid getting caught?"

Cheff thought about this, then asked, "Do you suppose if we could get the artifact and give it to Master Vessslu, it would give him some leverage with Attan?"

Kregg considered this. "That's hard to say, since we don't know what the artifact is. But it might, it very well might."

"I'd like to help the monastery, if we can," Cheff said.

"Strategy!" Sable said. "Invade or evade."

"Invade probably isn't an option," Kregg said. "We don't have the resources to tackle an entire contingent of soldiers."

"Evade it is, then," Cheff said. He scouted the landscape. "Where, exactly, can one hide out here in the Great Desert? It's so... flat!"

"Actually, it isn't," Jewell said. "It merely seems that way. There are a million places to hide out here, if you know where to look. And how to look. The problem is how to find a hiding place without leaving a trail for the soldiers to follow."

"Correct!" Kregg said. "And I know just the trick!"

"You do?" Buttons asked. "What is it? The ponies demand to know!"

"The ponies," Kregg said, "are going to have to wait and see. Meanwhile, Cheff, you and your people had best get your gear together. How is your gang at hiking?"

Cheff grinned. "For city kids, not too bad. We've done our share of walking."

Kregg pointed. "Look, we're a lot closer to that rock. What does it look like now?"

"It's a bear!" Button said. "That rock looks exactly like a giant bear! Awww…"

"What is it?" Cheff asked.

"Now I miss Mr. Grumbles." Buttons wiped away a tear with her sleeve.

"I'm sure he's fine," Cheff said.

"I know, Cheff. Still."

"Yeah, I get it," Cheff said, and gave her a little hug. "You all ready to jump?"

"Jump? I'm all packed, if that's what you mean."

"Kregg doesn't want to risk stopping, so he's only going to slow down. When he does, we're going to jump out of the bus."

"Jump out of a moving bus!" Mid said. "Are you crazy? Wait—I already know the answer to that."

"Drop and roll," Cheff said. "The sand will break your fall."

"Break my leg, more likely," Mid muttered.

"Everyone all set?" Cheff called out.

We were all ready, except for Tocette, who was still in the driver's seat.

"Do you want Tocette with you, Cheff," Kregg asked, "or should I keep her on the bus with me?"

"Well," Cheff said, "Tocette has come with us this far. I don't see why she shouldn't go the rest of the way." He sighed.

"Fair enough," Kregg went to the front, thanked Tocette for her driving, and told her to get packed.

"Packed? I am packed. Where're we going, Cheff?"

"It's time to get out and walk," Cheff said. "You up for it?"

"I am if you are," Tocette said. "Besides, Brex, I mean Miss Brex, said I have to keep an eye on you. I can't do that unless I'm with you, right?"

"Right," Cheff said. "Okay, hang on. We're waiting for an instruction from Kregg."

"It's coming right up," Kregg said from the driver's seat. "Be ready!"

Sable retrieved her tool belt from her valise and secured it around her waist.

Jewell grabbed the eight food packages the cooks at the monastery had made for us, and eight small canteens, and distributed them among us. Her brow was furrowed. "Please be safe, children."

"Desert survival training," Sable said.

"Say, what?" Cheff said. "You've had desert survival training?"

Sable gazed at him.

He smacked his forehead. "Of course you have. What am I thinking? It's a perfectly obvious course for a Naval Cadet. Still, you might have said a thing."

Sable shrugged.

"Okay, kids!" Kregg called out. "The Stone Bear is dead ahead. Get ready to jump! Hide in the shadows until the desert is clear, then head as fast as you can toward the sunset. Got it?"

We got it.

The Stone Bear loomed in the front window. Kregg said, "Okay, this is it." He closed the steam valve a little, then applied the brakes. "Go, go, go!"

The eight of us spilled out into the desert sands, dropping and rolling away from the bus. As soon as we were clear, Kregg cranked up the steam. The last we saw of the Great Desert Safari bus was Jewell, in the rear window, waving goodbye.

"Be safe, children," she called. "Be careful! We'll meet you at the tower, if we can."

# OPERATION SHIFTING SANDS

— **18** —

## SAND PIRATES

---

WHEN WE HAD all regained our feet and brushed ourselves off, Cheff said, "Let's see if we can find some shelter under the Stone Bear. We'd best be out of sight by the time the soldiers catch up with us."

So we explored the Stone Bear, walking around it clockwise, to see what sort of cover it offered.

Buttons looked up, shading her eyes with her hand. "It doesn't look much like a bear up close, does it?"

Cheff looked up, too. "Not much. It's bigger than I thought, though."

"A *lot* bigger," Mid said.

"Cave," called Sable, who was scouting ahead a little.

We found her standing at a narrow cave entrance. Cheff peered inside. "It's pretty dark in there. Mid, do you have your flashlight?"

Mid handed the light to Cheff, who peered inside again. "It's huge in there. It looks like there's room enough for all of us."

Buttons brushed past him and started to squeeze herself in.

157

"Not yet, Buttons," Cheff said. "Let's watch and see what the soldiers do. There might be no need to go inside."

Lhuk peered into the dark opening, then shivered. "I hope not. I don't like caves."

"I like caves," Mid said. "They're cool and dark."

"Tracks," Sable said.

"Right." Cheff pulled up a clump of desert brush and shook the sand off the roots, then used it like a broom to erase our tracks. "This will do the trick. Who wants to be the official track-eraser?"

"I… I can do it," Lery said.

"Good." Cheff handed him the brush. "Make sure you get them all, especially those near the bus tracks."

"Okay… Friend Cheff." Lery went back around the rock.

Sable climbed up the side of the Stone Bear.

"Where are you going?" Buttons asked.

"Lookout," she said.

Cheff said, "Excellent! Your desert training is paying off already!"

Sable was already halfway to the top. She looked down at Cheff. "Not training," she said. "Common sense."

Mid laughed. "Well, you've been told, haven't you, Old Man? What would you like the rest of us to do, Oh Senseless Leader?"

Cheff grimaced. "The rest of us should avoid making any more footprints. Stay up on the rocks, okay? And be ready to go into the cave at a moment's notice. Lhuk, you and Buttons stay where you can see Sable, and let the rest of us know if she signals."

"Okay, Cheff!" Buttons said. "The ponies will keep all four of their eyes on Sable at all times! Ready Lhuk? Let's get into position."

Tocette shyly approached Cheff. "Um, Cheff? I don't really understand what's going on. Why did we leave the bus?"

"It's hard to explain, Tocette, the Beautiful and Intrepid Great Driver."

Tocette said, "I did good, driving, didn't I?"

"Absolutely," Cheff said. "The thing is, while you were driving, you probably didn't notice that we were being followed."

"Oh," Tocette said. "Who was following us?"

"Um…" Cheff was stumped.

"Sand pirates!" I said, to everyone's surprise, including my own.

Tocette wrapped her arms around her chest. "Oh, no!" she wailed. "Sand pirates!" She paused, then asked, "Cheff, what are sand pirates?"

"What are sand pirates?" Cheff repeated. "Um… sand pirates are"—he scratched his head—"that's a good question, Tocette."

Mid grinned. He explained, complete with grand gestures, "Sand pirates are roving gangs of outcasts and outlaws who live away out here in the vast Great Desert. They are fierce and bloodthirsty, dirty and bearded. They attack and kill visitors to the desert!"

"Oh, dear!" Tocette wailed. "I don't want to be killed by a sand pirate!"

"No worries," Cheff said, getting into the spirit. "They only kill the men and boys."

"Oh. What do they do with the girls?" Tocette asked.

"You're too young to know," Mid said. "But you wouldn't like it."

"They keep the girls for ransom," Cheff said, giving Mid a look.

"Oh, dear," Tocette said again. "I don't want to be kept for ransom." She wrung her hands, then stopped. "Cheff? What's ransom?"

"They make your family pay to get you back."

"Oh, dear, I don't have any family. And the woman I live with is really poor. Besides, I don't think she likes me much. She'd never pay to get me back." Tears welled up in her eyes.

"Then we'd better make sure the pirates don't get you, right?" Cheff patted her shoulder. "It's all right, now, don't worry. We'll protect you."

"Oh dear, oh dear."

Lery came back around the rock, still sweeping away our tracks. He worked his way around to where we waited on a little rock ledge. "All done… Cheff."

"Good, excellent work. Sit up here on the ledge with us and catch your breath."

"Why… Cheff? Is… is my breath… running away?"

"Is your breath—Lery! You made a joke!"

"Yeah," Lery said, "a joke."

We laughed, a welcome break from the tension.

From her relay position, Buttons hissed, "Cheff! Sable is signaling."

Cheff ran over and looked up. "Are they coming our way?"

Sable nodded.

"Okay, come on down." He hurried back to the rest of us. "They're coming. Everyone into the cave. Buttons, you and Lhuk first."

"Okay." Buttons slipped through the narrow crack in the rock.

"Go, Lhuk," Cheff said.

Lhuk stepped up to the crack and peered inside. "I don't think so."

"Come on, Lhuk," Buttons called from inside the cave. "It's cool in here. You'll like it."

But Lhuk stepped away from the opening.

Mid stepped forward. "I'll go next." He wriggled about halfway in, then stopped.

"What's the matter?" Cheff asked.

"I don't fit. I'm stuck."

"No you're not," Cheff said, and with one strong push, he dislodged Mid like a cork from a bottle.

"Ow!" Mid said.

"Better… Better fit… than fat…" Lery said and guffawed.

"I heard that!" Mid said from inside.

"Lery!" Cheff said. "Two jokes in one day!"

Sable joined us at the cave entrance.

Tocette rushed up to her. "Did you see them? The sand pirates, I mean? Are they almost here?"

Sable looked at Cheff, eyebrows raised.

Cheff looked blank.

Sable shook her head. Without a word, she slipped past Cheff into the cave.

Cheff said to Tocette, "You're next."

Tocette, who was considerably larger than Mid, looked doubtful, but said, "Okay, Cheff," and plunged gamely into the crack. "Oh, dear, I'm stuck too. The pirates are going to ransom me! Pull me in, Sable!"

Sable pulled, but Tocette didn't budge.

Cheff and I pushed Tocette as hard as we could, but she still didn't move.

"Lery?" Cheff said.

Lery stepped forward, placed both his hands on Tocette's ample fundament, and we heaved together. Tocette exploded into the cave, but I think she left a few bits of skin and clothing on the edges.

Lery blushed furiously. "I… I touched… her… her… her…"

"Forget it," Cheff said. "Needs of the moment prevail. In you go."

Lery stepped through, and I followed him. After my eyes adjusted, I could see everyone dimly in the weak light coming in through the crack.

Lery carefully picked the bits of Tocette's clothing from the entrance.

I peeked outside. Cheff was trying to convince Lhuk to enter the cave. Finally, Cheff said, "Sorry, Lhuk, we're out of time." He lifted little Lhuk and shoved him bodily through the crack. "In you go!" Cheff squeezed in behind him. "Is that everybody?"

"All present and accounted for, oh Fearless Leader," Mid said.

"Good. How's Lhuk?"

"Not so good, Cheff," Buttons said.

Lhuk sat against one wall of the cave, curled up into a ball, eyes closed, rocking back and forth.

Cheff went to him. "I'm sorry, Lhuk, truly. If you had stayed out there, the, er, sand pirates would have spotted you and killed all of us."

"I know," Lhuk said, shivering. "I'm not mad. I don't know what I am. I've never felt like this before. I feel like I'm carrying tons of rock on my shoulders. I can't breathe."

"Try feeding Squeaky, or making him do some tricks," Mid said. "Take your mind off it."

"Long, slow, deep breaths," Sable said.

"Can you turn your flashlight on?" Lhuk asked.

"Not until we're sure we're safe," Cheff said. "Sorry, Lhuk."

"It's okay," Lhuk said. "I'll be fine." He took Squeaky out of his jacket pocket and opened his food bundle.

Buttons sat down beside Lhuk and got the ponies out of the backpack. Squeaky sniffed at Starry and Moka, then returned to his biscuit crumbs.

We heard a commotion outside the cave opening.

Cheff said, "Everybody away from the opening, hold still, be quiet. Sable?"

With her dark skin and black clothing, it was almost impossible to see her at all. She crept up to the crack and glanced out. "Nothing yet."

We waited silently in the dark. A century passed, then another, and another. Finally Sable whispered, "Here they come."

Sable moved away from the opening. The rest of us pressed ourselves against the cool rock walls, willing ourselves to be invisible.

We heard the clatter of carelessly handled weapons and hobnailed boots on the rocks outside.

"I found a cave!" one voice said in a Fessal accent.

"That's not a cave, it's a crack," a second voice said.

"Go in and check it out," an authoritative voice commanded.

"We can't, sir," the first voice said. "It's too small. Nobody could get in there."

"Lemme see."

A light shone through the crack and played about the cave. We covered our faces, barely breathing.

"Nah, nothing," the authoritative voice said. "It's impossible. Forget it, let's go."

The sounds outside faded into the distance.

We heaved a collective sigh of relief.

"That was close!" Cheff said. His voice shook. "If they had been more astute, it would have been the end of us."

"They're gone?" Lhuk asked. "Great! Let's get out of here." He bolted for the crack.

Cheff grabbed him by the arm. "Hang on, Lhuk, not so fast. And keep your voice down. They might still be out there."

"Second truck," Sable said.

"Right," Cheff said. "Don't forget there's a second truck."

"I wonder if they'll stop or follow the others," I said.

"I don't know," Cheff said. "But let's wait for… let's see, how far behind the first truck do you suppose they are?"

"Half hour, maybe?" Mid said. He checked his timepiece.

"Hour," Sable said.

"Okay," Cheff said, "mark the time, Mid. We'll wait two hours, to be safe, then Sable can have a look. It'll likely be dark by then, right?"

Mid checked his timepiece again. "Right. The sun should go down pretty soon. My, how time goes by when you're having fun!"

Lhuk groaned. "Two more hours! I'm not sure I can…"

"Sure you can," Buttons said. "The ponies and I will help you."

"Well," Mid said, "if it wasn't so dark in here, I'd have a look around."

"Glasses," Sable said.

"Oh, of course." Mid took off his dark glasses and returned them to his tech bag. "That's better! I forgot all about them."

Mid blinked a few times and looked around. "Hey! It's bigger in here than we thought. And I feel a breeze. I wonder where it's coming from?" He handed Lhuk his light. "Here, you keep this for me. I can see fine, now. Trohs have great night vision, you know."

"Okay," Lhuk said. "Thanks."

"Don't wander off," Cheff said, but it was too late. Mid's footsteps grew fainter and farther away.

"I'll go," Sable said. She had pretty good night vision, too.

"Right," Cheff said.

After a quarter of an hour, or so, they both returned.

"Cheff!" Mid said. "You have to see it! It's incredible!"

"What is?" Cheff asked.

"A little passage goes down, like a hallway," Mid said, "and at the bottom, there's a huge cave. It's enormous! With lights! And Cheff? That passage, it isn't natural. You can see and feel the excavation marks in it."

"Lhuk," Sable said.

"Yeah," Cheff said. "Lhuk might feel a lot more comfortable in a bigger room. Want to try it out, Lhuk?"

He returned Squeaky to his pocket, then got up, and brushed himself off. Sweat had soaked completely through his clothing. Sable handed him her canteen, and he took a long drink. "Better," he said. "I'm ready, I guess."

"It isn't far," Mid said, "and it's worth the trip."

We followed Mid and Sable down the corridor, inspecting the pick and shovel marks as we went.

"Definitely man-made," Cheff said. "I wonder how old it is."

"Look, Cheff!" Mid said. "Right here in the middle, there's a little jink. See? The walls don't quite line up."

"Why do you think that is?" I asked.

"They started excavating at both ends," Mid said, "and met in the middle. Almost, but not quite, perfect."

"But they could build the tunnel twice as fast," Cheff said.

"True," Mid said. "That's probably exactly the reason for it."

A little farther on, the tunnel made a sharp turn, then emptied out into a huge cavern. We stopped dead in our tracks. Thousands of little blue and gold points of light illuminated the entire dome. Far below, the reflection of those lights glittered and sparkled in what had to be a large body of water. From somewhere in the distance came the burbling sound of a stream or brook.

"No wonder the Great Desert is so dry," Buttons said. "The water's all down here!"

# — 19 —

## THE BELOWGROUND

---

"**N**ow, THIS IS more like it!" Mid said. "Doesn't blind a fellow like that desert does. Too much light up there, way too much." He sniffed the air. "It smells good down here. A fellow could get used to living in the Belowground."

"It looks like we found the Belowground again," Cheff said. "That's the second time today."

"Second time?" Tocette asked.

"We met a old Seph this morning," Mid said. "He lived in the Belowground under the monastery."

"Oh," Tocette said. "Is this the same Belowground?"

"I don't know," Cheff said. "It might be. From what little I've heard, the Belowground lies under a large part of Andaran."

"Most of the Belowground is natural formations," I said. "But some of it was excavated by people hundreds of years ago."

"Excavated?" Tocette said. "Like, with shovels?"

"Shovels, picks, wheelbarrows," Mid said. "Drills, maybe. I don't know if they had steam drills hundreds of years ago."

"The… the right tools…" Lery said. His hand strayed to the handle of his borrowed pipe wrench.

I searched my mental archives. "I never read of any steam drills, but there might have been. I do have a book that mentions that King Maghorn III was developing the Belowground as a major transportation route. Underground electric railroad."

"Oh," Tocette said. "Why did he want to do that?"

"Because snow and ice can interfere with the trains and other transportation. There's no weather underground."

"Oh," Tocette said. She shivered. "I can't imagine living and working down here all the time."

"I sure wouldn't mind," Mid said. "It's cool and dark. I like it. Maybe I'll get a job in the Belowground someday."

"I never even heard of the Belowground until today," Tocette said.

"Are you from Fellstone City?" I asked her.

"All my life. I don't remember my parents, though. They died, or ran away, or something, before I was old enough to remember."

"Well, that's why you don't know about the Belowground," Mid said. "Fellstone City doesn't have one."

"Oh," Tocette said. "Why not?"

"Yes, why not?" Buttons asked. "The ponies are curious."

Cheff said, "I think it has to do with mountains, but I'm not sure. Books?"

"My father had a Geography book," I said. "I used to like to look at the pictures. Give me a sec." I closed my eyes and called up the images of the book's pages. "Cheff's right. It has to do with mountains. According to the book,

> 'The vast system of underground caverns we call the Belowground came into being millions of years ago, at the time when the mountains of Andaran were forming. As thousands of volcanoes produced layers upon layers of lava, which eventually became the mountain ranges of Andaran, many pockets of volcanic gas-

*ses were trapped, making bubbles in the hot lava. When the lava cooled, those bubbles became the cave systems we know today collectively as the Belowground.'"*

"Wow!" Tocette said. "You remember all that? I can't hardly remember anything I read. I, well, I don't read so good, and it's such hard work that when I'm done with a page, I've already forgotten the beginning of it. You must be really smart, Books."

Cheff was giving me a stern look. "It's just a knack I have, Tocette. No big deal."

"Oh." She looked doubtful. "Okay, I guess, if you say so."

"Listen, Beautiful Tocette," Cheff said, "we'd appreciate it if you didn't mention Books' 'knack' to anyone else, okay? It could make him, um, *interesting*, to certain people, if you get my meaning?"

She stared at Cheff, then at me, then at Cheff again. "You mean like—" She imitated Brex's cold-eyed, thin-lipped, disapproving face.

We laughed.

"Exactly!" Cheff said.

Tocette thought this over, then she smacked me on my back. "Don't worry, little Booksie Buddy. Your secret is safe with me!"

"Thanks, Tocette. I appreciate it."

"No problem, Booksie Buddy." She squeezed me again, then let me go. "One thing, though: you have to promise me that you'll tell me more book stuff sometime."

"Sure," I said. "I'd be happy to."

This seemed to satisfy her. She wandered off to examine the walls of the passage we had come through.

Mid asked Cheff, "What now, oh Great and Fearless Leader? Should we go back up? The second soldier truck will have passed by now. Or do we go on? This cave, or cavern, or bubble, or whatever you call it, seems to go straight west."

Cheff considered. "Well, that's true, Old Son. And we'd be safe down here, from patrols and such. I doubt anyone's been here in a long time. On the other hand, there's no guarantee that we'd find another way out."

"Right you are, Old Man," Mid said, "but my guess is that we'll not only find another way back to the surface, but we'll find many of them."

"Why… why do you guess… that?" Lery asked.

"Simple: engineering!"

"How do you figure?" Cheff asked.

"Well, consider the purpose, the problem, and the solution. Books said that the people before The Fall, they were building a tunnel system, right? There's no point in having a tunnel system unless you can get in and out where you want."

"I get it!" Buttons said. "It would be like riding a bus that made no stops."

"Right," Mid said. "Second, the workers who built the connecting tunnels and whatever else is down here would need food and other supplies. There must be… openings… of some kind, to get food and water and tools to them."

"They didn't get a lot of food or water through the opening we came through," I said. "Too small."

"True," Mid said. "Maybe they never got that part finished. The little room we were in at first seems to be the end of this part of the Belowground. Maybe something happened that stopped the work before it was finished."

"Something like The Fall?" I asked. "That would have stopped everything, right?"

"Could be," Mid replied.

"Makes sense," Cheff said. "Anyway, what's the worst that can happen? If we don't find a way out, we'll have to come back here to the Stone Bear and get out the way we came in."

"And by then, the soldiers would be gone, for sure," Mid added. "So we win, either way."

"Let's vote," Cheff said. "I'm for going ahead through the Belowground. Everyone?"

Sable said, "Belowground."

Mid and Lery agreed.

Tocette called from the little passageway, "I don't care. I'll go wherever you all go."

Buttons consulted Starry and Moka. "The ponies say, 'Always forward, never backward!'"

"Lhuk, how about you?" Cheff asked. "Think you're up to it?"

Lhuk said, "I don't like it, but I'm better in this big room. It's the little room that got to me. I'll try it."

"I'm in," I said.

"Then forward it is," Cheff said. "Look out, Belowground, here we come! Mid, how about you and your flashlight take the lead?"

"Right away, Fearless Leader!" Mid clicked his light on and made his way cautiously westward along the south wall of the long cavern, following the edge of the big underground lake. After a hundred steps or so, he said, "Looks like this might have been a path or a trail or something. See? There are footprints."

"Footprints!" Cheff said. "How old?"

"How would I know?" Mid said. "Maybe Sable and her desert survival training can help."

Sable knelt to examine the footprints. "Unknown," she said. "Likely unknowable."

"Why, Miss Sable?" Tocette asked. "Can't you tell?"

Sable said, "No wind, no rain."

Cheff said, "Without weather, there's nothing to disturb the dust."

"Are you saying that these footprints could have been made hundreds of years ago?" Buttons asked.

Sable nodded.

"That's amazing!" Buttons said. "I'll be careful not to step in them."

"Don't worry," Cheff said. "If they were made that long ago, whoever made them isn't around to care anymore."

"I suppose," Buttons said. "Still."

"Caution," Sable said.

"Sable's right, Cheff," Mid said. "If we can't tell, we have to assume that they might be recent. 'Err on the safe side,' isn't that what you always say?"

"You're right, of course, both of you," Cheff said. "We must assume that we might have company down here. So let's use all caution, and keep our eyes and ears open." Cheff sagged a little.

"Fatigued," Sable said.

"I must be," Cheff agreed. "It's been a long day. It's probably getting dark on the surface. Maybe we should take a break."

Mid consulted his timepiece. "Right again, Fearless Leader. It's well past dinner time."

"I… could eat…" Lery said.

"Me, too," Tocette said.

"So could I," Cheff said, "but if you all don't mind, let's walk for a little while more. Maybe we'll find a nice place to camp."

"Water," Sable said. "Running."

"A campfire would be nice," Mid added.

"Okay, let's look for a spot," Cheff said. "It can't be too hard to find. On we go!"

As we walked along, enjoying the beauty of the cavern and the cool stillness of the air, Cheff scanned the rocky cavern floor. He periodically picked up a smooth round stone and put it in his front trouser pocket.

"Expecting a battle?" I asked.

"Maybe," he said quietly so Tocette wouldn't hear. He discreetly pulled a handful of items from his pocket and showed them to me. Besides the rocks, there were a dozen fat ball bearings. "I got these from Buttons. They were left over the last time she stuffed Starry. They'll pack quite a punch."

"But they're not enough?" I asked.

Cheff scowled. "That's the problem, Books, Old Son—we simply don't know what we're going to need. Better to be safe, right?"

"Right." I started looking for smooth round stones, too.

"What makes the lights?" Tocette asked after a while. She pointed at the roof of the cavern.

"Mushrooms," Sable said, "and bugs."

"Oh," Tocette said. "Bugs? I'm not crazy about bugs."

"As long as they stay up there on the roof, they won't bother us any," Cheff said.

It was true—for whatever bug reasons the bugs had, they seemed to prefer the top of the cavern to the sides, although in a few places, the tiny points of light came a little way down the cavern walls. In one spot, a lone golden light was low enough for us to examine. It was, as Sable had said, coming from the hindquarters of a long, winged bug.

"What makes it glow like that?" Tocette asked. "Is it on fire inside?"

"It's called 'bioluminescence,'" I said. "They do it with special chemicals inside them. It's their way of finding mates."

"Oh," Tocette said. "That's clever of them."

"Lots of animals have them," Mid said. "When my dad was alive, and we worked on the fishing boat in Settport, we sometimes saw whole schools of lighted sea creatures. In fact, my dad said that long ago, in the mines of Tumberland, dried fish skins were used to light the coal mines. It was some special kind of fish, I forget what he said it was. But even after the fish was dead, the skins would glow a little."

"Why not use electric lights?" Buttons asked.

"They weren't invented yet," Cheff said.

"Candles, then."

Mid said, "Because candles could, and sometimes did, ignite the coal dust, which killed the miners."

Buttons said, "Okay, that makes sense. Killing the miners is a bad thing."

Tocette was staring up at the roof of the cavern. "There must be millions of them! Why are some blue? Are the girl bugs golden and the boy bugs blue?"

"Mushrooms," Sable said, "are blue."

"Oh."

We hiked for another half-hour until we found ourselves by the side of an underground stream where it left the lake. It was only a little stream, but it was trickling cheerfully westward.

"This could be our spot," Cheff said. "What do you all think?"

"Could work," Mid said. "I smell ashes. Let me have a look around." He took his flashlight and scouted the area. "Look! Look here!"

"What is it?" Cheff asked. "Trouble?"

"No trouble," Mid said, "but it seems we're not the only ones to have the idea of camping here." He shone his light on the remains of a campfire—a few old charred sticks and some white, powdery coals. "And look at this—they must have been planning to come back." A few feet from the campfire ashes was a fair-sized stack of firewood.

"Great!" Cheff said. "I was wondering where we were going to find firewood down here. Mid, can you and Lery get a fire going? Let's keep it pretty small, barely enough to cook on." He tested the air with his hands. "It's not too cold down here, so I don't think we'll need the fire to heat us."

"Right away, Oh Fearless Leader," Mid said. "I'll use my Fire Cylinder."

"Yay!" Buttons said. "The ponies *love* watching you do that. Tocette! Lhuk! You haven't seen this yet. Come watch!"

They gathered around the fire pit and watched as Mid found some twigs and slivers of dry wood. He used his pocket knife to shave some tinder from a dry stick. From his tech bag, he retrieved his amazing Fire Piston and a scrap of K-cloth. He inserted the K-cloth into the tube. Next, he inserted the piston, smacked it with his hand, then shook the little bit of K-cloth, now smoldering, onto the pile of tinder. He picked up the tinder and blew on it gently. In seconds, a little flame licked eagerly at the centuries-dry tinder.

"Bravo!" Cheff said, and the rest of us applauded. "I never get tired of seeing that!"

Mid said, "It's yet another reminder of why we should always be nice to the techies among us. You never know what we might have in our tech bags! Nyah-ha-haaa!"

"How does it work, Mid?" Tocette asked.

"When you hit it with your hand," Mid explained, "the increased pressure in the cylinder makes it hot enough to ignite the K-cloth."

"Oh," Tocette said, frowning. "What's K-cloth?"

"Top secret!" Cheff said. "Mid invented it. It's a special kind of cloth that catches on fire easily."

"Oh," Tocette said again. "Can I try it sometime?"

"Sure," Mid said. "Next time we have a fire."

Tocette brightened. "I'd like that!"

Lery pulled his teapot, folding grill, and a few other items from his grub sack, and started a pot of felmoss tea for us. The rest of us sat around the fire and opened the food packages the cooks back at the monastery had put together for us. Even Squeaky joined the fun, nosing about for crumbs and scraps.

"These lunch packages are great!" Tocette said, spraying the area with food fragments. "Those cooks at Xan… Xerr… Pan… oh, you know, the monastery, really know how to pack a lunch!"

After we'd eaten and had some tea, we felt considerably restored. Lhuk seemed to have recovered somewhat from his claustrophobia. "How are you feeling?" I asked him.

"Better," he said. "I'm still uneasy, but it doesn't feel like the rocks are going to crush me the next second."

"Good," I said. "We're pretty safe, I should think. This cavern has been here for a zillion years, without falling in. It would be strange if it picked tonight to fall on us."

He gave me a funny look. "Yeah, strange. Thanks for the encouragement, Books. I think I'll try to get some sleep, if you don't mind." He gave Squeaky another morsel of biscuit, then wrapped his coat around himself and stretched out on the rock.

"Good idea," Cheff said. "Let's all turn in. We have a long walk tomorrow. We'll take turns standing watch, as usual. Sable, would you mind terribly taking the first watch? I'm beat."

Sable took her post standing up nearby. In a couple of hours, she would wake one of us to take a turn. I was pretty sure it wasn't going to be Cheff's turn next.

I found a place by the fire and wrapped my clothes around me as best I could. I didn't fall asleep right away, though. The Belowground was a strange and different world. It wasn't terribly cold or damp, but the bare rock felt like it was sucking all the heat from my body, and I didn't have a lot of extra heat to spare. Every small movement created an echo, as did the multitude of dripping sounds and the small noises the cave creatures made. I listened for a while to this other-worldly music, then I must have fallen asleep because in what seemed no time at all, I awoke to the sound of movement.

*"Now, this is more like it!"*

# — 20 —

# THE TOWER

It was strange to wake up in the darkness of the cavern. I had no idea how long I'd slept. I looked around and saw that Mid was sitting up, checking his timepiece.

"What time is it?" I whispered. "I didn't get a watch."

"I did, right after Sable. It's late. We've slept for over 10 hours. Cheff let you and Tocette and Buttons sleep. And Lhuk. I went overtime on my watch. Something about the cavern kept me awake."

"So it's tomorrow already?"

"Sure is. Midmorning, actually."

Cheff sat up and blinked. Mid pointed meaningfully at his timepiece.

Cheff stood up. "All right, everyone, rise and—well, rise, any-way. It's already late and we have a long way to go today."

"Do we?" Mid asked.

"Maybe," Cheff said. "Actually, we have no idea how far the tower is. For all we know, we've already passed it."

"I hope not!" Buttons said. "The ponies hate backtracking." She rubbed her arms. "I'm freezing, Cheff. We should have brought blankets or something. I'm sure glad Jewell told us to bring our jackets everywhere."

"You're right, we should have brought blankets. But who could have seen this coming?" Cheff gestured grandly toward the seemingly endless expanse of the Belowground.

We took care of our morning business, then filled our canteens from the burbling stream. Lery made another little fire and heated some felmoss tea. We huddled around the flames, trying to warm ourselves.

All of us except Sable, that is. Sable had wandered away a little and was examining the ceiling. After a while, she joined us at the fire.

"What did you see?" Cheff asked.

"Skylight."

"Say, what?"

We went over to where Sable had been and looked upward. Sure enough, a tiny patch of blue sky shone through the rock roof of the cavern.

"Why didn't we see it yesterday?" Tocette asked.

"Probably because it was already dark outside," Mid said.

"Oh."

"How far away do you suppose it is?" I asked.

"You mean, how far up?" Cheff said. "Too far, I'm afraid."

Mid took his flashlight and examined the floor of the cavern directly below the opening in the roof. "Look! There's a pile of stuff here."

"What kind of stuff?" Cheff asked.

"A bunch of rotten wood and twisted metal."

"I bet that's where the wood for the campfire came from," Buttons said. She picked up a chunk and held it for the ponies to examine. "It looks the same, anyway."

"It… it's… a ladder," Lery said.

"Not anymore," Mid said, and we laughed. "But I think you're right, Lery. It looks like it used to be. Maybe it's a supply place for workers like we talked about last night."

"Might be," Cheff said, "but it isn't going to do us any good."

"True," Mid said, "but now that we know there is one, it's a pretty good guess that there are more. If we keep looking, we might find one we can use."

"Good thinking," Cheff said. "So, I guess that's what we'll do. Everybody ready? Let's go. We can nibble on some of our monastery food while we walk."

We gathered our gear and off we went, following the pleasant little stream that ran along the edge of the cavern. It was easy going and fairly cool. The Belowground didn't seem to heat up during the day nor cool down during the night. After a few minutes of walking, we warmed up and were quite comfortable. Lhuk didn't seem much bothered by his claustrophobia.

From time to time, we passed something man-made, a wheelbarrow, a forgotten pick or shovel, or some empty food cans. Once we passed a fallen wooden sign with arrows pointing ahead and behind, and some writing next to each arrow. Mid picked it up and wiped the dust off with his sleeve.

"What does it say, Mid?" Tocette asked.

"Can't tell," Mid said. "The paint is nearly all gone."

"Let me look!" Buttons said. She pointed at one spot that still had remnants of paint. "That word, right there—it could be 'tower,' couldn't it?"

"Maybe," Mid said, "but I can't be sure."

"Well, the ponies and I are sure. It says 'tower,' and that means that the Belowground goes all the way to the tower we're supposed to find! All we have to do is keep going."

"You may very well be right," Cheff said. "And that's exactly what we're going to try. We're out of the heat and have plenty of food and water, and we don't have to worry about the Fessals down here. No offense, Lery."

"Stupid... Fessals," Lery said.

"Hey!" Tocette said. "I'm a Fessal, you know. And so are you, Lery!"

Cheff laughed. "We don't mean you, Tocette. It's a kind of a private joke between us and Lery. You see, even though Lery is a Fessal himself, most of the Fessals he has met in his life were soldiers, and they weren't very nice to him."

"Oh," Tocette said. She thought about this for a while. "I don't get the joke."

Cheff explained, "Like I said, it's a private joke."

"Oh. Well, maybe you can explain it to me, sometime. I like jokes, too."

"Maybe sometime," Cheff said.

And so the morning went on. We walked for several hours, stopped for a brief rest and another round of felmoss tea, then resumed our journey.

Finally, we came to the end of the cavern. The little stream disappeared underground somewhere, and the path we were following led to the entrance of another excavated tunnel.

Cheff went into the tunnel without hesitation, followed by Mid, Sable, and Lery. But when Lhuk got to the dark doorway, he stopped dead.

"I... I can't." Lhuk said. "I'm sorry, but I just can't."

"But, Lhuk," I said. "It's the only way. You can't stay out here, and if you go back, there's another tunnel."

Lhuk took a long, deep breath. "I know. Give me a minute, let me get myself together." He plopped down onto the rocky trail and hung his head.

Cheff and the others came back to where Lhuk was sitting.

"Tunnel giving you troubles?" Cheff asked kindly.

"I'm sorry, Cheff. I thought I'd gotten over it, and it took me by surprise."

"It's okay, Lhuk. Take your time."

After a little while, Sable took a black handkerchief from a little pouch on her equipment belt, then knelt in the dust beside Lhuk. "Try something? For me?"

Lhuk looked up at her green eyes shining from behind her jet-black bangs. "What is it?"

"Blindfold," Sable said.

"Will that help?" Lhuk asked. "Sure, um, okay. I guess so." He closed his eyes and turned up his face.

Sable folded the black cloth into a band and gently tied it over Lhuk's eyes. She looked at Cheff. "Tocette."

"Right," Cheff said. "Tocette, can you come over here, please?"

Tocette, who had been hanging back a little, said, "Sure."

"We need your help," Cheff said.

"My help? Um, what do I do?"

"We need you to be Lhuk's guide, okay?"

"Sure, I guess so. How do I do that?"

"Lhuk is going to walk behind you. He needs to hold onto your waist, and you need to go slow enough for him to keep up."

"Okay, Cheff, I can do that." She positioned herself in front of Lhuk.

Cheff and Sable helped Lhuk find handholds on Tocette's waistband.

"Ready, Lhuk?" Cheff asked.

"Sure, I guess."

"Right, then, let's see if it works," Cheff said.

He and Sable entered the tunnel again. This time, Tocette followed Sable, with Lhuk clinging tightly to her waist.

I followed Lhuk, and the rest of the gang brought up the rear.

After a dozen steps, Cheff called back, "How's it going, Lhuk?"

Lhuk said, "So far, so good. It's amazing."

"Great!" Cheff said. "It shouldn't be long. If my guess is correct, this tunnel will lead us to another cavern."

"Please, Cheff," Lhuk said, "don't remind me we're in a tunnel, okay?"

"Sorry," Cheff said. "Let's keep moving."

Cheff's guess was almost right, but not quite. He was right about the tunnel not being too long, but it opened, not into another cavern, but into a large, dimly lit room.

Sable untied Lhuk's blindfold. Lhuk blinked against the dim light radiating from a pair of gently glowing, milky white panels in the ceiling.

The stucco walls resembled the monastery's. Cool, red-clay tiles paved the floor. A large silver panel dominated one wall.

"Pretty fancy for a cavern, Old Man," Mid said.

"I'll say," Cheff agreed. "I wonder where we've come to?"

"It's the tower, Cheff!" Buttons said. "The ponies tried to tell you."

Cheff laughed, then tousled her hair. He gave each pony a gentle pat on the head. "Good ponies, smart ponies. I should have listened."

Buttons held the ponies up to her ear. "The ponies say, that's okay, but you should remember to listen next time."

"I will most certainly do that, ponies," Cheff said. "Now for the big question: where do we go from here?"

"Maybe that silver thing is a door, Cheff." Tocette ran her hands over the shiny metal surface. "Look! There's a button."

"Wait!" Cheff yelled. "Don't push—"

But it was too late—she'd already pushed it.

"Uh-oh," she said. "Sorry, Cheff."

We stood motionless, waiting and listening.

Nothing.

Cheff heaved a sigh of relief. "It's okay, nothing seems to be happ—"

*Clunk!* The loud, mechanical clunk was followed by a low rumble that grew steadily louder until the floor was shaking.

"Uh-oh," Tocette said again, edging back toward the tunnel entrance.

The rest of us edged with her.

The rumbling stopped suddenly.

So did we.

With a startling hissing noise, the silver panel split down the middle and became an open doorway.

We waited. When nothing happened, Cheff cautiously approached the new doorway and peeked inside. "It's a tiny little room. There's a row of buttons on one wall, with numbers on them. And—"

There was another clunk and the silver doors started to close.

"Cheff! Look out!" Buttons yelled.

The doors crashed into Cheff, then stopped and retracted back into the walls.

Mid was laughing so hard that the tears were running down his cheeks. Sable, too, was smiling. The rest of us were staring at Mid and Sable, too horrified to speak.

"What?" Mid said. "It's an elevator! Haven't you yokels ever seen an elevator before?"

None of us ever had, except Sable, who said, "Military base," and Mid, who was laughing so hard he could barely speak.

Cheff scowled and grumbled at Mid, "You couldn't say something?"

"You should have seen the look on your face, Old Man." And he laughed all over again.

At last, Cheff couldn't help himself and had to laugh, too. "No," he said. I've never seen one before. I've heard of them, of course. Where did you see elevators?"

"In the mines where my father worked, up in Toof-Toof," Mid said. "My father took me for a ride on one when I was a small boy. The mine shafts were hundreds of feet deep, too far for the miners to walk down."

"Don't they take a lot of power?" Cheff asked.

"Yes, they do," Mid said. "And elevators big enough for Seph aren't practical. That's why we didn't see any at the Iron Fortress. But you're right—they take a lot of power. Whatever this place is, it has some kind of power source. Maybe the underground river? Maybe a generator of some kind?"

Cheff stepped inside the elevator and looked around. "I suppose these buttons take you to different levels?"

"Right," Mid said, "but wait until we all get in."

"Okay. Come on, everyone."

We jammed into the little space, and the doors closed behind us. I felt Lhuk shudder, and I put my hand on his shoulder.

"I'm okay, I think," he said. "But you'd better push something quick, Cheff."

"Right," Cheff said, "but which one?"

"Any one," Mid said. "What difference does it make?"

Cheff raised his eyebrows. "Oh, sure, that's what you say *now*." He pushed the top button.

At first, nothing happened, then *clunk!* the elevator shuddered and started moving upward.

And kept going, and going, and going.

"Is it taking us to the moon?" Mid asked.

"Maybe we're going to pay a social call on the Great Fisherman," Buttons said, referring to one of Andaran's most recognizable constellations.

"You never know, Sis," Cheff said, "you just never know."

"Really, Cheff?" Tocette asked. "Are we really going to the moon?"

"No," Cheff said, "not really."

"Oh," Tocette said. She seemed disappointed.

After what felt like a long time, the rumbling stopped and the elevator was still. The doors slid open with another clunk, and we stepped out into a small, empty room, stuccoed and tiled like the basement. A single glowing ceiling panel provided dim light.

There was a door in the wall in front of us. Cheff boldly walked across and opened it, then stepped through.

"Andaran's bones!" we heard him call. "You'd better come have a look at this!"

188

— 21 —

# THE TOWER KEEPER

---

WE JOINED CHEFF on a balcony that ran completely around the four sides of the tower. The view was amazing! We could see for miles and miles in all directions.

The desert sun blazed directly overhead. The Stone Bear was clearly identifiable far to the east. Southward and westward there was nothing but desert and more desert, all the way to the horizon. Northward, the Imperial Highway was a golden ribbon running east-west, and beyond that, shrouded in purple mists, were the mountains. There was no sign of the Great Desert Safari bus or the soldiers' trucks, though we knew they were out there somewhere. I thought about what Jewell had said about there being plenty of hiding places in the not-so-flat desert.

"'Andaran's bones' is right, Old Man," Mid said. "I've never seen anything like this."

"Me, too," Buttons said. "I mean, me neither. It's beautiful!"

"I'm glad I got to come," Tocette said. "Thank you for bringing me with you, Cheff."

"Think nothing of it," Cheff said. "It is our pleasure."

As we absorbed the magnificent scenery, I could feel something move deep inside me, filling up an empty spot I didn't know I had.

Cheff evidently felt the same. "This is what it's all about," he said quietly.

"What?" Mid asked. "Climbing up onto high places and looking out?"

"Yeah, maybe," Cheff said. "It would be enough, wouldn't it?"

Mid didn't answer, but I guessed he knew what Cheff meant.

When, at last, we'd drunk our fill of the magnificent view, Cheff sighed. "I suppose we'd better locate the artifact, then be on our way. There obviously isn't anything up here at the top of this tower, so I suppose we'll have to try some of the other levels. Does anyone remember how many buttons there were in the elevator?"

"Starry does," Buttons said. Starry stepped forward and counted to twelve with her forehoof.

"Twelve, eh?" Cheff said. "Good pony!" He gave Starry a pat.

Lhuk had wandered back to the interior room. "Look at this," he called. "It's a Torph." He pointed to a highly stylized image of a man and a woman standing side-by-side, carved into the wall by the elevator. In spite of their simplicity, the little flat-faced stick figures were obviously meant to be Torphs.

"Interesting," I said. "Eleven floors, with the Torph room on top, assuming that the twelfth button was for the Belowground where we got on. Do you suppose that could be significant?"

"Why should it be?" Mid asked.

"Well, you know," I said. "Eleven floors, eleven Peoples."

"Could be a coincidence," Mid said.

"Easy enough to find out," Cheff said. "Let's go down one level." He pushed the elevator button.

The elevator doors opened immediately. It seemed that the elevator car had been waiting for us. We got in, and Cheff pushed the button right below the top one. Lhuk took a deep breath and reached for Buttons' hand, but this time the trip was brief. The elevator rumbled, then stopped and opened its doors.

We stepped out and looked at the wall near the elevator door. Sure enough, there was another man and woman standing side-by-side.

"Fruen species," Cheff said. "Look at the stripes in their hair."

"Interesting," Mid said. "Let's check the next one."

"Hang on," Cheff said. "We should look around a little, first."

This room was somewhat larger than the top, or Torph, level. It had windows, but no door leading to a balcony. It wasn't empty, like the Torph room. Papers, maps, and some strange instruments that I didn't recognize covered a number of tables. Some of the items looked old, extremely old.

A few large, leather-bound books lay scattered among the tables. I leafed through one of them. It was about astronomy, full of pictures of the sun, planets, the moon, and some constellations. A few pages explained the different types of clouds.

"Do you suppose they came up here to study the sky?" I asked.

"Who knows?" Cheff said. "Maybe. The Torph level would sure be a good place to see the sky from."

We poked around for another little while, then Cheff said, "Everybody seen enough here? Ready to go to the next level down?"

We were ready, but Sable came up to Cheff and said, "People."

"Do you think there are people here? In this tower?" He glanced around the room. "Hmmm, I suppose there might be. The room doesn't look abandoned. The tables aren't dusty. Let's stay alert. Everybody keep an eye out for anyone who might be here who isn't us, okay?" He pushed the elevator button again.

The next level down, the third from the top, also displayed drawings near the elevator door, this time of the Frae species. The room outside the elevator was small, with several doors in the walls.

"What's this place?" Tocette asked.

"Looks like a foyer," Cheff said.

"Oh," Tocette said. "What's a foyer?"

"You… make one… to cook on… outside." Lery said with a straight face.

Tocette frowned, then a grin slowly spread across her wide face. "Nooo, that's a *fire*. This is something else."

Lery grinned back. "I… was kidding."

"Oh."

"Didn't… anyone ever… kid you… before?"

"Not that I remember," Tocette said. "Not the funny kind like you did, anyway."

Lery blushed a little.

"Ehem," Mid said. "A foyer is a small room used as an entranceway to larger rooms."

"Oh." Tocette looked around. "I guess those doors must go to the other rooms, then."

"I guess so," Cheff said. "We'll have to check each one, so let's split up into teams. Let's see, there are four doors, so… Sable, Buttons, you take that one." He pointed at the door closest to the elevator. "Mid, you and Lery take the next one. Tocette and Lhuk take the third. Books and I will take the fourth. Okay? Let's be careful. If you meet anyone, come back to the foyer immediately and call the others."

Cheff waited until the other three teams had left the foyer, then he and I went through the fourth door into a large, dark room. As we entered, there was a clicking sound, and a pair of milky-white ceiling panels glowed softly.

"It knows we're here," I said.

"Seems to," Cheff agreed. "I wonder how it can tell. I've never seen anything like it. You?"

I shook my head. "Never."

Shelves lined the room from floor to ceiling. Messy heaps of all kinds of things covered a few tables: papers, books, plants, seeds, sticks, stones, man-made objects of all sorts, and a bunch of stuff

I couldn't identify at first glance. All manner of strange and peculiar items filled the shelves.

"What is this place?" I asked Cheff.

"I don't know. It looks like someone roams the desert, or maybe even beyond the desert, collects anything and everything, and hauls it back here."

"Look," I said. "Here's a book with handwriting in it. It looks like a kind of log or journal."

"Let me see." Cheff picked up the large volume, held it directly under one of the ceiling lights, then moved it close to his eyes.

*"Seventh month, second week, fourth day. Found three lightly speckled eggs in a nest almost hidden under a large rock. Possibly plover eggs. Seventh month, second week, fifth day. Came across the skin of a large snake, recently shed."*

"Hmmm." He gave the book back to me. "I think you might be correct, Books. It does look like someone goes out into the desert and brings stuff back. To what end, I wonder?"

"Maybe he's a scientist of some sort. A researcher, perhaps?"

"Is? Or was? Some of this junk looks pretty old."

I returned the book to its place. On the next table, a sort of round ball was mounted on a stand in such a way that the ball could turn. "Look at this, Cheff."

Cheff came over and gave the ball a spin. On one side there was a brown splotch, but the rest of it was greenish blue. "This spot looks like a map of Andaran." He dusted it off with his sleeve. "It *is* a map of Andaran. I recognize it from geography class in Basic School."

"It's a map of the world!" I said. "I've never seen one on a ball before."

"It's called a globe," Cheff said. "It's supposed to represent the entire planet. My father told me about them."

"It's the first one I've ever seen," I said.

Cheff made a sour face. "Another result of Pallador's vision of enlightenment. Years before I was born, he had all the globes rounded up and destroyed so people wouldn't realize that the world is round, or how big it is. Pah!"

"Then why does he allow maps?"

"If you think about it, Books, you'll realize that every map you've ever seen featured Pallador's activities."

"That's true," I said. "But the maps still show all of Andaran."

"Because Pallador has plans for all of Andaran," Cheff said.

"Makes sense. I don't see anything like a crystal sphere here, Cheff."

"Me neither. Let's go back to the foyer and wait for the others."

But when we got there, the others were already waiting for us.

"What did you find?" Cheff asked. "Anything interesting?"

"Bunch of junk on shelves and tables," Mid said.

"Same," Sable said.

"Us, too," Tocette said.

Lhuk said, "There was one strange thing. Some of the shelves were empty, and one was half empty."

"That's right," Tocette said. "Our room was full of boxes and packing stuff. Like they were in the middle of moving or something."

"Odd," Cheff said. "Where do you suppose they would move *to*? There's nothing else out here in the desert, at least not that we could see from the tower."

"Maybe somewhere in the Belowground?" Tocette asked.

"Yeah, maybe," Cheff said. "Good thinking, Tocette."

Tocette blushed. "Aw, thanks, Cheff."

Cheff continued, "But nothing like a crystal sphere? No? Okay, then, let's go down one more."

Cheff called the elevator again, and in we went. The next floor down had drawings by the elevator, the same as the other floors. This time they had the long arms and sloping foreheads of the Altaar species.

"Altaars!" Lhuk said. "We don't see a lot of Altaars in Fellstone City."

"I wonder why that is?" Mid asked.

"I… saw an… an Altaar… once… at… at the… Iron… Fortress…" Lery said. "He… died."

"Not good," Cheff said. "I wonder what our Beloved Emperor has against the Altaars."

"I… dunno… Friend Cheff," Lery said sadly. "I wasn't… supposed to… but… I talked to… to him… a little. He was… nice. Smart." He turned his face away and grew quiet.

The Altaar level's foyer was somewhat larger than the one on the Frae level. This time there were six doors.

"The tower must be getting wider as we go down," Cheff said.

"Gets narrower as it goes up, more likely, Old Man," Mid said.

"Say, what?" Cheff asked, then got it. "Oh, right. If we ever get outside again, we can test your theory, Old Son. Should be pretty obvious from the outside."

"Agreed," Mid said. "How do you want to explore this level?"

"Well, let's see," Cheff said. "Six doors, eight of us. We could make two teams of four each, and each team could take three rooms."

"We only needed two per team before, Cheff," Buttons said. "Why four this time?"

"You heard what Mid said," Cheff replied. "The levels are getting bigger."

The ponies considered this, then nodded. "Okay," Buttons said. "We can do it that way."

"Why, thank you, Buttons," Cheff said too sweetly. "I appreciate that."

"Don't mention it," Buttons said brightly. "The ponies are always happy to be of help."

"Hang on," Mid said, sniffing the air. "I smell something."

"You always smell something," Cheff said. "What is it this time?"

Mid sniffed again. "Sausage."

"What?"

"Someone's cooking sausage."

"So," Cheff said, "we're *not* alone. Where is it coming from? Can you tell?"

"Not sure yet. Give me a minute." Mid went around the foyer, sniffing at each door. Finally, he went back to the third door from the left. "This one. It's coming from here."

Cheff tiptoed over and tried the handle. The door opened. The squeak of its hinges shattered the stillness of the foyer.

Cheff froze.

We waited.

Nothing.

Quietly, Cheff edged into the room, motioning for the rest of us to stay put. In spite of this, Mid, then the rest of us, followed Cheff. He turned and gave us a look, then again motioned for us to wait.

We kept right on following.

This time, the ceiling panels didn't come on automatically wherever we went. We tiptoed as quietly as we could. On the far side of the room, a sliver of light sliced through the darkness. Cheff steered toward it.

The light came through the crack of a slightly open door. Cheff peered through the crack, then opened the door a couple of inches and peered again. "There's no one there," he whispered.

He opened the door the rest of the way, then slid into the lighted room. Once again, he motioned for us to wait, and once again, we ignored him.

The aroma of sausage was tantalizing. It had been a while since we'd had a hot meal. We seemed to be crossing someone's living quarters. A book rested on a little table next to a comfy-looking chair. A pair of reading glasses lay on top of the book. Behind the chair was a floor lamp, but it was turned off.

We crossed the room, then passed through another open doorway into a small kitchen. On the stove, a pan full of large sausages sizzled and crackled, maybe two dozen of them.

Mid whispered, "Whoever he is, he has a mighty big appetite."

Lery stifled a giggle.

Suddenly, an enormous figure darkened the doorway behind us. A large man, an Altaar, lurched into the kitchen. "WHAT ARE YOU CHILDREN DOING IN MY TOWER!"

Clerment

# — 22 —

## CLERMENT

---

I FROZE. LERY'S JAW dropped open. Sable assumed a combat crouch. Buttons nearly dropped the ponies.

Cheff recovered first. "I'm sorry, sir. We had no idea anyone lived here."

"That doesn't answer the question, young man."

"No, sir, I guess it doesn't. With respect, sir, before we can answer that question, we'd have to know a bit about you."

The Altaar glared at Cheff over his black-rimmed glasses, but Cheff held firm. Eventually, the Altaar's countenance softened, and he smiled a tiny smile. "Tight lips, eh? That's wise. All right, the lot of you, find seats at my table, and let's have some supper. Questions will wait, sausages will not."

We were still catching our breath, but we made our way to his long table and took seats there. The table was already set for nine, complete with plates, silverware, and crystal glasses full of ice-cold tonton juice. A plate laden with warm, freshly baked brown bread, sat next to a bowl of butter. A larger bowl held a variety of fruit. A plate of smoked salmon, covered in peppercorns, sat next to the fruit. I wondered how he got fish all the way out here in the desert.

The Altaar tended the sausages, rolling them around in the pan. He noticed me watching, and said, "You have to get the shade of brown exactly right, the shade of desert clay in the afternoon. One shade darker, and they're ruined."

A few minutes later, he held up a sausage on the end of a fork. "There, you see? Absolute perfection! Quickly now, let's get them on the plate." He emptied the pan onto the platter, then set the platter in the middle of the table. "Let them rest, children. They keep cooking a little after you take them off the fire."

We buttered some of the steaming brown bread while we waited.

"Do you like my bread, children? Eat it up! I make it myself. I even grind the grain, so you can be sure there's no jexan in it."

Cheff looked at him sharply.

"Oh my, oh my," the Altaar said. "I shouldn't have said that. I, well, I forget myself sometimes, I do. Getting too old for this job, that's what."

"Don't worry, sir," Cheff said. "We already know about jexan."

"In fact," Buttons said brightly, "Lery is the one who—oof!"

Cheff elbowed her in the ribs.

She looked up at him with misty eyes. "Andaran's bones, Cheff! I was about to tell—"

"Sorry, Mel. Didn't mean to hurt you." He glanced over at the Altaar. "But I do think it would be best to keep our own counsel for the time being. After all, we haven't even met our host yet—formally, that is."

"Quite right, quite right, young lady," the Altaar said in his peculiar lilting accent. "You can't be too careful these days. Permit me to introduce myself. I'm—oh, dear. You'll pardon me, but first, we should eat these sausages. It simply won't do to let them get cold." He dished out two sausages for everyone, including himself. "No, it simply won't do at all."

He seated himself, pinned down one of his sausages, then sliced off about an inch, which, on the end of his fork, he held up to his nose. "Ah, wonderful, wonderful! Can you smell the spices?" He took a bite, then closed his eyes blissfully, savoring the sausage without swallowing.

Lery followed the Altaar's example and sniffed carefully at his own bite of sausage. "I… recognize… the caraway… or is that… fennel?" He sniffed again. "Salt… pepper… and… and… I don't know… what that is, sir."

The Altaar looked delighted. "Desert sage, young man, desert sage. It grows wild in the desert around here. Wonderful, isn't it? Perfectly balances the fennel, don't you think? You would never know that you're eating—ehem. I mean, the meat takes the spice perfectly, don't you agree?"

Lery nodded, his mouth too full to answer. Cheff and Mid both froze with a forkful of sausage in mid-air. Cheff raised his eyebrows. Mid cautiously sniffed at his again, then shrugged and popped it in his mouth. Cheff hesitated, then followed suit.

"If you like it, young fellow, I'll gladly give you the recipe."

"Yes… please…" Lery said. "I'd like… that very… much."

We finished the sausages, then tucked into the smoked salmon and the fruit.

When we had polished off the last savory morsels, the Altaar said, "I suppose it's time for formal introductions, now, eh, what? Introductions are better on a full belly, I always say. I shall begin. My name is Clerment. I am, as you can see, a member of the Altaar People. I am the tower keeper here. Now you."

We introduced ourselves one by one, then Cheff asked, "Please sir, judging by this fine supper, I am guessing that you were expecting us. How could that be?"

"That's true, young… Cheff, is it? Right. But you should hardly be surprised, you know. You've been banging about in the Belowground for a day and a night, and rummaging around in my tower all morning. Of course I was expecting you! A bit of supper was my way of breaking the ice, so to speak."

"What place is this?" I asked.

"Why, this is Isomet Tower. It once was, and still is, for that matter, a kind of desert research station, among other things. It was built hundreds of years ago, I believe. Although, the elevator and electrical power were added recently, no more than a hundred years ago, or perhaps a bit more. Right before The Fall, you see."

"Are you a hundred years old, sir?" Buttons asked.

Cheff hissed, "Buttons!"

But Clerment laughed. "No, no, young lady. I'm not anywhere near that old. Altaars don't live any longer than the other species—that's merely a myth."

We looked at each other. No one had heard that myth before.

"However," Clerment continued, "my father was the tower keeper before me, and his father before him."

"And his father before him?" Tocette asked.

Clerment removed his spectacles and polished them with the edge of the tablecloth. "Yes, and his father before him, as far as I know."

"Oh," Tocette said. "What about *his* fath—"

Lhuk broke in. "Did you collect all the things?"

"I did, or, rather, we did, my forefathers and I, with the help of many others. As I said, Isomet Tower was built as a desert research facility before The Fall. We saw no reason to discontinue the research after The Fall. Later, however, Isomet took on another role. Many of the rooms are filled with things that people brought here, secretly, to keep from falling into the hands of that nasty Pallador fellow. Unpleasant chap, even for a Seph. Smells bad, too." He wrinkled his nose.

The ponies exchanged a glance, then  shook hooves with each other.

Clerment observed this procedure, then asked, "I say, what was that about?"

Buttons said, "The ponies not only agree with your assessment of the Emperor, but are most pleased to hear you say so."

"I see. I'm glad to hear it. Sadly," Clerment said, gesturing broadly at the tower all around, "it's all about to come to an end. So sad, you know, but, as they say, all good things, eh?"

Tocette brightened. "I know—come to an end, right? That's what all good things do."

"Exactly, Miss Tocette. Well said."

Mid asked, "*Why* is it coming to an end?"

Clerment considered this. "Since The Fall until now, Isomet Tower has escaped Pallador's attention. He has confined most of his activities to Fellstone City and other cities along the east coast. Now, however, he is beginning his westward expansion. It's no secret that he plans to rebuild the Imperial Highway and extend his Imperium all the way to the West Coast. He already has his agents installed at Xanparthur Monastery. Do you know it?"

"We came from there," Cheff said.

"Through the Belowground?" Clerment asked. "How… odd. But I suppose you have your reasons. As I was saying, that Attan fellow is about to make things most unpleasant for those poor monks. Did you happen to run into him during your visit?"

"He's the one who sent us out here," Tocette blurted.

Clerment's eyes widened. "I say, do you mean to tell me that you're all here on a mission for the Emperor?"

Cheff smiled. "Well, when you put it that way, technically, yes."

Clerment frowned. "Oh my, oh my! That's not good, not good at all."

"Don't worry," Cheff said quickly. "We don't work for Pallador or Attan. It's only a coincidence."

Clerment sighed in relief. "I'm so glad to hear that, so glad indeed!" Then he frowned. "However, I must say, I don't quite understand."

"Before we tell you any more about ourselves," Cheff said, "we'd like to ask you a few questions, if that's okay with you."

"Certainly, Cheff. I can't promise to answer them all. I have my secrets, too, you know."

"Yes, sir," Cheff said. "First question: you mentioned that Isomet's time as a refuge from Pallador is coming to an end. What will happen to all the things stored here?"

"Why, they'll be moved, of course. You must have noticed that the top floors are already empty?"

"Yes, sir," Mid said. "Where is all the stuff going?"

"That's one of the secrets," Clerment said. "There's only one way to keep a secret, you know—don't tell anyone, ever. I'm sure you children would never tell, but accidents happen. It simply wouldn't do if Pallador found out where it's all going, or even that it's been moved from here."

"He doesn't know about Isomet?" Buttons asked. "How can that be?"

"Oh, I suppose he knows the tower is here," Clerment said. "But as for what is in it, maybe, maybe not. He likely believes it's a research station for things of nature, as it has always been. Most of the items on display are readily found in the desert."

"If he knew you were moving all the things, would he come to take it, or destroy it, or whatever he does?" I asked.

"He might," Clerment said. "Then again, maybe not. He might save it for his own people to examine. This is a relatively safe place, being so isolated."

"What sort of stuff is it?" Buttons asked.

Clerment thought about that. "I suppose I can tell you that much. Especially since it will all be moved soon. There's quite a variety. Works of art, rare books, antiques of all sorts. Those items are *not* on display."

"The sort of things that don't exist in Pallador's new world," Cheff said. "Is that what you're saying?"

Clerment nodded at Cheff. "Precisely, young man. Isomet is one of several places in Andaran dedicated to the preservation of pre-Fall culture, art, and science. Xanparthur Monastery is another such place, and there are others, too. We believe that a time will come when it will once again be safe to share these things with the world."

"'We?'" Cheff asked.

"Oh my, oh my," Clerment said. "I'm definitely not all that good at secrets, am I? Too much time alone, I suppose. Let's say that there are others like me who would hate to see the rich cultural heritage of the Sixth Kingdom vanish into the mists of the Dark Century that is coming. Especially at the hands of that vile Seph miscreant, Pallador!" He wiped his forehead with a tiny white handkerchief with frilly edges. "I'm sorry, children. I tend to get a bit worked up sometimes."

"Don't worry," Mid said. "A lot of us are passionate about our work." He flicked his eyes toward Cheff.

"I see," Clerment said, then smiled.

Cheff smiled back. "You're keeping these things safe until the heir to the Sixth Kingdom is found, aren't you?"

Clerment gasped. "How… how do you know about that? Wait, don't answer, I already know. There's only one possible answer to that, and—"

"—it's a secret!" we said in unison, and laughed.

Clerment peeled an orange as he thought this over. "So, then, you're *not* on a mission for the Sephs, are you?" He handed sections of the orange to Buttons and Sable and began peeling another.

"No," Cheff said, "but Attan thinks we are."

"Nor for the monastery, either, correct?"

"Correct, sir. However, Master Vessslu—do you know him?— knows about what we're doing and why we're here. He didn't say anything about you. Although," he reflected, "he might not have wanted to mention you in front of Attan."

"Without doubt," Clerment agreed. "Master Vessslu is cautious. He knew you'd find me when you got here. Meanwhile, it's best you don't know anything you don't need to know, you see?"

"Yes, sir," Cheff said.

"Vessslu and I go back quite a few years," Clerment said. "In fact, some of Xanparthur's valuables are here now, awaiting shipment to… the safe place I mentioned. Vessslu no doubt intended for me to help you, or he wouldn't have sent you to me. What were your instructions, if you don't mind me asking?"

Cheff flicked his eyes toward Tocette.

Clerment raised his eyebrows and nodded slightly. "Miss Tocette, how would you like to see some of the Treasures of Xanparthur?"

"Treasures!" Tocette said. "I want to see treasures!"

"Very well," Clerment said. "Follow me."

He led her out through the foyer and into a side room. Their voices echoed back to us. "There you are," Clerment told her. "You may touch whatever you wish, but please be careful. Some of the treasures are quite valuable."

Tocette clasped her hands behind her back. "I won't touch anything, I promise. I'm only going to look."

"Good for you!" Clerment said. "We'll call you when we're ready to go exploring." He quietly closed the door to the foyer, then returned to us, still seated at the breakfast table. "Now, then, Master Cheff, can we talk freely?"

"Yes, sir."

"Good. You were about to explain your instructions from Masters Vessslu and Attan."

"Yes, sir," Cheff said again. "We're to find a certain object and return it to the monastery. I'm not sure I should tell you, sir."

"Cheff," Buttons said, "if he's going to help us find it, he's going to have to know what it is."

Sable said, "Safe."

"I… trust him…" Lery said.

"Tell him," Lhuk said. "We need all the help we can get."

"Agreed," Mid said.

"I'm in," I said.

"Fair enough," Cheff said. "We're supposed to find an *artifact*."

— **23** —

# THE ARTIFACT

CLERMENT STOOD UP so abruptly that his chair fell over backward. "Artifact? *An* Artifact? *The* Artifact? *Who told you about an artifact?*"

We stared at Clerment.

He took a deep breath. "I'm sorry, children. Let's start over, shall we?"

No one said anything.

"Maybe it would be best if you were to fill me in on how you came to know of the artifact."

"Okay," Cheff said, "we can do that, but we don't know all that much."

"I understand," Clerment said. "Simply do the best you can to help me understand, and I promise I'll do my best to help you however I can."

"It's like this," Cheff said. "We were looking for Master Vessslu in the monastery. Instead, we found an old Seph. He asked us to go into the Great Desert, find an artifact, and bring it back to him. That's pretty much the whole thing."

"I see," Clerment said. "Did he say where to find it?"

"We were to go south until we reached the Stone Bear, then turn west until we found the tower," Cheff said. "This tower, your tower."

"Yes," Clerment said. "This artifact, did he tell you what sort of artifact you were to look for?"

"A spherical crystal artifact," Buttons said.

"I see," Clerment said. "Are you sure?"

"That's what Kahph said," Buttons said.

"Kahph! That old villain?" Clerment said. "I didn't know he was still alive."

"You know him?" Mid asked.

"No, not personally," Clerment said, "but I know of him. One of my ancestors knew him quite well, in fact. Kahph was one of the great forces that precipitated The Fall, you see. Kahph, Pallador, the Cult of Callor. To a large extent, Kahph is responsible for the shape of the world today."

"Callor?" I said. "Kahph said that Callor was one of his names."

"That pretentious old menace!" Clerment said. "He probably belonged to the Cult of Callor, but I'm sure that was never one of *his* names. No, indeed!" Clerment thought this over, then asked, "Why did you children agree to help him?"

"We didn't, exactly," Mid said. "It's as we said before: we went to ask Master Vessslu about what Kahph had said and Attan was there. It was Attan who insisted that we go find the artifact and return it."

"Master Vessslu agreed," Cheff said, "but I think he was acting under pressure from Attan."

"He said that no one would notice a bunch of kids," Buttons said.

"But... someone... did notice..." Lery said. "Because... soldiers were... following us."

"Soldiers!"

"Yes, sir," Cheff said. "We left Xanparthur as tourists aboard the Great Desert Safari bus, with Kregg Setnar and Jewell. Do you know them, Mr. Clerment?"

"Oh, yes, I've known them for a long while. From time to time they stop by here and bring me something nice to eat, or something interesting that they found in the desert. Good people, Kregg and Jewell."

"Then why," Lhuk asked, "did they act as though they'd never heard of you or of your tower?"

"They did tell us how to get here," Buttons said.

"True," Lhuk agreed, "but they never mentioned Mr. Clerment or said that they knew him."

"Don't know, can't tell," Sable murmured.

"That's it exactly!" Clerment said. "They knew that if you found me, you'd find out everything you needed to know. And if you were captured, well, you can't tell what you don't know, as Miss Sable said."

"I guess that makes sense," Lhuk said grudgingly.

"Please continue," Clerment said.

"Fessals," Sable murmured. "Soldiers."

"They were chasing you?"

"It seems so," Cheff said. "Kregg Setnar thought so, anyway."

"I see," Clerment said. "Well, he would know, I suppose. Then what happened?"

"Then," Cheff said, "the eight of us jumped out of the bus when we got to the Stone Bear."

"What happened next?" Clerment asked.

"Claustrophobia is what happened next," Lhuk grumbled.

"We found a crack in the base of the Stone Bear," Cheff said. "It led to a cave. Inside the cave, we found a tunnel that led us to the Belowground. We followed an underground stream for a while, then found the basement of the tower."

"We didn't know anyone lived here," Buttons said. "Nobody said anything about you. No offense, sir."

"None taken, Miss Buttons."

"We started searching the tower," Cheff said, "looking for the artifact, you see. Then we found you."

"Thank you, children. I believe I have a good picture of what happened. One question: why did you agree to help the Sephs?"

"We didn't agree to anything," Mid said. "We were given orders."

"We did want to help," Cheff said, "but not necessarily by finding an artifact."

"Oh? How, then?"

"We figured out that Pallador sent Attan to make sure that the Xanparthur Sephs support Pallador's 'Path of Enlightenment' program."

"We don't want that to happen," Buttons said, "because the monks are trying to preserve knowledge, but Pallador is trying to erase knowledge. Right, Cheff?"

"That sums it up," Cheff said. "We figured, and Kregg Setnar agreed, that if we found the artifact, there might be some way for the Xanparthur monks to use it as leverage against Attan and ultimately Pallador."

"You children figured all that out?" Clerment asked. "Impressive." He thought it over, then said, "Well, it seems to me that if Kahph and Attan are both so interested in an artifact, we had better give them one."

"Nooo!" Buttons said. "You aren't going to give Kahph the artifact? Please say you're not! The ponies would be heartbroken!"

"Now, now, little Buttons," Clerment said. "I said we ought to give them *an* artifact, not *the* artifact."

"*An* artifact?" Buttons asked. "Do you mean there's more than one?"

"Not at all, Miss Buttons. And let me assure you, the ponies' hearts are safe."

"I don't get it," Mid said. "Are you going to give them the artifact or not?"

"Certainly not!" Clerment said. "What kind of man do you think I am? Even if I had the artifact, I'd never give it to a demented Kahph or a power-mad Attan."

"I'm glad to hear that," Cheff said. "You had me worried for a minute there."

"No need for worry," Clerment said. "As far as I know, no such artifact exists. Oh, there have been rumors about an artifact for decades. Centuries, even. Some say it was found before The Fall, then lost again. Others say it never existed at all. But there are some, Attan included, it seems, who not only believe that the artifact exists, but that whoever possesses it will have great power, power beyond imagining. Attan probably believes that the artifact will somehow make him the Emperor instead of Pallador."

Cheff said, "No doubt Kahph believes the same."

"On the bright side," Clerment said, "neither Attan nor Kahph seems to know what the artifact looks like."

"A spherical crystal," Buttons said. "That's what he told us."

Clerment snorted. "Nonsense, of course. If there were such an artifact, it wouldn't be some sort of crystal ball. There is only one kind of true power in this world, and that is Truth. With a capital T."

"Truth first," Sable said.

"Indeed, Miss Sable, quite. I would think that the real artifact, if such exists, would be a book, or a scroll, or some drawings or diagrams, or some such. However…"

"Yes?" Cheff said.

"However, if a crystal sphere is what Kahph wants and what Attan expects, it seems to me that we should get them one. Don't you agree?"

"Um, sure, I guess," Cheff said. "Where are we going to find one of those?"

"Where, indeed? But before we go looking—" He ducked back into the kitchen and returned with a small envelope, which he gave to Lery. "Here you go, young fellow. Desert sage for you to take back to Fellstone City."

"Thank… thank you… sir. I'll make… good… use of… it."

"I'm sure you will," Clerment said. He led us back to the foyer and called, "Come, Miss Tocette. We're going to see more treasures on the floor below." He pressed the elevator button. "Next stop: Kreff Level."

We went one level down, and sure enough, near the door, were figures of a tall, lithe Kreff man and woman.

"Look, Sable," Tocette said. "Maybe they were some ancestors of yours! The woman looks like you."

"Perhaps," Sable said.

There was no foyer on the Kreff level. Instead, there were rows and rows of crates and boxes stacked from floor to ceiling. Clerment led us among the containers. He opened the lid of a narrow wooden crate and held up a painting, a portrait, to the light for us to see.

"Who's that?" Buttons asked. "He has a crown. Is he a king?"

"Not anymore," Clerment said. "He's been dead for nearly five centuries. That has cut into his kingship, somewhat. This is the only known likeness of King Maghorn I, the founder of the Sixth Kingdom."

"Maghorn I," I said. "Amazing!"

"You've heard of him, then?" Clerment asked.

"Heard of him!" I said. "Master Vessslu gave me an entire book about him. And I read about him in some old history books my father had, before he… before… Well. Before."

"All right, young man, easy does it. I'm sorry to hear about your father. These are bad times."

"Yes, sir," I said and swallowed hard. "Anyway, I read that King Maghorn was the one who built the highways and bridges, and was developing the Belowground, and… well, lots of things."

"Quite correct. You can still see plenty of his works even today, such as the Royal Highway, or Imperial Highway as Emperor Pallador would have it."

Lhuk examined the portrait. "He's a Torph."

"He looks like you," Buttons said. "Except older. And fatter. A *lot* fatter."

"Andaran prospers when Torphs rule," Lhuk said. "That's what Master Vessslu told me and Books yesterday."

"It's quite true," Clerment said. "Maghorn's rule was the beginning of Andaran's Golden Age."

Lhuk continued contemplating the portrait, until Clerment said, "Well, let's see what else we can find, shall we?" He led us on the most wonderful tour of the entire tower, poking into boxes, searching shelves and cabinets, and, from time to time, showing us a marvelous work of art, a rare book, or an unusual specimen from the Great Desert.

Once, under a small glass dome, a hairy jumping spider, larger than Lery's hand, looked like it was about to jump. Another time, he found a stuffed and mounted desert pup.

Buttons hid the ponies' eyes. "Don't look, ponies! And whatever you do, don't breathe a word of this to Mr. Kip!" The ponies promised to keep their own counsel.

We spent hours searching for the 'artifact' with Clerment. Each new floor was bigger than the floor above, and they were all named after one of the Peoples—eleven floors, eleven Peoples. From the top down they were: Torph, Fruen, Frae, then Altaar, where we found Clerment. Next came Kreff, Lildur, Lora, and Troh. The last three were Sevro, Fessal, and finally Seph, at ground level.

"You were right, Books!" Buttons said. "Eleven floors, eleven species! The ponies are most pleased!"

We never made it to the Seph level. It took us quite a while to search the Fessal level, as it was large. Clerment kept opening boxes, doors, and drawers, all the while saying things like, "Oh my, oh my, it must be here somewhere," and "Wherever could I have put it?" and "It can't have grown legs and walked away, now, could it?"

At last, Clerment tripped over a small wooden crate. A round object wrapped in a blanket rolled across the floor. Clerment chased it down and picked it up. "Aha! There you are! We've been looking all over. Come, children, back to the elevator, and let's look at this in the light."

At the elevator, Clerment unwrapped the blanket, revealing a large, round, transparent sphere, bigger than a man's head. It glistened and sparkled in the artificial light.

"Is it crystal, Mr. Clerment?" Buttons asked.

"Well, er, no, it's not," Clerment said. "It's only glass. See the bubbles trapped inside? True crystal doesn't have bubbles in it like that, or streaks, or ripples. True crystal is, well, it's crystal clear."

We laughed.

Cheff asked, "Won't Kahph notice the difference?"

"Maybe, maybe not," Clerment said. "We all have a tendency to see what we want to see, do we not? Besides, who knows if Kahph has ever seen a crystal sphere this big, eh?"

"So," Cheff said, "your idea is to pull a fast one on Kahph and Attan? You think it'll work?"

"It's what we have," Clerment said. "Unless you can think of something better. No? Me neither. Well, then, come on back to my quarters. We can have a snack and discuss how best to use this 'artifact.'"

But when we got back to Clerment's quarters, a strange scuffling noise came from the kitchen. Clerment motioned for us to stop, then called out, "Who's there? Who is that?"

No one answered, but the scuffling noise continued. Clerment held his walking stick in both hands, like a club. "Show yourself, I say. Come out of there at once!"

Nothing.

"Last chance," Clerment called. "Who are you and what do you want? Speak up, now!"

The scuffling stopped and a plaintive voice said, "Treeeeeats? Caaaaaandy?"

"Mr. Kip!" Buttons said, and brushed past Clerment into the kitchen. Mr. Kip stood up when he saw her, then leaped across the room onto her shoulders. "Treeeeeeats?"

— **24** —

## DESERT TREK

BUTTONS FOUND THE remnants of the tonton fruit Clerment had squeezed for breakfast and gave a large piece to Mr. Kip, who promptly busied himself digging out the remaining bits of savory pulp.

"How did you get here?" Buttons asked Mr. Kip, but he was too busy to reply.

"If Mr. Kip is here," Cheff said, "then so are Kregg and Jewell. Let's go find them."

"They're probably outside with the bus," Mid said.

"Oh, good!" Tocette clapped her hands. "Maybe I'll get to drive again!"

We went back to the elevator, but as Cheff was about to press the call button, a metallic clatter came from somewhere below, and someone shouted something, then the elevator rumbled.

"Sounds like Kregg and Jewell are coming to find us," Buttons said. "The ponies will be glad to see them."

"I don't think so, Miss Buttons," Clerment said. "That sounds like the clatter of weapons to me."

Later, I'd wonder where and how the gentle Clerment had learned to recognize the sounds of war, but right then we were much too busy. In less time than it takes to tell, Clerment whisked us out of the elevator area, through his apartment, and into a stairwell via a door that had been hidden from view by a large tapestry.

"Back door," he said, pushing our recently acquired artifact into Cheff's hands. "Go down to the ground floor, go out the door, and find Kregg and Jewell. Hurry, now!"

"What about you?" Buttons asked. "Will you be okay?"

"Oh, I'll be fine. Fessal patrols have been stopping by every few months for years, now."

"Thank you," Cheff said, "for everything!"

"Especially the sausage!" Tocette said.

"You're welcome, most welcome, but go, go quickly, now."

Buttons threw her arms around Clerment's waist and gave him a quick hug. "The ponies hope we'll meet again," she said.

"As do I," Clerment said, "as do I. Goodbye, Miss Buttons. Goodbye, ponies. Goodbye, *everyone*, now!" He herded us into the stairwell and closed the door behind us.

We tiptoed as fast as we could down the stairs, found the exit door, and spilled out into the desert. It was late afternoon, and the heat hit us like a blow.

Kregg and Jewell waited in the Great Desert Safari bus only a few yards from the door. We ran for the bus as fast as we could.

"Hurry children!" Jewell said. "Soldiers in the tower! Must get moving!"

Kregg said, "This will never do. Those Fessals will soon realize you're not in the tower and come looking. The Great Desert Safari bus is fast, but military vehicles are faster—much faster. It's only a matter of time before they follow our tracks and catch up with us."

Cheff was momentarily stunned, then he rallied. "Excellent idea, Kregg! Everyone, come with me!" He jumped off the Safari

Bus and ran to the military vehicle. "Load up, everyone," Cheff yelled. "Fast!"

"You're kidding," Mid said. "You're going to steal a military vehicle?"

"Only a little bit. Hurry up!"

We all boarded the military truck except Mid, who merely stood there watching. Finally, he shrugged and jumped aboard.

"Can I drive?" Tocette shouted. "I'm a really good driver! Mr. Setnar said so."

"Sure," Cheff said. "Why not?

Mid looked at Cheff like he'd lost his mind.

Cheff said, "Let's get the water and coal flowing. Mid? Lery?"

Lery took Mid by the elbow and led him to the engine deck where they started fiddling with the controls.

Kregg and Jewell looked on in shocked disbelief.

Cheff waved at them. "We'll meet you back at the monastery," Cheff shouted. "Don't worry—if they catch you, you'll have no passengers!" Then to Tocette, "Okay, Beautiful Intrepid Good Driver, let her rip!"

Tocette, with a little help from Buttons and the ponies, coaxed the military vehicle into gear, then opened the throttle all the way. The truck leaped forward like a racehorse from the gate. For a few minutes, Tocette was busy steering around rocks and cacti and other desert obstacles.

I watched out the back window as the soldiers came out of Isomet Tower just in time to see us drive the vehicle away. The Great Desert Safari Bus was also on the move, only a short distance behind us. The soldiers shouted orders at Kregg and Jewell to stop and pick them up, but the Safari Bus was already far ahead of them and accelerating rapidly. I wondered how the soldiers would get home, but I didn't much care.

Buttons and the ponies kept watch behind us. "I can't see the Safari Bus anymore, Cheff."

"That's okay, Sis, they know where we're going and we'll meet up with them later." Cheff was busy making sure that Tocette was, in fact, actually driving the vehicle. She seemed to have a knack for it and was expertly avoiding obstacles.

Mid and Lery reported that the steam was functioning at optimum levels. "At this rate," Mid said, "we might be back to the monastery by bedtime."

We grabbed handholds as the vehicle lurched over a clump of cactus. "Wheee!" Tocette yelled. "This is really fun!"

Cheff said, "Maybe we should slow down a little so we don't lose Kregg and Jewell."

"We sure lost those soldiers though, didn't we?" Tocette said. "Haw haw, they'll have to walk home."

From the rear window, Buttons said, "Or maybe they'll take the other military truck back to the monastery."

"What other truck, Sis?" Cheff asked.

"The one that's following us."

"The one that—" He hung out the passenger door to get a good look behind us. "Andaran's Bones! There *is* another vehicle following us. And it's gaining on us fast." He leaned over and cranked up the speed control. "Lery! Mid! More coal! Tocette— faster, as fast as you can go!"

"Okay, Cheff. But why are the soldiers chasing us?"

"They think we're the sand pirates! We can't let them catch us!"

"Okay, Cheff! Wheee! This is fun!"

Of course, it couldn't last. We stayed ahead of the second vehicle for a good half hour, but they drew closer and closer. When they were almost even with us, Tocette drove over a rather large boulder. Our vehicle surged one last time, then came to rest with its broken axle perched on the boulder. The other vehicle stopped.

"Run!" Cheff shouted. "Run to the top of that rock formation!" He pointed to a large, rocky mass dead ahead.

We grabbed our gear and sprinted across the sand barely ahead of the soldiers. When we reached the rocks, we scrambled straight to the top. That was it. We were done for, cornered, with no way out, nowhere to go.

Our pursuers wore the green-and-gold uniforms of the Silver Palace Facilitators—they were Attan's flunkies.

"Hide in the rocks if you can!" Cheff said. "Hurry."

One soldier stopped at the edge of the rock formation and whistled. "Over here! Tracks!"

The entire batch of soldiers, twenty-two in all, converged on the whistler. They examined the tracks, then looked up at our rock formation.

"Up there!" said the whistler. "They're hiding in those rocks."

So much for concealing ourselves. I looked at the northeast horizon. Twenty-two soldiers comprised two platoons—they must have picked up the platoon whose vehicle we commandeered. Maybe that's why they looked so angry.

It was then that I noticed Lhuk, curled into a ball, chin tucked into his chest, his eyes closed. He seemed to be concentrating hard.

"What are you doing?" I hissed.

He didn't answer, only scrunched his eyes tighter.

Out of the corner of my eye, I caught a movement near the rock I was hiding behind. I watched and was rewarded by the sight of a colossal jumping spider making its way toward Lhuk.

A second later, I saw another jumping spider scramble over a formation near Cheff.

"Are you doing that, Lhuk?" I asked, but Lhuk didn't answer.

The soldiers came closer and closer. They were eager to climb up and capture us.

"Okay, men," their platoon leader said. "Let's bring them down. And remember, Attan wants them all dead. All eight of them, got it?"

"Got it, Sarge," one of the soldiers said. "Those kids got nowhere to go. It'll be a cinch!" He unslung his rifle and worked the bolt.

"But don't start shooting until you have the artifact in your hands! Understand? Now, go!"

As soon as a soldier started to climb the rock, an enormous jumping spider lived up to its name and jumped smack on his face.

"Aiiieee! They got me!" He writhed and twisted and beat at his own face. The spider, however, had long since slipped away and was approaching the next soldier to climb the rock.

"Arrgh!" The second soldier found himself trying to pull the jumping spider off his long Fessal nose.

Suddenly, dozens of spiders leaped from the rocks onto the faces of the oncoming soldiers.

I glanced over at Lhuk. He was laughing quietly to himself. Which was all well and good, but the spiders couldn't be more than a temporary distraction. After they were gone, we would be sitting ducks.

One at a time, the Fessals stomped the spiders into the sand. When, at last, our little corner of the Great Western Desert was spider-free, the soldiers resumed climbing the rocks, this time in earnest.

I looked over at Lhuk and raised my eyebrows.

He shook his head and shrugged. He was out of tricks. I wondered if being shot would hurt much.

*"Soldiers in the tower! Get moving!"*

# Operation Shifting Sands

# — 25 —

# BATTLE

---

THE SOLDIERS WERE upon us. Sable assumed her fighting stance. Lery unhooked his borrowed pipe wrench from his tool belt and stood ready.

Mid had taken something out of his tech pouch. I couldn't make it out, but I guessed it was his flashdark. It was also his regular flashlight, but when it was in flashdark mode, it sort of sucked the light right out of the air, wherever it was pointed. It had come in handy in the past.

Buttons tucked Moka away safely into her special pony-carrying backpack, then took hold of Starry's hind feet and smacked Starry against her palm.

"What are you doing that for?" Tocette asked.

"Starry's going to protect me," Buttons said.

"Oh," Tocette said. "She is? Wait—Starry's going to—how's she going to do that?"

"She's no ordinary pony, you know," Buttons said.

"Oh," Tocette said, then frowned. "I don't get it."

"Remember, on the bus, when I told you about Starry going swimming? And that's how her stuffing got shriveled?"

Tocette nodded.

"Well, when I went to put more stuffing into Starry, I didn't use regular stuffing."

"Oh," Tocette said. "What kind of stuffing did you use?"

"Let's just say that Starry is more substantial than she used to be."

"Oh," Tocette said, then shouted, "Look out!"

A soldier had made it to the rock where Buttons and Tocette were hiding. When he poked his ugly face over the top, Buttons swung Starry upside his head. *Whomp!*

The Fessal fell backward and rolled down to the sand, where he lay motionless.

"Good pony!" Buttons handed Starry to Tocette.

Tocette hefted Starry in the palm of her hand. Her eyes widened. "Oh," Tocette said. "*Now* I get it. What's in there, rocks?"

"Rocks, ball bearings, pieces of scrap metal." Buttons grinned wickedly. "Among other things."

The soldiers climbed the rock with great determination, and we were all suddenly rather occupied.

Lery swung his pipe wrench time after time, and each time a soldier rolled back to the sand below.

Mid carefully aimed his flashdark at each soldier in turn. When he pressed the button, the soldier he was aiming at grabbed at his eyes, and stumbled around, blind, until the effect passed.

Buttons swung Starry again, and another soldier fell. Tocette grabbed him and flung him away.

"We make a great team!" Buttons said.

"Oh," Tocette said. "We do?"

"Sure! I smack 'em, you attack 'em!"

"Oh." Tocette beamed. "I like that."

Sable lashed out with a long, lithe leg, and *wham!* another Fessal rolled down to the sand.

Cheff had a handful of smooth, round rocks in his left hand, and his trusty hunting sling in his right. He whirled it around his head. *Whizzzzz, thump!* A soldier starting up the rocks changed his mind, and instead staggered in circles, wiping the blood from his eyes.

Lhuk had a peculiar look on his face and the beginnings of a smile. He gazed at a soaring bird wheeling majestically overhead as it rose in a thermal updraft. The bird screeched and dove at a soldier, gripping his face with its mighty talons and beating him about the head and shoulders with its wings. Lhuk grinned and scanned the sky for another bird.

As for me, I was too small to do much hand-to-hand combat, but I chucked every loose rock I could put my hand on. I like to think I did my fair share.

For a while, we seemed to be winning, but ultimately, it could only end one way. The eight of us kids were no match for two platoons of Imperial soldiers.

The soldiers regrouped near their truck. The sergeant was giving them instructions of some sort, but we couldn't hear them from our perch on the rocks.

Without warning or apparent command given, all the soldiers made a rush for the rocks. This was it! But as they began to climb, a truckload of monastery facilitators in their distinctive red and gold uniforms roared up, spraying sand everywhere, and screeched to a halt right in front of the other military vehicle.

The entire truckload of monastery facilitators, armed with rifles, swords, and daggers, sprang from their vehicle and formed a skirmish line. They arranged themselves in two rows, the row in front kneeling, all rifles trained on Attan's sergeant.

"Vessslu," Sable said.

"It's Master Vessslu's Facilitators," Cheff said.

"They seem well armed," Mid observed.

"Disciplined," Sable said.

"That, too," Cheff agreed.

The leader of Master Vessslu's facilitator troops strode up to Attan's sergeant. "Have your men stand down, if you please, Sergeant. You are ordered to cease all hostile activity and return to Xanparthur Monastery where you will report directly to Masters Attan and Vessslu."

Attan's sergeant drew himself up to his full height, arms crossed over his barrel chest. "By whose authority?" he demanded.

"By my authority," the lieutenant replied mildly, "or haven't you noticed that I outrank you?" He tapped the lieutenant's insignia on his shoulder. "And by the authority of those sixteen rifles pointed at your head. Do you wish to challenge their authority at this time?"

The sergeant sneered. "You wouldn't dare!"

"Wouldn't I? Of course, I would never order my men to fire on fellow soldiers. But they are feeling a little twitchy at the moment. It's probably the heat. But keep this in mind: the Great Western Desert is vast and exceedingly dangerous. Any number of accidents could befall a troop of imperial soldiers out here, and who would be surprised?"

The lieutenant paused to let this sink in, then continued, "Well, sergeant? What shall it be? Will you relinquish these children to my care and be on your way? Or shall I step aside to afford my riflemen a clear field of fire?"

I almost felt sorry for the sergeant. Almost. He looked at his men, then at Vessslu's riflemen, then back at the lieutenant. The sergeant's face had turned a deep purple, and the veins on his forehead were swollen and throbbing.

"Very well, Lieutenant." His voice was hoarse. "You have the advantage this time, so we'll play it your way. But I promise you, you haven't heard the end of this! There will be a reckoning, or my name isn't—"

"No one cares about your name, Sergeant. Now gather your men and run along. Chop chop!"

If looks could kill, the lieutenant would have dropped down dead on the spot. The sergeant ordered his men into their truck and drove away.

"Good riddance," the lieutenant said to no one in particular. "Unpleasant fellow, wasn't he?" He wrinkled his nose. "And could have used a bath, too. At ease, men. Well done!"

He stepped up to the bottom of our rocks. "All right, children. You're safe now. Come on down, and we'll take you to the monastery. Master Vessslu is most anxious to have a word with you."

We climbed down the rocks and assembled at the bottom. The lieutenant, who was busy inspecting his fingernails, said, "Oh, by the way, children, I neglected to mention you're all under arrest. Take these handcuffs and put them on each other. Chop chop, now."

We couldn't believe our ears. Handcuffs? What kind of rescue *was* this, exactly?

The Great Desert Safari bus rounded the rock and came to a stop next to the Facilitators' vehicle. Kregg and Jewell stepped off and approached the lieutenant. "The handcuffs won't be necessary, Lieutenant," Kregg said. "These children were, and still are, in our custody. We'll take them from here."

"Oh?" The lieutenant's eyebrows arched. He thought it over. "You do have a great deal more room on your… vehicle… than we do in our personnel transport. I suppose, if you can give me your personal guarantee of safe delivery, I could go along with such an arrangement." He looked us children over, his eyes twinkling. "What about it, children? Do I have your word you will report directly to Xanparthur, no detours, no delays?"

"Yes, sir," Cheff said. "We were going there anyway until that other bunch crowded us."

"Good," the lieutenant said. "I shall take you at your word."

"Thank you, sir," Cheff said. "We'll do our part."

The lieutenant's laughing eyes betrayed his stern face. "I have every confidence in you." He turned to his men. "All right, you men. Load up! A brilliant performance, well done! Let's go get some supper, shall we? I've only recently learned that a little establishment in Kell's Junction is now serving last year's vintage of tonton wine."

His men didn't exactly wriggle with pleasure at his praise, but it was clear they were pleased. They loaded themselves into their truck, and with a roar of engines and a spray of golden desert sand, they were gone, headed straight for a certain establishment in Kell's Junction, no doubt.

Jewell came over and inspected each one of us, including Tocette. "Are you all right? Are you okay? Is anyone hurt? Did those soldiers do anything to you?"

Eventually, we were able to make it clear to Jewell that we were all unscathed, and, for that matter, only mildly shaken.

"All right, all right now," she said, over and over. "Let's get on board. I have some juice ready and some snacks. Get yourselves settled."

She seemed to be of the opinion that ice-cold tonton juice would cure most anything. She may have been right.

When we'd all found our seats and stowed our gear, Kregg said, "You did well, children. I take it you found what you're looking for?"

"Yes, sir," Cheff said. He held up the blanket-wrapped bundle that held the 'crystal artifact.' Your friend, Clerment, helped us find it."

"But it's only a—" Buttons started.

Kregg held up a hand. "Don't tell me, Miss Buttons. The less I know, the happier I am."

Jewell said, "Kregg and I have lasted so long out here by being overly careful about how much we don't know about Seph business. I strongly recommend you do the same."

"Yes, Miss Jewell," Cheff said. "Only, in this case, it's rather too late for that."

"It's all right," Jewell said. "I'm sure Master Vessslu knows what he's doing."

"I hope so," Tocette said, "because I sure don't. I'm not really sure what's going on at all."

Cheff gently punched her shoulder. "Don't worry, Beautiful and Intrepid Tocette, the Great Driver, you did fine. We're all hugely proud of you."

Tocette looked happier than I'd ever seen her look before.

Kregg mounted the driver's seat. I was happy to see Mr. Kip settle into his lookout perch on the dash—we'd lost track of him when we left the tower. Kregg shoved the Great Desert Safari bus into gear, pointed her nose directly northeast, and off we went, with a spectacular desert sunset behind us.

We arrived at Xanparthur as the sun touched the horizon.

Kregg and Jewell hugged each one of us as we disembarked. "Goodbye, children. Let us know how things turn out, okay?"

We promised we would. Buttons gave Mr. Kip a final farewell pat, then we watched and waved as Kregg and Jewell and the Great Desert Safari bus pulled away.

Cheff sighed. "Well, that is that. Good people, Kregg and Jewell."

"They certainly are!" Buttons said. "And nice, too!"

Mid said, "I suppose it's time we report to Master Vessslu."

"I suppose," Cheff said. "I'm not looking forward to it, though."

"Me neither, Cheff," Tocette said sadly. "I'd rather be eating supper. Pallador's Bounty, you know."

"Why not?" Cheff said. "*We* have to report to Master Vessslu, but you don't. You should report to Brex and get some chow."

Tocette brightened. "Really, Cheff? You wouldn't mind? I'm starving!"

"Not at all," Cheff said. "If we need you, we'll know where to find you."

"Thanks, Cheff!" Tocette ran off toward the dining hall.

"I can only imagine what her report to Brex will be like," Mid said.

"I'm not worried," Cheff said. "First, I'm not sure she knows anything at all. Second, it's unlikely that Brex is going to believe her, no matter what she says."

We laughed.

"I hope she doesn't get in trouble," Buttons said. "But I suppose, with Brex, that's inevitable."

We came to a stop outside Master Vessslu's office. Cheff took a deep breath. "Everyone ready? Great! Let's go in and face our fate!"

He raised his hand to knock, but Master Vessslu called from inside, "Come in, children. I've been waiting for you."

We went inside and looked around cautiously.

"Don't be concerned, children," Master Vessslu said. "Attan is not presssent at thisss time."

"Good," Cheff said. "You know, don't you, that Attan sent soldiers to kill us?"

"Of courssse, young Cheff," Master Vessslu said. Then, in a low voice, he confided, "Attan is not to be trusssted."

"No worries on that score," Mid said. "We don't."

"That'sss why I sssent my lieutenant and hisss men," Master Vessslu said. "Did you sssee them?"

"Did we ever!" Buttons said. "Attan's men tried to kill us. Your men saved us."

"I am mosssst gratified to hear thisss newsss," Master Vessslu said. "Now, tell me, asss I am eager to know: did you find the artifact?"

But before Cheff could answer, there was a knock at the door. Tocette stuck her head in.

"Come in, come in," Master Vessslu called.

"I thought you were going to supper," Cheff said. "You said you were hungry."

"I was hungry," Tocette said. "I still am. But after everything that happened today, I uh… well… um…"

"You wanted to sssee it through to the end?" Master Vessslu suggested.

Tocette nodded.

"Admirable," Master Vessslu said.

Tocette looked at Cheff.

Cheff said, "Admirable means good, extra good."

"It doesss, indeed, Misss Tocette. Pleassse come in and clossse the door." After Tocette got settled, Master Vessslu said, "Now, let me sssee, where were we? Ah, yesss, I had jussst asssked if you found the artifact. Did you?"

"For a while, we seemed to be winning..."

## — 26 —

## VIEWPOINTS

"WE FOUND AN artifact," Cheff said.

"Show me," Master Vessslu said.

Cheff unwrapped the blanket and held the sphere for Master Vessslu to examine.

"Pleassse, hold it up to the light."

Cheff complied.

Master Vessslu examined the sphere thoroughly, turning his head this way and that. When he was completely satisfied, he said, "Thank you, Cheff."

Then he started to laugh his peculiar Seph laugh. He laughed for a long time. "Thank you, thank you, children," he said. "I haven't laughed ssso hard in a century!"

"Excuse me, Master Vessslu," Buttons said, "but the ponies don't get the joke."

"It'sss glasss," Master Vessslu said, "and not very good glasss, at that. See the bubblesss? And the cracksss?" He laughed again. "Who gave thisss to you?"

"Clerment, sir. The tower keeper."

"Ah, old Clerment. Did you happen to tell him what you wanted it for?"

"Yes, sir, we did," Cheff said. "It seemed the right thing to do, at the time."

"The tower was much too big for us to search on our own," Mid said. "Mr. Clerment seemed to know where everything was."

"Quite right," Master Vessslu said. "You did well. I am mossst pleasssed."

"What happens now?" Cheff asked.

"I couldn't explain when you were here lassst, children, becaussse Attan was alssso presssent."

"We guessed as much," Cheff said. "We talked it over, sir, and we believe that Attan is trying to undermine Xanparthur in the name of Emperor Pallador's 'Path of Enlightenment' program."

"You are correct, young Cheff, but it's worssse than that. Attan is under ordersss to either bend Xanparthur to the Emperor'sss will or dessstroy it utterly."

"Why?" Tocette blurted. "It's a *good* monastery! I like it here! Why would anyone want to ruin it?"

"Enlightenment, dear child, is a ssstrange and peculiar concept," Master Vessslu said. "It dependsss a great deal on the persssonal viewpoint of the one being enlightened."

"Oh," Tocette said, frowning. "What does that mean?"

"Look around you, at your friendsss. What do you sssee?"

"I see Cheff and Mid and Buttons and Sable and Books and Lhuk and Lery. Hi, Lery." She waved.

Lery waved back. "Hi… Tocette."

"Now come here, to me," Master Vessslu said.

"To you? You mean, over there? By your cushion?"

"Yesss."

"Um… okay." But she didn't move.

"What isss it, child?" Master Vessslu asked.

"I'm afraid," Tocette said. "I'm sorry."

"No apology isss necesssary, child. It isss right to fear the Seph. Neverthelesss, come to me. I ssshall not harm you."

"Okay." Through sheer force of will, Tocette moved her feet, one by one, until she stood next to Master Vessslu.

"Clossser."

Tocette shuffled forward a smidgen.

"Clossser."

Tocette managed another inch.

"Put your cheek on my cheek." Master Vessslu lowered his head until his huge, scaly cheek was at Tocette's eye level, then held perfectly still.

Tocette scrunched her eyes closed, then slowly brought her cheek up to touch Master Vessslu's. At the first touch, she jumped back a little. "You're cold!"

"Yesss," Master Vessslu said. "The Seph are cold-blooded. That isss why we love our cushionsss so much. Try again, child."

Tocette gathered her inner resources and laid her cheek firmly against the Master's.

"Now look at your friends again," Master Vessslu instructed.

Tocette opened her eyes and blinked at us from across the room.

"Sssee? Thisss isss what your friendsss look like from my viewpoint. Tell me how you sssee them now."

Tocette shivered. "They look different. Bigger, maybe. No, that's not it. Stronger? More like a…"

"Team?" Master Vessslu suggested.

"Yes, that's it," Tocette said. "I still see each one separately, but now I see them all together, too."

"Excellent, child. You have done well. You may return to your friendsss."

Tocette beamed. "Thanks!" she said, then reached up and patted Master Vessslu affectionately on the cheek before returning to us.

Master Vessslu seemed surprised, but not displeased. "I sssee the sssame thing you sssaw, Miss Tocette. A team. A ssstrong and powerful force in Andaran." His eyes unfocused and he stared at the ceiling a while. "We can ssspeak more of thisss later. For the presssent, my intention wasss to demonstrate how a change of viewpoint can determine what constitutesss 'enlightenment.'

"Emperor Pallador hasss a visssion, children. He sssees one future for Andaran. Hisss vision is bright, and he desiresss everyone in Andaran to share it."

"And he's not terribly concerned about the viewpoints of others, is that it?" Cheff asked. "Or about what's true and right, either, I suppose."

"That isss it," Master Vessslu said, "exactly. Pallador isss right to educate hisss people, to instill his vision in all his subjects."

"*His* vision?" Buttons asked. "I bet it's not a nice vision, is it?"

"No, little Buttonsss, it isss not. In Pallador'sss visssion, the Seph rule all of Andaran. The other Peoplesss exissst only to ssserve and feed the Seph. Legend hasss it that, long ago, long before King Maghorn, the entire world wasss that way, until the Torph arossse and freed the other ten Peoplesss. I do not know if the legend isss true. It wasss long before my time."

"And Xanparthur, the monks, and the library, all give the lie to Pallador's vision?" Lhuk asked. "Like the lie about Torph Camps?"

Tocette said, "Wait—what about Torph Camps?"

"There are no Torph Campsss," Master Vessslu said.

"Oh," Tocette said. "Then where are your parents, Lhuk?"

Lhuk didn't answer.

"Oh," Tocette said again. "Oh."

"If the truthsss sssafeguarded here in Xanparthur were to become widely known, Pallador'sss visssion would be no more. He might be asssasssinated. Certainly hisss empire could not exissst in a climate of truth."

"So why not tell everyone," Mid said. "Why all the secrecy? Can't you print pamphlets and have them distributed or something?"

"You have hit on the dilemma in which we exissst," Master Vessslu said. "Four, nearly five, generationsss have lived and died sssince The Fall. Many alive today sssimply accept Pallador'sss rule as The Way Thingsss Are, without giving much thought to it. Othersss are too tired, hungry, or poor to care—they ssspend all their time and energy merely sssurviving."

"Some even like it this way," Mid said. He didn't say it, but we knew he was referring to the guard who sold his little sister to a rich Fessal woman to be her slave.

"That isss true," Master Vessslu said. "There are alwaysss thossse few who, through lack of compunctionsss and conss-science, rissse to the top and prosssper at the expenssse of the many. They would hate to sssee Pallador'sss government crumble—another viewpoint."

"Some people don't object to Pallador because they're dead," Lhuk said. "It cuts into their complaining, you see."

"Exactly," Master Vessslu said. "Thossse in power musssst control the thoughtsss of othersss in order to maintain a visssion basssed on liesss."

"So why not tell the truth and have done with it?" Mid asked again.

"If we believed it would help, we would do ssso, of courssse," Master Vessslu said. "But if we told all we knew, we would sss-soon be dessstroyed. Worssse, sssuch a revelation could lead to rioting, and many might lossse their livesss. Alssso, without a Torph heir to the rightful throne, we would have no new government to offer."

"Anarchy," Sable said.

"Utter chaosss," Master Vessslu said. "More dessstruction and losss of life."

"So, what, then?" Buttons asked. "Do nothing?"

"We wait for the right time," Master Vessslu said. "And while we wait, we work to prepare Andaran for the changesss to come."

"How do we do that?" Lhuk asked.

"Here at Xanparthur, we do that by pressserving the true hissstory and knowledge of Andaran. Othersss"—he looked directly into Cheff's eyes—"sssearch for the heir. Still othersss do what little they can to foil Pallador'sss schemesss and ssslow his progresss toward world domination."

"I want to do that!" Buttons said. "The ponies want to help, too!"

"From what I heard, Ssstarry wasss mossst helpful today."

"She's a good pony," Buttons said. "So is Moka, her sister. They both believe that telling people the truth is important." She held them to her ear and listened. "But they understand about waiting for the best time."

"So," Cheff said, "how are we going to convince Attan to not destroy Xanparthur?"

"A fine quessstion, young Cheff. I'm sure you and your friendsss will come up with sssomething. Meanwhile, it is time for me to ressst." He lowered his head onto his topmost coil and closed his eyes.

"I?" Cheff asked. "And my friends? *We're* supposed to come up with a plan? I wouldn't know where to start!"

Master Vessslu opened one eye. "I recommend you ssstart by going to the dining hall and having sssome sssupper. I find that I think better after I've eaten, don't you? After that, maybe you ssshould take Massster Kahph hisss artifact." His eye closed, and his breathing became regular.

We tiptoed out.

$$— 27 —$$

# SQUEAKY

---

A FACILITATOR, NOT SNARD, escorted us to the dining hall. While we filled our trays and found an empty table, Tocette joined Brex and the other Bluebands across the room. It looked like Brex was making Tocette report about her last two days with us. Brex didn't look happy. But then, she never did.

"I hope Tocette doesn't talk too much," Mid said. "She saw some stuff she probably shouldn't have, this trip."

"Not much we can do about it," Cheff said. "But let's keep an eye on Brex."

We finished our excellent supper, stuffed to the gills with fine food.

"These… monks… sure know how… how to… to eat," Lery said. "Maybe I can… can get… some recipes from… the cooks."

I glanced over at Tocette, being careful not to appear interested. "Cheff," I said, "judging by her arm movements, Tocette is telling them about the glass ball. Er, I mean, the 'crystal sphere'. Oh, yes, she's pointing our way."

"Brace for incoming," Cheff said, as he gently nudged the glass ball, still in its blanket, under the table.

Brex rose to her feet, gathered her Blueband thugs, and marched our way.

By the time they got to our table, Cheff was leaning back in his chair, rubbing his stomach with one hand, and picking his teeth with the little finger of the other. "Why, hello, Miss Brex," he said affably. "What brings your lovely presence to our table?"

With his foot, Mid slid an empty chair in her direction. "Won't you join us? It would be an honor."

Brex almost sat down, but caught herself in time. "Never mind that, Karfendek! Cadet Moron has given me her report. I wish to examine the object you brought back with you."

"Why, sure!" Cheff said. He retrieved the artifact from the floor and plopped it, still wrapped in the blanket, in the center of the table. "It's an ancient artifact from before The Fall," Cheff said. "Are you sure you want to see it?"

"Get on with it!" Brex snapped. She stood at the edge of the table opposite Cheff. Her thugs crowded behind her, straining to look over her shoulder.

"Certainly." Cheff started unwrapping the blanket. "I guess a Blueband leader such as yourself wouldn't put any stock in the legends."

"Legends?" Brex asked. "What legends?"

"About the effects of this artifact on the Torph brain structure. Ready? Brace yourself." He said to her followers, "You'd better back up, just in case." He made motions indicating that his head was exploding. "It's probably only folk tales, but you can't be too careful. Anyway, it only applies to Torphs with the Ability."

"Shut it, Karfendek. You know I don't have the Ability." Brex looked uncertain, but she couldn't afford to back down in front of her troops. "Open it. Now!"

"Okay, if you insist. But before I take the blanket all the way off, maybe you should have a little peek, okay?"

Behind his back, he gestured for Mid to use his flashdark. Mid took it out of his tech bag, then hesitated. Concealed from Brex's sight by the folds of the blanket, Mid slid the flashdark into the bundle until it touched the glass.

"Okay, here goes." Cheff lifted a corner of the blanket and motioned for Brex to look.

At the same instant, Mid switched on the flashdark, so that when Brex looked in, all she saw was a swirling mass of black nothingness. She stared, transfixed, for a long time, then forced herself to back away, blinking and rubbing her eyes.

"That was… um… it, uh… Yes. Very nice. Excellent find."

"Would you like another look before I put it away?" Cheff said. "We're under orders to deliver it to one of the Sephs as soon as we finish eating. Which, as you can see, we just did."

"No, er, no need to look again. I'm… it's… fine."

Cheff shrugged. "If you say so, Miss Brex."

She glanced uneasily at the artifact, which Mid was re-wrapping in its blanket.

Squeaky, Lhuk's pet mouse, who had been nosing around for crumbs under the blanket, chose that particular moment to stick his head up above the artifact's horizon.

Tocette let slip an involuntary yelp, then covered her mouth.

"Filthy rodent!" Brex swatted Squeaky off the artifact with the back of her hand. The poor little creature bounced off the wall behind Mid and Lhuk and fell to the floor. His little body quivered once, then was still.

Lhuk tried to rush toward his little friend, but Cheff and Mid held him back. Lhuk was trembling from head to toe. He struggled briefly, then was still.

Brex took no notice of Lhuk, only dusted her hands off. "I wonder how he got in here, the nasty vermin." She turned to Tocette. "Cadet Moron, find a dustpan and take that disgusting mess outside."

"Yes, Miss Brex," Tocette said. She glanced at Lhuk sadly, then padded off to the kitchen.

Brex whipped around and screamed at us, "The rest of you go deliver your artifact. Now! You do *not* want to keep the master waiting." She spun on her heel and strode out of the dining room, her contingent of bullies right behind her. Before she had gone five steps, she caught one foot on a chair and fell sprawling on her face, scattering the dining chairs every which way.

Her thugs rushed to her aid and helped her back to her feet with what little dignity she could muster. She strode from the room without looking back.

Then I noticed Lhuk. His face had the expression it took on when he was using his Torph Ability to make Squeaky do tricks. "Lhuk!" I whispered, "did you make Brex trip?"

Lhuk looked coolly at me, lips set in a tight line. "Of course not. You know Torph Ability doesn't work on sentient species. I wish it did. Best I could do was move that chair a little with my foot."

"I'd laugh," I said, "except that if you got caught we'd all be in serious trouble. Anyway, it's the least you could do for poor little Squeaky. But be careful, okay? The last thing you need is to become Brex's special interest."

Tocette came back from the kitchen bearing a dustpan and dust brush. She stopped and looked around the room then, satisfied that Brex was gone, shyly approached Lhuk. "I'm sorry she did that, Lhuk. I know Squeaky was your friend. I wish… I wish…" A huge tear spilled over and ran down her cheek.

Sable took the dustpan and dust brush away from Tocette, who covered her face with her hands. Sable examined the motionless mouse, then shook her head sadly. She found a large handkerchief in her mission bag and tenderly wrapped poor Squeaky in it, then handed him to Lhuk. "Burial tomorrow," Sable said, "with honors."

Lhuk accepted the somber bundle, which he tucked carefully into Squeaky's accustomed pocket. His whisper was barely audible. "Thank you, Sable." He turned and stepped a few paces away.

Cheff touched Lhuk on the shoulder, then said, more gently than I'd ever heard him speak, "When you're ready, we should take this artifact to Master Kahph. But only when you're ready."

"I'm ready right now, Cheff," Lhuk said, his face completely expressionless. "Why wouldn't I be? Let's go. He's waiting for us." He grabbed the artifact from the table and led the way out the door.

# Operation Shifting Sands

## — 28 —

## DINNER WITH KAHPH

---

WE EXCHANGED WORRIED glances, then fell in behind Lhuk. He navigated the corridors and slitherways as though he'd been born and raised in the monastery.

At one point, Buttons asked, "Lhuk, how do you know where you're going?"

"Are you kidding?" Lhuk asked. "Can't you feel him?"

"Him who?" Buttons asked.

"Kahph," Lhuk said. "He knows we're back, and he knows we have the artifact, and he's impatient." He made a sharp right turn and led us down another little maze of twisty corridors that all looked the same. All of a sudden, we were outside Master Kahph's door. Lhuk hesitated, then knocked tentatively.

"Come in, come in," Kahph said through the door, and we did.

*"Ah, at lassst!*

*"I regain my passst,*

*"Show me my sssphere,*

*"If you've brought it here."*

"I have it, Master Kahph," Lhuk said. "Here it is." He placed his bundle on a low table in front of Kahph's cushions, then threw off the blanket. "There you are, Master," Lhuk said agreeably, but his lips were grim, and the knuckles on his fists were glowing white dots in the gloomy room. He took a step backward.

Kahph stretched his neck in order to examine the artifact up close. He resumed his weaving and swaying.

*"There you are,*

*"My ssshining star,*

*"You come to me*

*"From oh, ssso far!"*

The ponies were exchanging glances again, but refrained from making 'crazy' gestures.

*"Thank you, thank you,*

*"Friendsss of mine,*

*"For bringing me*

*"This gift ssso fine."*

"You're, uh, welcome," Cheff said. "I hope it's everything you expected. We, uh, we'll be going now, Master Kahph. It was nice to meet you."

*"Not so fassst,*

*"My little friendsss,*

*"You mussst not leave*

*"Until dinner endsss."*

"Thank you, sir," Mid said, "but we already ate at the dining hall."

Kahph's rumble grew louder and more demanding.

*"I must inssssissst,*

*"That you perssssissst*

*"As guestsss at my table*

*"Asss long asss you're able."*

"Certainly, Master Kahph, as you wish," Cheff said. "We are honored by your invitation."

A Fessal Facilitator, eyes glazed over, came in leading a young goat on a rope.

The ponies looked at each other in horror. "No, Cheff," Buttons said. "Oh, please, no."

"Steady, Sis," Cheff said. "It looks like we're stuck here for the moment. Hang on as best you can."

"Okay, Cheff." She lowered her voice. "But I'm not sure the ponies can handle this."

"Sure they can," Cheff said. "The ponies are a lot tougher than they look."

The poor little goat took one look at the enormous Seph and bleated pitifully. Its entire body was trembling.

"Nooo," Buttons said, turning her face away. "The ponies don't want to see this." She took Cheff's hand and squinched her eyes shut.

The rest of us steeled ourselves for the inevitable. I didn't want to see it either, but I couldn't seem to tear my eyes away.

The Facilitator returned, this time bearing trays of sandwiches and fruit, which he set before us. Then he fled.

*"Eat, my children, eat.*

*"Until you are replete*

*"With the very bessst treat*

*"My cooksss can complete."*

"Yes, sir," Cheff said, then swallowed hard. "Thank you."

Master Kahph did not reply. Instead, he swayed, wove, and bobbed his head, all the while staring into the little goat's eyes.

The little goat relaxed completely and stared back into the Master's huge eyes. Back and forth, back and forth, and then the poor creature reluctantly took a few stumbling steps toward Kahph.

Kahph unhinged his jaw and lowered his head until the jaw touched the floor. The goat took a few more steps, stopped briefly, then walked right into Kahph's open mouth. *Snap!* Kahph's mighty jaws closed around the goat. We heard the muffled sounds of frantic bleating coming from inside the giant Seph.

Kahph's head lunged forward once, twice, and a third time, and the goat became a bulge in Kahph's neck. After one last despairing cry, the bleating stopped.

Buttons hid her face in Cheff's chest. Lery's face was bone white. His eyes were closed. He was sweating and trembling all over. Lhuk wore the same empty expression he had in the dining hall. I suppose the rest of us—Tocette, Mid, Sable, and I—were in shock. We merely stood and watched as the lump in Kahph's throat gradually made its way toward his belly.

After a while, Kahph emitted an enormous belch. The metallic stench of blood and goat and death was overwhelming. "Why, children," he said in a completely normal voice, "you haven't touched your sssnacksss."

"Um, well, we, uh, ate upstairs," Mid said, turning green. "I'm sorry, sir—I tried to explain earlier."

"Ssso you did, ssso you did," Kahph said.

"But we thank you for the meal, sir," Cheff said. He looked even greener than Mid. He gulped, then said, "It's time we headed back upstairs." He turned to us. "Ready, gang?"

*"Not so fassst,*

*"Let's make this lassst.*

*"You mussst not leave,*

*"Lessst I should grieve.*

*"For, you all should sssee,*

*"You mussst ssset me free."*

"Set you free," Cheff echoed, then rallied. "Wait—what?

*"Now I have my cryssstal sssphere,*

*"It'sss time for me to disssappear.*

*"I have the ancient artifact—*

*"Now I must leave and not come back."*

"We can't let you go! To start with, I don't think you'd fit through this door."

Kahph resumed his hypnotic weaving.

*"Not through the door,*

*"That'sss not what it's for.*

*"Inssstead use the wall,*

*"It's big enough for all."*

"The wall?" Cheff asked. "What wall?"

Kahph stopped weaving and lowered his head to Cheff's eye level. "The wall behind me, fool! It's a great big door. How did you think I got in here? There'sss a lever in the corridor, where I can't get to it. Go pull that lever. NOW!"

"I'm sorry, Master Kahph," Cheff began, "but I don't think—" He stopped in mid-sentence and stared off into space.

Kahph resumed weaving, looking at Cheff in much the same way he'd looked at the little goat a few minutes ago.

"Ability," Sable said. "Resist!"

The air in the room grew heavier and heavier. Then, for one brief heartbeat, the heaviness lifted.

"There!" Lhuk shouted. "Take that!"

"Why, imagine!" Kahph said. "Little Torph boy isss a *man*! Who would have thought?" In a flash, Kahph's tail lashed out and dashed Lhuk against the wall. Lhuk looked surprised, then he closed his eyes and slid to the floor.

"Would anyone elssse care to try me?" Kahph asked. "I didn't think ssso."

The heaviness returned, and grew heavier and heavier, until at last it became a warm, dark, comfortable sea of molasses, in which we were all drowning. Lery and Tocette succumbed first, but soon we all suffered the effects of Seph Ability.

"Now, then, boy," Kahph said to Cheff, "weren't you about to do sssomething for me?"

"Yes, Master Kahph," Cheff said in a monotone. He stumbled into the corridor and pulled the lever. The wall behind Kahph split in the middle. Both halves slid open to reveal an unfinished corridor in the native rock of the Belowground.

Cheff returned. Without expression, he asked, "Would you like me to carry your artifact for you, Master?"

"No need, boy, no need." Kahph unhinged his jaw again and swallowed the artifact in a single gulp. He laughed at our expressions. "Don't worry—I'll sssee it again sssoon enough."

"Yuck!" Buttons whispered.

Then, much more swiftly than you might imagine a Seph of his bulk ever could, he slithered out the wall-door and disappeared down the rocky corridor, presumably into the Belowground. After a long time, the heavy feeling lifted sufficiently for us to attend to Lhuk. He was dazed, but apparently unhurt. And he was furious.

"I'm sorry, everyone," Lhuk said, rubbing the rapidly growing knot on his skull. "I underestimated him."

He lurched to his feet, then staggered, but Lery caught him. "It's… okay… Lhuk… He was… rather powerful. I know."

"He sure was," Tocette said. "Whew!" She wiped her forehead with her sleeve. "Made me feel like… like… like that time I ate too much Bounty. Remember?"

We remembered.

"Easy does it, Beautiful and Intrepid Tocette," Cheff said. "Give yourself time to recover."

Tocette pouted. "You forgot 'Great Driver,'" she said, and sniffled.

"And Great Driver Tocette," Cheff said dutifully. "Now rest a little, then we need to get upstairs and let Master Vessslu know that Kahph is gone. Preferably before something worse happens."

But it was already too late. There was a rustling in the corridor, then Attan's ugly face poked through the door. "Where is Kahph?" he demanded, looking at the open wall-door and the empty Seph cushion. "More to the point, where is my artifact?"

Mid snorted. "*Your* artifact? That's a good one."

"I beg your pardon?" Attan asked incredulously.

I was pounding Mid on the shoulder, begging him to keep quiet, but he shook me off.

"Why, sure," Mid said. "After all, who went out into the desert to retrieve it? Huh? Who did? WE did, that's who."

"Mid, *stop*!" I said.

"Why?" Mid asked. "It's true, isn't it?"

"Forgive him, Master Attan," Cheff said. "Kahph used his Ability on us all. We haven't recovered all the way."

"I see," Attan said. "That explains much. Stand down, Troh boy. It'll wear off in a little while. But do this for me, will you, while you're waiting?"

"What's that, sir?" Mid asked.

"KEEP QUIET!" Attan roared.

"Well, sure, okay," Mid said in a hurt voice. "You don't have to shout." He staggered off to where Cheff and Sable stood.

When the room grew quiet again, Attan said, "Excellent. Now we can discuss your treason, and, of course, your sentence. Death, naturally."

# — 29 —

## TREASON

---

"NATURALLY," MID SAID. "Wait—what?"

I gulped. "Treason, sir?" I said, with some difficulty, as my mouth had gone dry.

"Of course," Attan said. "You delivered a valuable artifact to an enemy of the Imperium, then helped him escape with that same artifact. Do you deny this?"

"Well, no," Cheff said, "we don't deny it, exactly. But there's more to the—"

"Excellent," Attan said. "You plead guilty. That will save us much time and trouble."

"Guilty? Not me! I'm too cute to be guilty!" Buttons said. "The ponies object!"

"Hey!" Mid said. "We didn't confess to anything!"

Attan slowly turned his gaze on Mid. "I thought I told you to keep quiet."

"Why should I, if you're only going to kill us anyway?" Mid asked.

It seemed a fair question.

"Why, indeed?" Attan said. "For one thing, we haven't yet discussed the means of your deaths. It could be quick, possibly even painless, or relatively so. On the other hand, you could end up like that little goat I sent to Kahph earlier this evening. I had one myself. He was delicious. I love it when they wriggle inside. But he was so small, and I'm so sharpishly hungry." He opened his jaws wide enough to show his fangs, then flicked his forked tongue almost into Mid's face. "Mmm… Troh! It's been a long time since I tasted a chubby little Troh boy!"

"Hey!" Mid said.

"Master Vessslu is expecting us," Cheff said. "You'll never get away with it."

"Get away with it?" Attan asked. "Me? You mean Kahph, don't you? I assure you, I will be most sincerely sad when I report that Kahph devoured the lot of you before escaping." He chuckled. "Oh, yes, I can see it now. How sad we'll all be to learn that the old villain, Kahph, has once again taken sentient lives. I'm sure that the memorial service will be quite… touching."

Cheff was stumped—we all were. Then once again I felt the sensation of being drowned in honey. Attan was using his Ability. I tried to move but my feet felt as though they were stuck to the floor.

"Go ahead, eat me, I don't care," Mid said. "You don't scare me, you big bully! I hope I get stuck in your throat and you choke!"

"I don't frighten you?" Attan asked. "What a pity. You must either be exceptionally brave, or consummately stupid. Or maybe you simply don't care about yourself. I wonder how much you care about your friends." He lowered his head until his face nearly touched the end of Buttons' nose. His ugly purple tongue flicked again. "How nice! A little girl, a little Lora girl. I hope you don't taste too much like fish. Loras always taste fishy."

Cheff was struggling to break free of Attan's Ability, but to no avail. "You filthy cannibal!"

"So, you care about this little one, do you? That's good to know. Is she your nest mate? Your sister, perhaps? All the better! I shall begin with her. "Step inside, little girl.""

He unhinged his jaw and lowered it until it touched the cold stone floor of the corridor. At first, nothing happened. Then Buttons, in spite of her struggling, took a step forward, then another, then she put her head inside Attan's mouth.

"Don't do it, Buttons!" Cheff yelled. "Don't let him make you do anything."

"I can't help it, Cheff. My feet won't listen to me anymore." She lifted her right leg and put a knee inside.

Attan was clearly enjoying her discomfort. He drooled until it spilled over his scaly lips onto the floor.

Buttons lifted her other knee and put it inside, too. "Help me, Cheff!"

"I can't move!"

Attan ran his slimy tongue over her face. "Mmm… delicious."

"Lhuk! Do something!" Cheff yelled.

"Like what? I'm stuck, too."

"Use your Ability! Make him not want to eat Buttons!"

Lhuk's eyes were scrunched tight. "I'm trying, I'm trying. It's not working."

"Try harder!"

"I can't! He's too powerful!"

"Forget that, make him not want *anything*!"

Lhuk's eyes scrunched tighter, and his face grew red. "No good! I'm sorry, Cheff!"

"Concentrate!"

Attan's slavering jaws started to close. Buttons screamed. "Nooo! Don't. Hurt. My. *Ponies!!!*"

Attan laughed at that, nearly spilling Buttons out of his mouth. He must have relaxed his Ability for a fraction of a second, for Buttons hauled Starry back and bashed him on the end of his reptilian nose. It seemed to be a sensitive spot because Attan roared in pain, then the massive jaws slammed shut, trapping Buttons inside.

"Nooo!" Cheff screamed. "Buttons!" He tried to run to her, but he was still immobilized. "Lhuk!"

A muffled *thump* came from inside Attan's closed mouth, then another, and another. Attan roared again, but kept his mouth closed. His Facilitators answered his silent summons and came running, carrying knives and short swords.

There was one final *thump!* inside his mouth, then Attan reared up, screaming in pain. He collapsed into a heap on his own coils, motionless.

I was free. I looked around—the others were moving, too.

Cheff shook his head to clear it, then asked Lhuk, "What did you do?"

Lhuk shrugged. "What you said."

"What I—"

"You said to make him not want anything. Now he doesn't."

"Oh. Oh, I see. Then the danger's over?"

"I guess." Lhuk nodded toward the motionless Attan. "From *him*, anyway."

We breathed a collective sigh of relief.

From inside Attan's mouth came a series of rather rude remarks about Attan's family, ancestry, and personal habits, ending with a pointed opinion about boys in general, brothers in particular, especially those who stand around asking silly questions when their sister is being eaten, all of which was punctuated by intermittent crashing sounds.

"I think she's trying to tell you something, Old Man," Mid said, grinning. "But I can't quite make it out."

Cheff put his ear to Attan's still-closed jaws. "I see what you mean, Old Son. She's definitely on about something."

"Hard to hear through his closed mouth," Mid said.

Sable pushed past the two of them. "Lhuk!"

Lhuk wiped the smile off his face and said quietly, "Attan, open."

The great jaws gradually opened, and Buttons slid to the floor, dripping with Seph spit and smelling sour.

Cheff ran to her and took her in his arms. "Are you okay, Sis? No cuts or bruises or broken bones?"

Buttons and the ponies assured him that she was uninjured.

He held her tightly until she complained that the ponies couldn't breathe.

Next, Mid and Lhuk hugged her, one on each side, while Lery petted the ponies, all heedless of the Seph spit.

Finally, Tocette and Sable came and cleaned her up with Sables' mission handkerchief as best as they could under the circumstances.

When they were finished, I took her hand and held it briefly. "I'm sure glad you're okay."

"I am too, Books. Thanks!"

I gave each of the ponies a pat on the head. "You are the best ponies in the whole wide world," I said, "and I can lick anyone who says otherwise!" I made fists and punched the air, and that made Buttons giggle a little.

Buttons jabbed her finger toward Attan. "I'm afraid he's going to need a trip to the dentist," she said, giving Starry a pat. "Good pony."

"I've never thought of Seph dentists," I said.

"You didn't?" Buttons asked. "With all those teeth, it seems pretty obvious to me."

"I suppose so," I said.

"What did you do to him?" Tocette asked.

"Me? Nothing. But Starry found a cavity, a nasty, deep cavity, and decided that extraction was indicated."

"Oh," Tocette said. "What's extraction?"

"It means to pull out a tooth," I said.

"Oh." Tocette considered this. "Don't you need special pliers for that?"

"The… the right… tools… for the…right… job…" Lery said.

"Well, yes," Buttons said. "But Starry left her pliers back in Fellstone City. Since it was an emergency, she decided to proceed with the tools at hoof." She gave Starry another pat. "Clever pony!"

"Attan lost his concentration for an instant," Lhuk said, "and that's all I needed."

"Is he dead?" Tocette asked softly.

"No," Lhuk said. "I didn't kill him. I only… improved… his disposition a little."

"Oh," Tocette said. "What's a disposition?"

"I made him nicer," Lhuk explained.

"Oh. That's good. He wasn't very nice, before."

"He certainly wasn't," Cheff said. "Good work, Lhuk!"

"I suppose so," Lhuk said, but he was frowning.

"What's the matter, Lhuk?" Mid asked.

"I, um, didn't mean to break his brain," Lhuk said. "I just meant to make him stop eating Buttons. But he hurried me, and when I felt his distraction, I pushed as hard as I could."

"Pushed?" Cheff asked.

"Inside, with my Torph Ability. It's hard to explain. But I think maybe I pushed too hard."

Mid sauntered up to the massive Seph and kicked him in the head a couple of times. "Yeah, maybe. I think he's lost his appetite."

"I think he may have lost it forever," Lhuk said. "Like you told me, Cheff, I made him stop wanting anything."

Attan twitched and opened one eye. Mid backed away. "He's awake!"

"Hello, Attan," Lhuk said.

"Hello, children." Attan's voice came out funny because his mouth was stuck open. He delicately explored the inside of his mouth with his forked tongue. "My tooth hurts. Are you here to fix my tooth?"

"Sure." Lery unhooked his oversized pipe wrench from his tool belt and started toward Attan, but Cheff held him back.

"I think we'd better let his Facilitators handle it," Cheff said. "They're probably used to things like that."

"Okay… Friend Cheff." Lery looked disappointed, but he returned the wrench to its place on his belt.

"Speaking of Facilitators…" Cheff approached Attan's Fessals, who were shuffling around in the corridor, dazed. "You there!" Cheff said in his best command voice. "What are you about? Don't you have somewhere to be?"

"I… I don't know?" said the one who seemed to be in charge. I recognized him as Wert, the one who had spoken to us on the first morning at the monastery. "We were doing… something… and now we're… not." He jerked his large thumb toward the prone Seph. "What's with him?"

"Oh, he's resting," Mid said. "He has a toothache. Isn't there something you could do for a toothache?"

"Well, sure. If I wanted to. But why should I? Let him fix it for himself. Come on, men, let's get some chow. And I need a shower. Then I'm going to catch the first bus back to Fellstone City and see my family. The rest of you can do what you want." He led the Facilitators out of the room and away down the corridor, leaving their knives and short swords on the flagstones.

Buttons ambled over and casually picked up one of the short swords the Facilitators had left behind. She hefted it and took a couple of practice swings.

Sable approached Buttons and gave her a look.

Buttons replaced the sword on the floor and took Sable's hand.

Mid asked, "What now, oh Fearless Leader?"

"I was asking myself that same question," Cheff said. "I suppose we ought to report to Master Vessslu."

"Sounds right," Mid said.

"Wait, Cheff," Lhuk said. "I want to try to do something for Attan."

"You know how to fix a cavity?" Tocette asked.

"No. I meant I want to fix his mind."

"Oh," Tocette said, looking at Attan curiously. His mouth remained wide open. "Has he still got one?"

"That's what we need to find out," Cheff said. "What did you have in mind, Lhuk?"

"I hate leaving him empty-headed. He needs a new purpose in life." He put his hand on Attan's scaly snout. "Attan, can you hear me?"

Attan opened his eyes slightly. "Of course, Torph boy. I'm not deaf, you know. What can I do for you?"

"You can start by closing your mouth," Lhuk said.

Attan's jaws slowly came together. He raised his head a few inches above the stony corridor floor.

"We came to give you some important information," Lhuk said. "You need to know that Emperor Pallador is mistaken—there's no need to destroy or control Xanparthur Monastery. The monks here are good and peaceful and serve the Emperor faithfully."

"Oh," Attan said. "That's nice. Think of the trouble that will save me." He closed his eyes again.

Lhuk continued, "You must report regularly to the IID and your Emperor that all is well here at the monastery. You should make Master Vessslu the Grand Master again and do everything he tells you."

"Artifact," Sable said.

"Ah, yes," Attan said. "I'm supposed to get an artifact for Pallador."

"There is no artifact," Lhuk said. "There never was."

"No artifact? Oh, that's nice." He closed his eyes again.

"What about us?" Cheff whispered.

"Attan," Lhuk said. "I want you to look at us."

One eye opened and surveyed the room. "Hello, children," he said again. "I think I'm supposed to eat you, or at least kill you, right? But I'm so tired now. Can it wait until some other time?"

"Look at us carefully," Lhuk said, "and remember this: you're not looking for us anymore, nor any other children. Ever."

"I'm not? Well, that's fine."

Sable murmured, "Dark food."

"Right," Lhuk said. "And Attan, no more eating people, of any species. Eating people is wrong. Got it?"

"Got it," Attan said. "I should get some sleep now."

"All right," Lhuk said. "Get some sleep. When you wake up, you'll feel better than you've felt for a long time. You'll know, deep down inside, that supporting Grand Master Vessslu is the best way to serve Pallador."

Attan didn't answer.

"Will that work?" Cheff asked.

"Yes, it will work," Lhuk said.

"Then why are you so sad?" Buttons asked. "You saved me! You saved us all! You should be happy!"

"I am happy that you're all okay and that you didn't get eaten. But I'm afraid I did a bad thing, something that I can't fix."

"What's that?" Cheff asked.

"I… emptied him. He's not Attan anymore—Attan's gone. And I don't think he'll be coming back, not anytime soon. Maybe never."

"And good riddance," Mid added.

"Him or us," Sable said.

"I know," Lhuk said. "It had to be done, but it feels bad. It's not the way Torph Ability should be used. And I'm afraid Master Vessslu is going to be disappointed with me."

Cheff put his arm around Lhuk's shoulders. "Maybe so, Lhuk, maybe so. But *we're* not disappointed. You saved us all, and we're all proud of you."

Lhuk nodded, but didn't seem to be cheered up.

"All right, everyone," Cheff said. "Let's go find Master Vessslu."

"*Grand* Master," Buttons said, grinning.

"Right," Cheff said. "I wonder if he stays up this late."

"I do, indeed," Master Vessslu's deep voice rumbled, as he came down the corridor with his Facilitator, Snard. He looked around the corridor, then shook his head sadly. "Oh, children, what have you done?"

"Buttons took a step forward, then another…"

# OPERATION SHIFTING SANDS

## — 30 —

# THE UNBINDING

---

NO ONE KNEW quite what to say. Lhuk hung his head. We moved aside as Master Vessslu peered into Kahph's chamber at the open wall-door, Kahph's empty cushion, and the remnants of our 'supper.' Then he inspected the inert Attan sprawled on the bare rock floor of the corridor.

Finally, Cheff stepped forward. "We delivered the artifact to Kahph, as you directed."

"And where is the artifact now?"

"Kahph took it when he escaped," Mid said.

"He ate it!" Tocette said. "Swallowed it whole!"

"I sssee," Master Vessslu said. "And how did Kahph manage to essscape?"

"Ability," Sable said.

"Kahph used his Ability?" Master Vessslu asked. "Inside the monastery? I can't say I'm truly surprisssed, though he did give me hisss word that he wouldn't ussse it here. I ssshould have known better."

"We didn't even know there was a wall-door," Mid said. "Until he made us open it."

Master Vessslu nodded toward Attan. "And what is this all about?"

Facilitator Snard nudged the somnolent Attan with the toe of his shiny boot. Attan opened one eye and peered at Snard. When he noticed Master Vessslu behind Snard, he opened both eyes. "Oh, hello!" he said cheerfully. "It's so nice to see you, Grand Master Vessslu. Is all well?"

Master Vessslu snorted. "Go back to sleep."

"All right," Attan said, and did so immediately.

"What happened to him?" Master Vessslu inquired.

"He used his Ability, too," Cheff said. "He wasn't happy to discover that Kahph and the artifact were gone."

"He was eating me!" Buttons said. "And the ponies, too!"

"Attan made Buttons climb into his mouth," Tocette said. "She got all slimy!"

Master Vessslu nodded toward Attan again, and again Snard nudged Attan with his boot. Attan opened his eyes.

"Did you try to eat thisss little girl?" Master Vessslu asked.

"Why, yes, indeed I did."

"That's horrible!" Master Vessslu said. "What a disgusting thing to do! Civilized sentients don't eat one another. *Ever*!"

"I couldn't, though. I tried, but I couldn't eat her."

"And why isss that?"

"My cavity hurt. A lot. I have a cavity in my tooth." He ran his forked serpent tongue around the inside of his mouth. "Also," he jerked his chin toward Lhuk, "*he* wouldn't let me."

"Let you what?" Master Vessslu asked.

"He wouldn't let me eat the little girl."

"I sssee. And how, exactly, did he ssstop you?"

"I used my Ability, sir," Lhuk said. "I was immobilized like everyone else at first, but when Buttons, um, she, uh… anyway,

Attan got distracted by his cavity, and I took advantage of the opportunity."

"You usssed your Ability inssside Xanparthur?"

"Yes, sir."

"And why you would do that? You know the rulesss here."

"Yes, sir, I do. But, you see, he was eating Buttons, and it seemed like a good idea, at the time. Only—"

"What isss it, young Lhuk? Ssspeak up, child."

"I think I did something bad."

"You *did* do sssomething bad," Master Vessslu said. "We do not permit the ussse of Ability, Seph or Torph, within the mon-assstery walls. You knew that, didn't you?"

"Yes, sir, but that's not what I mean. I mean, I think I broke him. Inside, in his brain."

"What did you do, exactly? Tell me."

"When I was scared, deeply scared, for Buttons, I wanted him to stop wanting to eat us. That's what I pushed at him, with my Ability—to stop wanting anything."

"Well," Master Vessslu said, "it looksss like that'sss exactly what happened. Thisss isss not good, not good at all."

"Can you fix him?" Lhuk asked.

"No, child. When a Seph is blasssted that hard with Torph Abil-ity, he never recoversss. Why, Kahph was only partially blasssst-ed during the battle at The Fall, and you sssee what he became. What you did to Attan is much, much worssse. I'm afraid you have shattered Attan permanently."

Cheff frowned. "Why in the world would you even *want* to fix that… that… horrible being? He was scheming to destroy you and your monastery, and bring all your work to nothing. And—he was *eating* my *sister*! He snapped his jaws shut around her. It's a wonder she wasn't bitten in half. If you ask me, I'd say Lhuk has made a significant improvement to his personality."

"All right, children," Master Vessslu said, "I've learned every-thing I need here. Let'sss continue thisss conversssation in my office. Snard, would you be ssso kind asss to run ahead and arrange for some blanketsss, some felmosss tea, and some cookiesss."

"Certainly, Master Vessslu."

"The ressst of you follow me. Have you ever walked with a Seph before?"

"You can walk?" Tocette blurted, and examined Master Vessslu's undercarriage as though she expected him to sprout legs.

Master Vessslu laughed. "No, I'll be ssslithering. You'll be doing the walking."

"Oh."

"We never have," Cheff said. "Walked with a Seph, that is. The few we've seen have been on cushions."

"I mussst caution you, then," Master Vessslu said. "Ssstay in front of me. Do not, under any circumstancesss, get between me and the wallsss. It's easssy to get crushed, and I probably wouldn't even feel it. Undersssstood?"

We understood.

"That's funny," Tocette said. "We follow from in front." She giggled a little.

"That'sss right, Miss Tocette. And I ssshall lead from behind."

* * *

In Master Vessslu's office, eight chairs stood in a half-circle around Master Vessslu's cushion. A nice warm fire burned cheerfully in the hearth. A little side table held tea, cookies, and tonton juice.

"Help yoursssselvesss, children, while I get sssettled. If you require anything elssse, jussst asssk Facilitator Snard."

Even though we had eaten not long before, we were famished after our encounters with Kahph and Attan. But the warm fire and the sweet treats soon restored us somewhat.

It was wonderful to watch Master Vessslu coil himself on his enormous red and gold cushion. He started around the back of it, got his head up first, then went around and around, making a perfect stack of coils, with his head resting on the topmost.

"Now, children, I'm afraid I have sssome bad newsss for you: I can not permit Lhuk to remain here at Xanparthur. For hundredsss of yearsss, thossse who have usssed the Ability within these wallsss have been expelled and never permitted to return."

"But Lhuk was acting in self-defense," Cheff said. "He saved Buttons, and all the rest of us too. Why should he be punished?"

"That's a good question," Mid said.

"Yes," I said, "especially in light of the fact that only two days ago, in the library downstairs, you explained to Lhuk and me that Torphs ruled Andaran for centuries because they have the Ability, and that even now people are searching for the true Torph Heir."

"And you told Lhuk that, then expected him not to use his Ability, even in self-defense?" Cheff asked. "I don't get it. How is that in any way fair or just?"

"You misssundersssstand me, young Cheff. We at Xanparthur are not againsssst the proper ussse of Torph Ability. To the contrary, I explained to Lhuk that when Torphs rule, Andaran prospersss."

"Then... then what's the... the big deal?" Lery asked. "I'm glad... Lhuk did what he... did...I'm a Fessal... you know... and we feel it more."

"We do?" Tocette asked. "Oh. I guess that's why I couldn't move at all, and Buttons still could, a little."

"It's funny," Buttons said. "At first, I could only do what Attan made me do. But when I was inside his mouth, I couldn't feel his Ability anymore."

"No wonder those who are eaten are given plenty of jexan," Mid said.

"Goat," Sable said.

"Attan sent Kahph a goat to eat right in front of us," Mid explained. "And Kahph did."

"That poor little goat," Buttons said.

"I'll bet that goat didn't get any jexan first," Cheff added. "Attan said he liked the way his food wriggled inside."

"Attan sssaid that to you?" Master Vessslu asked. "I'm ssso sssorry, children. Seph eating habitsss can be distresssing to the other Peoples."

"You can say that again!" Buttons said. The ponies nodded emphatically.

"Normally," Master Vessslu said, "Sephs eat privately. Throughout hissstory, thossse Seph all throughout Andaran who wished to live in harmony with the other species have consssidered it cruel and uncivilized to eat live prey." He shook his massive head. "We've heard rumorsss of eating live prey and even cannibalism, the so-called 'dark food,' but thisss isss our firssst actual confirmation. It is extremely distressing that such has occurred under our own roof! I did not know that Attan permitted such—it certainly didn't happen while I was Grand Master. It seems that the degradation of sssociety under Seph rule is accelerating fassster than we here at Xanparthur imagined. Unchecked power alwaysss, *alwaysss*, corruptsss."

"They aren't rumors," Buttons said. "We've seen it."

"Ssseen what, child?"

"Sephs in The Fel eating live prey." She glanced at Tocette. "And… other places, too."

"Truly? You mussst tell me that ssstory sssometime. Sssometime sssoon."

"And not only goats, either."

"Buttons!" Cheff warned.

"I don't care, Cheff. Master Vessslu needs to know."

"What do I need to know?"

No one spoke at first, then Sable said quietly, "Dark food."

Master Vessslu was visibly shaken. "Are you sssure?"

"Quite sure," Cheff said. "One of the victims was my uncle!"

"My father," Sable said.

"They had a friend of ours in a cage, ready to eat," Buttons said.

"They did?" Tocette asked.

"Yeah, but we got her out," Cheff said.

"Oh. That's good."

Cheff said, "Master Vessslu, you still haven't explained why you're punishing Lhuk."

"Oh, dear children, dear young Lhuk, we are not punissshing you. No one isss angry with you about what you did to Attan. He wasss a bad perssson and needed to be ssstopped. The problem isss that you did it inssside Xanparthur. We ssserve a ssspecific role in Andaran, and we are all dedicated to keeping the monassstery free."

"Keeping the monastery free?" Cheff asked. "How's that going for you, do you think? Maybe we should have invited Attan outside before we stopped him from eating Buttons? We would have, but we were a little pressed for time. Anyway, it was Sephs, Kahph and Attan, who introduced dark food into the monastery, and you did nothing—*nothing at all*—to stop them. You should be giving Lhuk a medal, not kicking him out!"

"Easy, Cheff," Mid said. "Take a breath. Maybe several breaths."

"I agree with you in principle, young Cheff," Master Vessslu said. "But in practice, as Grand Massster, I must uphold the tenets that comprise the foundations of Xanparthur."

"How about Attan?" Mid asked. "Are you going to throw him out, too?"

"Attan hasss been damaged beyond repair. We will care for him here."

"Great, just great," Lhuk said bitterly. "I use my Ability to *save* lives and you throw me out. Attan used his Ability to eat my friends, and he gets to stay. Where's the justice?"

"I'm sorry, young Lhuk, but that isss how it mussst be. Xanparthur standsss for many thingsss, but above all we ssstand for each individual'sss right to ssself-determination. The Ability interferesss with self-determination. In Attan's cassse, you took away his ssself-determination for the ressst of his life. He hasss already paid the ultimate price. He will need conssstant care and sssupervision. We call what you did to him 'the unbinding.' You have unbound hisss mind from hisss life. He'll get hungry, but won't eat unlesss directed to do ssso. He'll get cold, but won't move to the fire. And ssso on. Thisss isss your doing, Lhuk, and you mussst live with the consequencesss for the ressst of your life."

"I don't like it," Cheff said. "Something feels wrong about what you said, but I can't put my finger on it."

"Tenets," Sable murmured. "Principles."

"I don't undersssstand," Master Vessslu said.

"That's it!" Cheff said. "What Sable means, and I agree, is that your tenets should uphold and support your principles, not undermine them. Why should Lhuk, a Torph, be the only one keeping your Seph monastery free of the evils you dread? And being penalized for it, to boot? Lhuk is an invited guest in your monastery, and, as such, should have been afforded your protection. Instead, you're treating him like a schoolboy being expelled for defending himself from a bully."

"There is much merit in what you sssay, Cheff," Master Vessslu said. "We, all the Seph here at Xanparthur, will consider it. Formally, in council. We acknowledge that we are indebted to Lhuk."

Cheff glowered, but said no more.

"Exiled or not, I'm not going to stop using my Ability," Lhuk said. "There's no point in having it and not using it. But I do want to use it only for good, never for bad."

"That isss a good ssstart, Lhuk," Master Vessslu said.

"I didn't mean to break Attan," Lhuk said. "I didn't even know it was possible. I only learned I had some Ability last year, and that was only to make Squeaky—" His voice broke.

"In the old daysss," Master Vessslu said, "during the Sssixth Kingdom, ussse of Torph Ability was consssidered a necesssary skill for the Torph kingsss and queensss. There were trainersss, older Torphsss who had massstered the Ability, who trained princesss, princesssesss, and other Torphsss to use their Ability sssafely. I wish we could keep you here, Lhuk, and train you ourselvesss. But that would not only be against the rulesss, it would be dangerousss for you and for usss. As much asss we don't alwaysss like it, the rulesss are there for a reassson. Sssnard!"

Snard appeared. "Yes, Master?"

"We have jussst received terrible newsss from Fellstone City regarding dark food, eating live prey, and society in general, via these children. Conditionsss are deteriorating much fassster than we expected. Asssemble all the monksss. We mussst move the library at once! If the Imperial sssoldiersss find our library, it will be dessstroyed. And they *will* come, and they *will* sssearch every nook and cranny. We mussst be sssure they find nothing. Oh, Sssnard, while you're down there, pleassse bring me the book I mentioned to you earlier. The one about Torphsss. Thank you."

Master Vessslu turned to us again. "How isss it that you children have learned sssuch things? Wait—don't tell me. I don't need to know. Lhuk, as I mentioned to you in the library, your Torph Ability is far stronger than average, especially for one so young. Few Torphs throughout history were capable of the Unbinding. In light of this, I have three assignmentsss for you: firssst: you must learn to use your Ability well and precisssely. Second, you must learn to conceal your Ability perfectly—your life dependsss on it. And third: you must ussse it only to defend yoursssself and othersss againsssst the misussse of Seph Ability. Can you do that?"

"I will do my best, Master Vessslu."

"Good. As for the ressst of you, well, jussst keep doing what you are doing. Andaran needs youngstersss like you, and I feel that in the near future, Andaran will need you even more. And one more thing, Cheff: you and your friendsss take good care of Lhuk. He isss going to need you and your protection in the daysss to come."

"Yes, sir," Cheff said. "We will."

"Very well," Master Vessslu said. "It'sss late, children. You ssshould try to catch a few hoursss sssleep. You have a long busss ride tomorrow."

"Okay," Cheff said. "And thank you, sir."

Snard came back, a fat book with a black leather cover in his hands. He held it up for Master Vessslu to see. "This one, right? Good. Here you go, Lhuk."

"Thank you," Lhuk said. He opened the cover and read the title. "*On the Ability—A Treatise* by Master Trainer Felmor. Sounds interesting."

"Felmor trained kingsss and queensss three hundred years ago," Master Vessslu said. "He, like you, had exceptional Ability. I met him once, a long time ago. He wasss a tiny little Torph, quite bald, as I recall. Lovely golden ssskin with beautiful Torph markingsss. Lived to a ripe old age." He sighed. "Run along, now, children. I'm tired. If you think you're tired now, wait until you're four hundred yearsss old. If I can, I'll come sssee you off in the morning. Snard, would you pleassse essscort these children to the dormitory. No, take them to one of the guessst roomsss instead. No point in arousssing the entire dormitory."

"Excuse me, Master Vessslu," Lhuk said, "but there'sss one more thing I need to tell you."

"And what isss that?"

"Well, the, um, unbinding isn't all I did to Attan."

"Not all you—Andaran'sss bonesss, youngsssster, don't you think unbinding him wasss enough? What, exactly, did you do?"

"Well... you might find that Attan is under the impression that you and all of Xanparthur Monastery are loyal subjects of the Emperor and are serving him faithfully. He's going to have a desire to write many good reports about you and send them to his bosses at the IID."

Cheff added, "Also, he's not concerned about the artifact anymore."

Mid said, "And he's decided that you should be the Grand Master again."

Master Vessslu stared at us, then threw back his head and started to laugh. Then he laughed some more. "Oh, my," he said. "Oh, my!"

The last thing we heard as Facilitator Snard led us down the corridor was Master Vessslu's laughter echoing throughout the monastery.

— **31** —

## With Honors

---

**B**EFORE DAWN, I awoke to a soft knocking on the guest-room door. Facilitator Snard entered. "Wake up, children. Come with me."

"Okay," Tocette said, rubbing the sleep out of her eyes. "Where are we going?"

"Quickly, now," Facilitator Snard said.

We followed him into the dark corridor and out into the Courtyard of the Seven Gardens. We crossed the lawn to the section that represented the Fellstone region. Jewell and Kregg were waiting for us there, next to a small, square hole in the garden bed.

Jewell held a little pasteboard box, which she opened to reveal a small square of light blue material. She held it out to Lhuk.

Lhuk stared at it, uncomprehending.

"With honors," Sable said.

Lhuk got it. He gently removed Squeaky's body from his coat pocket, still wrapped in Sable's handkerchief, and handed him to Jewell, who respectfully wrapped poor Squeaky in the blue cloth. She stroked the little bundle once.

"Goodbye, Squeaky," she said, her tears flowing freely.

One by one, as Jewell held the box, we each said goodbye to the little mouse. Lhuk was last. He put his hand on Squeaky one final time. Whatever goodbye he had to say, he said silently. Which was right.

At last, he took the box from Jewell. He hesitated, then took a deep breath, bent down, and placed the box carefully into the tiny grave.

Kregg said, "When you're ready."

"Ready," Lhuk whispered.

Kregg gently covered Squeaky with the rich, fresh earth of Xanparthur.

When Kregg finished, Jewell covered the bare mound with a bouquet of fresh flowers she had picked before we arrived.

Cheff whispered, "Sable?"

Sable glanced at Lhuk, who nodded. She stepped forward. "Today we lay to rest the first of us to fall in the line of duty. Squeaky was a fine mouse and a good friend. He lived well and died bravely. Though he was small, he had the heart of a lion. Farewell, comrade. Rest in peace." She stepped back.

I was astounded—that was a long speech for Sable.

"Thank you, Sable," Lhuk said, and then to Kregg and Jewell, "and thank you both, too." But then his composure began to slip, so Cheff put his arm around Lhuk's shoulders and walked him away from our little group.

The rest of us stood respectfully in silent contemplation until Facilitator Snard said, "I'm sorry children, but it's time to go. The buses will be here soon."

So, our hearts heavy, we gathered Cheff and Lhuk and made our way back to the guest room we'd slept in. On the way, Lhuk asked, "Facilitator Snard, how did you know?"

"Master Vessslu told me, and asked me to arrange things."

"Master Vessslu knows about Squeaky? But, how?"

Snard smiled a little. "Well, young Lhuk, Master Vessslu doesn't miss much of what goes on here at Xanparthur. How else would he have become the Grand Master all those years ago? We're all glad that he is the Grand Master once again."

Lhuk smiled a little, too. "I hope I have a chance to thank him before we leave."

Back in the guest room, Facilitator Snard said, "Pack what little you have. Be especially careful to pack certain items well out of sight of prying eyes."

We made sure that Lhuk's black book, the one he'd gotten from Master Vessslu the night before, and the red book Master Vessslu had given me in the Library, were both well concealed. I put *The Life and Times of Maghorn I* deep into my pack, but Lhuk's pack wasn't big enough for *On the Ability—A Treatise* by Master Trainer Felmor.

"Would you like me to put it in with the ponies?" Buttons asked. "They won't mind. In fact, they'd be happy to help."

Lhuk silently handed her the book.

"Oof, it's heavy!" Buttons said. "But not *too* heavy," she added quickly. She handed Moka to Lhuk. "Moka says it's too crowded in there. She wants to ride with you."

Lhuk looked into her eyes briefly, then accepted Moka without a word.

"Cheff?" Tocette said. "There's something I don't understand."

"What's that?"

"Sable said—"

Cheff motioned for her to lower her voice.

"Sable said," she said, much more quietly, "that Squeaky died in the line of duty. What does that mean? What duty?"

Cheff patted Tocette on the shoulder. "Well, Beautiful and Intrepid and Great Driver Tocette, it's like this: there are some things I simply can't tell you."

"In fact," Mid said, "You've seen quite a few things on this trip that you shouldn't have."

"Oh," Tocette said. "You mean like the artifact?"

"Yes, and other things, too," Cheff said. "Ancient books, Seph Ability, Attan trying to eat a living person."

Tocette looked at Lhuk. "Torph Ability."

"Yes," Cheff said. "And Torph Ability. You saw Lhuk's in action. Brex is going to expect a full report. What do you think will happen if you tell her about these things?"

Tocette thought about this, then her eyes widened. "She'll have Lhuk sent away to a Torph Camp!"

"But you learned something about Torph Camps, too, didn't you?" Mid asked.

"Oh, no!" Tocette wailed. "She's going to have Lhuk killed, maybe eaten!"

"Yes, good," Cheff said. "Smart girl."

Tocette smiled slightly at that, then darkened. "But I don't want Lhuk to be eaten. He… he's my friend!"

"I'm glad you see it that way," Lhuk said. "I don't especially care to be eaten, either." He laughed, but Tocette didn't see the humor in it.

"But, Cheff—isn't it my duty to tell Brex? That's why she sent me. If I don't tell her, won't I be a traitor?"

"Duty," Sable said. "Who decides?"

"Well…" Tocette was stumped. "I don't know. I never thought about it before."

"That's okay," Buttons said kindly. "Most people never think about it."

"That's true," Cheff said. "Most people go through their lives letting everyone else tell them what their duty is—parents, teachers, the government."

"Emperor Pallador," Mid said.

"Brex!" Tocette said. "She is always telling me what my duty is, and how to do it."

"The truth is, Tocette," Cheff said, "that no one can tell you what your duty is. That's a question that everyone must decide for themselves. Especially when they've seen the world the way you have in the last few days."

"Seen the world?"

"Sure," Cheff said. "How many people, including Brex, have seen what you saw on this trip? An Altaar tower keeper. Sephs who are dedicated to self-determination. An evil Seph in Pallador's service. Buttons nearly eaten. Torphs have been Andaran's traditional and rightful rulers. Forbidden books going home with us. An awareness that Pallador's 'Path of Enlightenment' isn't exactly what he says it is. That kind of knowledge makes you powerful."

"Powerful?" Tocette thought about that. "I've never been powerful before."

"Well, you are now," Cheff said. "Any one of those things, were they to become known, could have us all put in jail, or even executed."

"And most likely eaten," Buttons added.

"Oh, no!" Tocette cried. "I don't want to be that kind of powerful!" She turned to Lhuk and got down on one knee to be at his eye level. "Can't you make me forget, Lhuk? Like you did to Attan?"

Lhuk regarded her soberly. "No, Torph Ability doesn't work that way. But even if I could, I wouldn't. You see, I've learned something on this trip, too, from Master Vessslu. It's not right to fool around with other people's minds or control their thoughts. Everyone should be free to think his or her own thoughts."

"Oh, dear," Tocette said again. "What are you going to do about me, then?"

"Nothing," Cheff said.

"Nothing?"

"Nothing. We're going to trust you to figure out what your duty is and then to do it."

"Trust me?" She considered. "What if I'm not trustworthy? What if I say something accidentally? I do that, sometimes, you know."

Cheff shrugged. "Then you do, and we, and you, will suffer whatever consequences come of it."

"I see, I guess."

"Sometimes," Sable said, "duties conflict."

"Oh," Tocette said. "What does that mean?"

"It's like right now," Cheff said. "You have a duty to Brex, another duty to Emperor Pallador, and maybe a duty to us, your friends. And the different duties argue with each other. Tell Brex or keep your friends safe. See how it works?"

"Oh. Yes, I see."

"There are other kinds of duties, too," Cheff said, "that you can choose for yourself. Duty to the Truth. Duty to yourself. Duty to do good and not do bad. You can, and should, choose for yourself which duties you will assume."

"Oh. This is hard."

"Yes," Sable said.

"Will you help me?"

"No," Cheff said. "We've already helped you as much as we can. Now it's up to you."

We left Tocette to her thoughts while we finished getting ready. As we shouldered our respective packs, bags, and, for Sable, her mission bag, Tocette said, "Well, I thought of something."

"That's good," Cheff said. "What is it?"

"If I tell Brex something, I can never un-tell her."

Sable smiled. "True."

"Brex gets to pick her own duties, too, right?" Tocette asked.

"Yes," Cheff said, "she does."

"Her duties might, what did you call it? Argue, with mine, right?"

"Right," Mid said. "I think you have the idea. Well done!"

Tocette smiled at that, but she wasn't finished yet. "If I don't tell Brex anything, I mean about the stuff you said before, then her duty won't have anything to argue with mine about, right?"

"That's right," Cheff said.

"Good," Tocette said. "That settles it, then."

"What did you decide?" I asked.

"My duty to my friends comes before my duty to Brex," Tocette said, then whispered, "I don't *like* her, you know. She calls me Cadet Moron. I know I'm slow sometimes, but I'm *not* a moron, and it's not nice to call me that."

"No, it isn't!" Buttons said. "The ponies don't like her much, either. Anyway, it isn't true."

"Oh," Tocette said. "What isn't true?"

"You're *not* a moron," Buttons said. "You're fine. Brex is just plain mean."

"Thank you, Tocette," Cheff said. "That's good to know—about your duty to your friends, I mean. I see we did well to trust you."

"I will do my best to be as trustworthy as I can," Tocette said. "I still have a lot to think about, though. About Pallador and… other things. Like Xan… Xen… Par… you know, the monastery."

"Good," Cheff said. "Thinking is a good thing."

"TBA," Sable said. "Think Before Acting."

"Oh," Tocette said. "TBA—I like that."

"Always a good plan," Cheff said. "It looks like we're about to leave. Ready to head out, everyone?"

We were ready, and just in time, too. Facilitator Snard returned and led us to the parking area out front. "I'm sorry, children, but you missed breakfast. I had the cooks pack you some snacks. I know it's not the same, but it's better than the alternative, I should think."

We thanked him and got in the queue for our bus. We were at the tail end of the line of students waiting to get on. Jewell came over. "Come with me, children. There's something you need to see in the Great Desert Safari bus."

We followed her to the bus, where Kregg let us in. "We've had a bit of a surprise with Mr. Kip. I'm afraid he's not Mr. Kip anymore."

Lhuk's eyes went wide. "He's not… not…"

"Oh, no, he's fine," Kregg said. "But it seems that *he* turned out to be a *she*."

"Has been all along, I should think," Jewell said, mostly to herself.

"How can you tell?" Lhuk asked.

"Come see." Kregg led the way to the juice station where, in a small wooden crate on the floor, the desert pup was serenely suckling a litter of four tiny newborn pups, their little eyes tightly closed.

"I guess we'd better call her *Mrs.* Kip from now on," Lhuk said, which made everyone smile.

"Treeeeeats?" Mrs. Kip asked. "Caaaaandy?"

Jewell slipped some tonton fruit into Lhuk's hand. He knelt by the crate and handed the fruit to *Mrs.* Kip, which she accepted eagerly. "Taaaaank youuuuu, Lhuuuuuk!"

"Well, how about that?" Kregg said. "That pesky little creature finally learned some manners."

"Oh, hush," Jewell said, smiling.

"I guess we should go," Cheff said, peeking out the window of the Safari Bus. "Our bus is almost loaded."

"Right," Kregg said. "Don't want to miss the bus."

"One more thing, before you go," Jewell said. "Lhuk, I know you're always going to miss Squeaky, but if you'd like, you can have one of Mrs. Kip's pups, when they're old enough."

Lhuk brightened. "That would be nice," he said. "I'd like that. But how will I get him? I don't think I'll be coming back here anytime soon."

"It takes about six weeks until they're weaned and ready for a new home," Kregg said. "By then, I think we can arrange to get him to you in Fellstone City."

"You can?" Cheff asked. "How?"

"You don't need to know that," Kregg said. "Let's just say that I spoke to Harleen, and he knows your innkeeper, Meltern. Those guest-house keepers all seem to know each other. Anyway, no need to worry about that, okay?"

"Okay," Cheff said.

"Thank you," Lhuk said. "I'll be looking forward to it." He gave Jewell a quick hug and was out the door and across the parking area to our own bus.

The rest of us said our goodbyes to Kregg and Jewell and followed Lhuk.

*  *  *

The instant we boarded, Brex screamed, "Cadet Moron! Get over here at once!"

Tocette ignored Brex completely, to our astonishment, and sat by herself in the middle of the bus.

"Are you deaf, Cadet Moron? I said get over here, *now!*"

Tocette appeared not to have heard.

Brex's face turned a deep, raging purple. She stormed over to where Tocette was sitting. "WHAT IS THE MATTER WITH YOU? I'M TALKING TO YOU, CADET MORON! ANSWER ME!"

"My name is Tocette. Tocette Crindel." She stood up as close to Brex as she could without actually stepping on her toes.

Brex involuntarily backed up a step.

"You can call me Tocette, or Cadet Crindel, if you wish. Hmmm, Cadet Crindel—nice ring to it, don't you think? My duty to you, and to the emperor, does not include being called a moron. Call me by my name, or don't bother calling me at all." She sat down. "I'm not one, you know—a moron, I mean. I'm fine. And I don't like being called that. I never did. Now go away. I need to think." She closed her eyes and left Brex sputtering in the aisle.

Brex made her way back to her own seat. "Shut up!" she yelled at her thugs, even though no one had said a word. She flounced into her seat and crossed her arms across her chest, her eyes glowing like coals in a campfire.

"Well, now," Sable murmured.

"Yeah," Cheff and Mid said in unison.

The bus rumbled out of the parking lot and turned toward Fell-stone City. Mid immediately tore into his package of food.

"Easy does it, Old Son," Cheff said. "Remember what happened last time on the curvy road."

"But I'm hungry," Mid said through a mouthful of tonton pastry. "Missed breakfast again, you know."

Lhuk came over and took a seat next to Cheff. He cradled Moka on his lap and stroked her absently. He looked around to make sure no one was listening. "I've been thinking," he said quietly.

"Yes?" Cheff asked.

"About what you told Tocette about choosing which duties we will be bound by."

"I see."

"I never thought about it before. I was… going along, I guess, like Buttons said. But watching all of you in action made me think—about a lot of things."

"Oh?"

Lhuk lowered his voice. "Like my Ability. All my life, I was taught that having the Ability is a bad thing, something to be ashamed of. But I do have it, and I don't see any sense in pretending I don't."

"It did come in pretty handy yesterday," Mid said.

"It sure did," Cheff said. "In fact, I owe you—we all owe you—a formal thank you for saving our lives with your Ability. We don't care what Master Vessslu says—to us, you're a hero."

"And to the ponies," Buttons said. "You saved them, too, you know."

"I couldn't have done it without Starry's help." Lhuk smiled. "If I'm going to have the Ability, there's no point in not using it. And if I'm going to use it, I want to use it well, as my ancestors did before The Fall." He paused briefly. "Do you think that BSI of yours will still want me, now that I have the Ability in full force?"

"I think the BSI will want you especially *because* you have the Ability," Cheff said. "We're all extremely proud of you, Old Son!"

Lhuk smiled. "I was hoping you'd say that. How about, on the ride home, you tell me more about the BSI, and what a Torph boy would have to do to join?"

*"Though he was small, he had the heart of a lion."*

# Operation Recall

Clang! Clang! Clang!

Buttons and I looked up from weeding the tonton-fruit bed. "Is that Cheff?" Buttons asked.

"I don't know," I said. "Why would Cheff need to knock?"

"Why would *anyone* need to knock?" Buttons asked. "Maybe the hatch is stuck again."

Clang! Clang! Clang! Clang!

"We'd better go see," I said.

We brushed the sand off our hands and clothing, then headed to the supply room that served as our foyer. Mid, Lery, Sable, and Lhuk were already there. Mid motioned for all of us to get out of sight. We lined up along the wall on the hinge side of the door. Lery, closest to the door, unhooked the giant pipe wrench he carried on his belt. Sable pulled her long black hair into a ponytail. Buttons slapped Starry, her ball-bearing-filled pony, against her palm.

Clang! Clang! Clang! Clang! Clang! Clang! Clang! Clang! Clang!

"Are we sure it's Cheff?" I asked.

Mid raised his eyebrows. "Impatient, whoever it is." He glanced at Sable.

Sable nodded.

Mid gently pushed the hatch open. "Andaran's bones, Cheff! You don't have to beat the door down. It wasn't even locked — Hey, you're not Cheff!"

It was a mysterious stranger, complete with a black trench coat and a wide-brimmed black fedora pulled low over his eyes. The dark stranger growled, "And you're not a little Torph boy, fatty!"

At the word 'Torph,' Lhuk faded into one of the side rooms and quietly closed the door behind him.

"Hey! That's not nice," Mid said. "Who are you, and what do you want?"

"Get out of my way, fatty!" The stranger gave Mid a shove that sent him sprawling.

As the stranger stepped through the hatch, Lery clipped him neatly with his pipe wrench on the base of his skull. He collapsed into a rumpled heap on the floor.

Sable stepped up, a coil of rope in her hand. "Chair," she murmured to Lery.

Lery picked the stranger off the floor, carried him to the main room, and deposited him into a chair.

Sable tied the stranger firmly to the chair, then tied the chair to a table leg. The stranger wasn't going anywhere anytime soon.

Mid jabbed the stranger in the ribs with his thumb, then growled, "*And don't call me fatty!*" He turned to Lery and Sable. "Well done. That was smooth, rock smooth!" He hesitated. "Now what?"

"We wait," Sable murmured.

So we waited.

Sable slid into a chair across from the unconscious stranger. The rest of us sat around the table, too, even Lhuk.

Lery made some felmoss tea to help us stay awake and baked a batch of pleasantly sweet cookies to go with the tea. We got our flour and honey from our friend, Zeek, who got it from his farmer friends north of Fellstone City. They grew their own wheat and ground it themselves, so we knew there wasn't any jexan in it.

After he served the tea and cookies, Lery sat next to the stranger and kept his pipe wrench in his lap.

Buttons found Moka, Starry's sister pony, and danced them both around the table top.

Miss Whiskers, Lhuk's pet desert pup, jumped into Lhuk's lap. "Treeeeeats?"

"These aren't treats. These are cookies," Lhuk told her.

"Treeeeeats!" Miss Whiskers insisted through a mouthful of crumbs.

For the next hour, the stranger didn't so much as twitch.

Mid asked Lery, "Exactly how hard did you hit him?"

"Not… not too… hard, Brother Mid. A little… love tap… is all… He'll… wake up… soon… I think."

Mid took off the stranger's hat and pulled his wrinkled overcoat away from his face. He lifted an eyelid, then let it fall. He slapped the stranger lightly on both cheeks. "I don't know, Lery. He's not moving." Mid put his hand on the stranger's chest. "He's breathing, though, and I can feel his heart beating. Any of you recognize this guy? He's of the Sevro people. Do we know any Sevros? Where do you suppose Cheff's gotten to?"

"All I know is what you know," Buttons said. "He went into Old City to meet with Meltern to see if there's another mission for us yet."

"Careful what you say, Buttons," Mid said. "Our guest might be faking it."

"It's been almost four months since our last one," I said.

"Why do you suppose he"—Buttons jerked her thumb at the inert stranger—"said that Mid wasn't a little Torph boy?"

"Mid isn't… a little… little Torph boy," Lery said, smiling.

"Very funny," Buttons said. "But Lhuk is. Do you think he came here to find Lhuk? The ponies are concerned. They don't want Lhuk to be taken to a Torph Camp."

"There are no Torph Camps, remember?" Mid said. "We learned that on our trip to The Fel. Torphs don't go to camps. They get killed, and probably eaten."

We stared at Mid. Sable shook her head sadly.

"Well, they do," Mid mumbled.

Tears welled up and ran down Buttons' face. The ponies hid their faces with their hooves.

Sable said, "Mid. Stop talking. Now."

Mid stared at his lap.

The hatch clacked, and Cheff stepped in from the storm drain.

"Oh, Cheff!" Buttons ran to her brother, flung her arms around him, and buried her face in his chest.

Cheff patted her on the back. "What's all this? I was only gone a few hours."

"I don't want Lhuk to be taken away and killed and eaten," she sobbed.

Cheff raised his eyebrows and looked at us inquiringly. Lery pointed at Mid. Mid hung his head again.

"I see," Cheff said. He gently disengaged Buttons' arms. "Who's going to take Lhuk away to be eaten?"

"*Him!*" Buttons pointed at the stranger, still slumped in his chair. As slumped as he could be, anyway, with that much rope around him.

"Him?" Cheff noticed the stranger for the first time. He grabbed a handful of the stranger's hair, lifted his head, and peered into his face. "Who is he? And what's he doing here?"

Mid briefly recounted the stranger's arrival.

"And he's been unconscious since then?" Cheff asked. "How long?"

"An hour," Sable said.

"I see," Cheff said again. "Has Zeek been here?"

"Zeek?" Mid asked. "No, why would Zeek be here? Zeek never comes here. Not once. What's going on, Cheff? Do you know who this guy is?"

"Maybe," Cheff said. He took a seat at the table.

"Wait… Friend Cheff," Lery said. He went to the kitchen and brought another teapot, a cup, and a plate of cookies.

"Treeeeeats?" Miss Whiskers asked. Lhuk broke a cookie and gave her a piece. "Taaaaank youuuuuu!"

Cheff took a big swig of felmoss tea and a bite of cookie. "I met with Meltern. He's back from Tumberland."

"Did he give us a you-know-what, Cheff? A job?" Buttons asked.

"No, not exactly. But he did have another task for us. A short one. It concerns Lhuk."

Lhuk put Miss Whiskers down and gave her the rest of the cookie. "What's up, Cheff?"

"It seems that when we submitted your name and information as a potential… friend, it set some unusual wheels in motion. As a Torph with above-average Ability, you're of great interest to certain people. Your name eventually made its way to the special agent in charge of locating the Heir. An older fellow named Noddak. He wanted to interview you, and the top boss gave the go-ahead." He glanced at the motionless stranger. "Meltern said Noddak's a Sevro, by the way."

"Uh-oh," Lery said.

"The plan was that I would escort the special agent to Zeek's place, then the three of us would come here together. But, apparently, he got impatient and took off. I tried to catch up with him before he got here, but I couldn't. He must have been moving pretty fast."

"Must have," Mid agreed. "It doesn't seem to be working out for him, though. How in Andaran did he manage to find our headquarters? It's supposed to be top-secret."

"I don't know." Cheff's expression said that he would surely find out.

"Look, Cheff!" Buttons said. "He moved. Maybe he's waking up now."

The stranger twitched, then moaned. He tried to move. When he discovered he was tied, he started to yell. "Untie me at once, you delinquents! What's wrong with you? Don't you know who I am? How dare you interfere with an agent of—" He stopped abruptly. "Why am I tied up? Who are you people? Whoever you are, you're in a lot of trouble. When I get loose, I'm going to—"

Cheff pulled a rather untidy handkerchief from his vest pocket and unceremoniously stuffed it into the stranger's mouth.

The stranger's eyes went wide, then narrowed into slits. "Mmm mmmmm mmmmf mmmmfle mmm!"

We couldn't help it—we broke into laughter.

While we were laughing, there came a gentle knocking on the hatch, then our friend Zeek stepped in. Zeek was a huge bear of a man. He boomed, "Ah, Cheff, there you are. I waited for you, but when you didn't come, I thought I'd better check on everyone. Hello, children!"

We smiled and waved.

The stranger was struggling and trying to spit out the handkerchief.

Zeek stared down at him, arms crossed on his chest. "Noddak, you fool! You've been up to your old tricks again, haven't you? I told you these weren't ordinary children, didn't I? Now look at the sorry state you've come to."

Noddak commenced shouting at Zeek through the handkerchief. We couldn't tell what he was saying, but he seemed unhappy about something.

Zeek shook his head sadly and took a seat next to Sable. He helped himself to a cookie. "Say, these are good. You make them, Lery?"

Lery nodded happily and went to fetch another teacup.

Buttons brought the ponies to shake hooves with Zeek, then climbed into Zeek's lap and nestled contentedly.

"So you know this guy, Zeek?" Cheff asked.

"Oh, I've known him for many years. I don't see him often, because he's usually on some far-away assignment. But he comes through town from time to time, and we have a special dinner with plenty of Meltern's cider, the grown-up kind, and catch each other up with all our doings. Needless to say, his stories are generally a great deal more entertaining than mine. Although," he reflected, "I was looking forward to telling him all about our little salvage operation a few months back. There aren't many people I can tell my stories to, but old Noddak here is cleared for anything and everything. Makes for a great dinner companion, eh?" He reached over and elbowed Noddak in the ribs, which caused Noddak's face to turn red and his struggling to intensify.

"Easy does it, old friend," Zeek said. "You keep on like that, and you'll do yourself an injury."

Noddak didn't actually shoot daggers out of his eyes, but certainly gave the impression of a man who, for two pins, would so shoot.

"I'm not going to let you go until you calm yourself," Zeek said. "It's more than likely your own fault you're in this fix. Let me guess—instead of following Meltern's plan, you took it upon yourself to show up unannounced at a top-secret location. Instead of introducing yourself, you shouted some demand comprehensible only to you, probably implicating little Lhuk, here. Then you made some precipitous move, and lights out! Am I right? Of course I'm right."

We all laughed. Even Sable smiled.

Buttons looked up into Zeek's face. "The ponies say that's about the gist of it."

"They do, do they?" Zeek asked. He patted each pony on the head. "Well, they are extremely smart ponies. What did you expect, Noddak? I told you—these aren't ordinary children. They also happen to be well-trained and highly effective FRM operatives. And I'm sure your official report will include glowing commendations for their effective neutralization of an unexpected threat, without resorting to lethal force."

Noddak raised his eyebrows.

"Or," Zeek continued, "would you rather stay tied to that chair all night? It's up to you, old friend."

Noddak took a long, slow, deep breath. Then he nodded once.

Zeek removed the handkerchief and threw it on the floor.

"Do you think," Noddak asked politely, "that you could have the big one put that pipe wrench away?"

"Of course, of course, old friend," Zeek said. "These are good children. I'm sure there are no hard feelings. In fact, I'd bet they'd even be willing to share their tea and these excellent cookies." Zeek helped himself to another.

"All right," Noddak said. "I promise to be calm. Now would you please let me go?"

Sable silently consulted Zeek and Cheff, then untied Noddak's bonds.

Lery fetched yet another teacup and another plate of cookies, hot from the oven. He offered a cookie to the liberated Noddak, who accepted, tasted, and confirmed, "Zeek's right, Lery, is it? These are the best cookies I've had in ages. Maybe ever. May I have another?"

# About the Author

Liam Kincaid was born to parents of Scottish descent on December 30, 1953, in a boxcar in the high Sierra Nevadas during a raging snowstorm. After graduating from high school, Liam declined a medical scholarship to Stanford University and a musical scholarship to Julliard.

Instead, Liam served for a time in the United States Air Force, then traveled the world working at many jobs, including professional woodworker and stilts maker, maintenance supply specialist for Pacific Southwest Airlines, kelp processor for Kelco, hot-air balloon pilot, cow clipper (for one day), house painter, time-share salesman in Mexico, hospital housekeeper, school bus driver, wrestling-arena peanut vendor, street musician, English teacher in the Dominican Republic, ranch hand, e-zine publisher, bio-diesel manufacturer, carpet cleaner, pig photographer, and computer programmer.

When his roaming days were over, he longed for the wholesome science-fiction adventure stories of his youth, so he decided to try his hand at writing some. Having raised four sons, he was inspired by the powerful, astounding feats a group of intelligent, determined children can accomplish.

Liam welcomes correspondence from his readers and does his best to answer each one personally. E-mail him at: LiamKincaid@WorldHeartEpic.com

# ABOUT THE ARTIST

Daniel Wood is a freelance artist and illustrator based in Richmond, Virginia.

He honed his skills at Virginia Commonwealth University, where he earned a Bachelor of Fine Arts degree in Communication Arts. Drawing is the love of his life, so much so that he often spends his spare time drawing the day away.

Skilled in many forms of illustration, including concept art, comic art, book illustrations, and game art, both colored and black-and-white, he specializes in fantasy, science-fiction, and all of their more specific subgenres. Every project is a joyful challenge to transform the author's concepts into compelling visual imagery.

Daniel welcomes discussions regarding new projects. See more of his work at DanielWoodArt.com, or e-mail him at woodillustration@gmail.com.

# We Need Your Help!

Dear Reader,

We depend on your reviews and word-of-mouth.

If you enjoyed this book, please help spread the word through Twitter, Facebook, and other social media, and please consider giving us five stars and writing a brief review on Amazon.com and Goodreads.com, or your favorite book-review venue.

Thank you very much!

Liam Kincaid

North California Coast,

March 2024

To view full-size, full-color maps and illustrations,
and to learn more about Fellstone and its peoples, visit:

https://FellstoneTales.com

www.ingramcontent.com/pod-product-compliance
Lightning Source LLC
Chambersburg PA
CBHW060243100726